Real Love

by

Graysen Morgen

2020

Triplicity Publishing, LLC

ISBN-13: 978-1-970042-08-5
ISBN-10: 1-970042-08-7

Printed in the United States of America
First Edition – 2020

Cover Design: Triplicity Publishing, LLC
Interior Design: Triplicity Publishing, LLC
Editor: Megan Brady - Triplicity Publishing, LLC

Also by Graysen Morgen

Playing the Game

Mission Compromised

Boone Creek (Law & Order Series: book 1)

Castor Valley (Law & Order Series: book 2)

Never Let Go (Never Series: book 1)

Never Quit (Never Series: book 2)

Meant to Be

Coming Home

Bridesmaid of Honor (Bridal Series: book 1)

Brides (Bridal Series: book 2)

Mommies (Bridal Series: book 3)

Crashing Waves

Cypress Lake

Falling Snow

Fast Pitch

Fate vs. Destiny

In Love, at War

Just Me

Love, Loss, Revenge

Natural Instinct

Secluded Heart

Submerged

Special thanks to my editor, Megan Brady, for dealing with the monotony of my mistakes! *Muchas gracias!*

For my wife.
Amo la vita con te.

Chapter 1

One of the fluorescent lights overhead buzzed, indicating it was going to give out at any moment, but no one bothered to change it. The nurses had enough on their plates, and the doctors certainly weren't going to do it. That left the maintenance crew, who were already days behind fixing the rest of the issues in the dilapidated old building. Nevertheless, people kept coming for appointments, emergencies kept arriving, and the employees kept going about their daily duties at County General Hospital.

"If one more doctor tells me to take care of his patient in such and such room, I'm going to shove this electronic device so far up his ass, Alexa will announce when he passes gas!" Leigh growled, slamming her tablet onto the desk at the nurses' station. "And why are my shoes squeaking like I'm on a basketball court?"

"Girl, that's one of the perks of being a nurse practitioner. They give you their shit work instead of utilizing you for the skills you're licensed to perform," her friend Abby replied, adding, "they waxed the floors last night, by the way. Must be a new company. My shoes are squeaking too." Her shoulder-length, copper-colored hair shifted back and forth, and her thin lips formed a grin. "At least you don't get the shit work the rest of us regular nurses get. I'm not a CNA, but I've changed three bedpans already this morning."

"Yeah, well I'm over it," she grumbled, running her hand through her long, dirty blonde hair before pulling it back in a ponytail.

"You're a little more on edge than usual. What's going on?" Abby asked, moving closer.

"Nothing." Leigh sighed. "I don't know. I'm just frustrated."

"You sound burned out, hun." Abby looked at her friend. Leigh Myer was beautiful, and could easily pass for Jennifer Aniston's doppelgänger. She'd turned forty a few months earlier and Abby had noticed a shift in her friend's normally upbeat personality. "Why don't you take some of the vacation days you hoard and go up to that cabin I own. I'm sure you could get a little R&R up in the mountains."

"What cabin?"

"The one I got from asshole in the divorce. I've never been there, but supposedly his family used it for hunting. Anyway, it wouldn't hurt to get away for a bit. I think it's about three hours from here." Abby shrugged.

"I don't know." Leigh's grayish-blue eyes closed as she shook her head. She'd never been to a mountain cabin.

"Well, my offer stands."

"Myer, I have a patient in three who needs a catheter and order a CBC," one of the doctors said in passing.

"Seriously!" Leigh growled. "Get a nurse to do it. We have a full waiting room."

"You *are* a nurse," he replied snidely.

"I'm licensed to diagnose and treat illnesses and injuries, not insert catheters and order blood work!" she called to his back as he kept walking.

"He's an ass. Don't let him get to you," Abby said.

Leigh blew out a breath in frustration. "I need a break from this place," she muttered. "That cabin's sounding better by the minute," she added as she stepped away, heading towards room three.

"It's available!" Abby called.

Leigh waved her hand in the air before entering the room.

*

By the time her shift ended Leigh was exhausted, and she'd barely done anything remotely close to her duties as a nurse practitioner in one of the busiest hospitals in Vermont. She wasn't tired because of her work. No, it was deeper, and leaning dangerously towards depression. Abby was right. She *was* burned out. In the fifteen years that she'd been in her field, she'd never 'burned out.' She'd also never battled depression.

As she walked across the long parking lot towards her car, freezing because it was in the low forties and she'd forgotten her jacket inside the hospital, she thought back to Abby's offer. She loved her friend, but the idea of spending a week of her vacation time in a hunting cabin in the woods up on some mountain, sounded crazy. She lived in the city, and had never been 'to the mountains,' nor had she ever dealt with snow, other than the foot or two they got in the city, which was cleared right away by snowplows before she ever went outside. It was mid-February and the mountains certainly had more snow. If it wasn't already several feet deep, it would be soon.

"She's crazy," she mumbled to herself as she slid behind the wheel and closed the door. Her phone beeped with a text message as she turned the key and pressed the button for the heated seat.

Going to Nelly's. Figured a glass of vino was on your mind too!

"You know me too well," Leigh laughed. She grabbed the phone and texted back as she waited for the car to warm up.

Need to go change…but YES!

The drive to her apartment was short, and the tiny one-bedroom unit on the second floor was nothing to get excited about. She had thought about buying a house over the years, but the idea of owning a big house that would mostly be empty, wasn't appealing to her. However, the idea of a place of her own that she could call home, was.

Leigh quickly discarded her scrubs and stepped into the bathroom to look in the mirror as she brushed her hair out. The color was the epitome of dirty blonde with highlights that lightened even more in the sun, and completely natural. People stopped her often to ask where she had her hair done.

She sprayed a little perfume to ward off the hospital stench since she didn't have time to shower, and dressed in a pair of tight blue jeans with a wide black belt and a black turtle neck that hugged her full B cups. She finished with a waist-length, black leather jacket and a pair of black pointed-toe, suede boots that she tucked under her pant legs, almost like short, cowgirl boots. She pulled her hair free of her jacket and fanned it out over her shoulders where it fell to the top of her breasts.

*

The drive to Nelly's Bar and Grille took less than ten minutes. Leigh pulled into a space a few down from Abby's car. She shoved her phone into her small purse before getting out. The temperature had dropped into the thirties and was threatening to go well below freezing during the wee hours of the morning. She zipped her jacket to ward off the chill as she walked through the lot.

"I ordered a bottle," Abby said with a grin while holding her glass up. Dark red liquid sloshed back and forth.

"Wonderful!" Leigh replied, taking a seat next to her at a high-top table in the bar area. She hung her purse on the back of the chair, then removed her jacket, adding it to the chair as well. "It feels like it's getting colder out there."

"Yeah, supposed to go down to the teens. You look great, by the way."

"I just threw something on."

Abby laughed. "Girl, you could prance around in a brown paper sack and people would notice you. I've seen at least three women look your way since you walked in, and this isn't a gay bar."

Leigh laughed. "I'm not interested."

"That's because you don't date!"

"I do, just not often."

"I've known you for five years, through the end of my marriage and a nasty divorce, and getting back into the dating world after ten years, and I've never seen you go on a date."

"They are few and far between. Sadly, that shitty hospital takes up all of my time, running me ragged until I'm too tired to do anything but binge-watch TV."

"Don't you miss sex?"

"Of course," Leigh blurted, nearly spilling her wine.

"I think you've let that hospital run all over you for too long."

"You're right. Honestly, I think I'm getting burned out. It scares me."

"That's not good."

"I know." Leigh sipped her wine and picked at the appetizer plate. "How far away did you say that cabin was?"

"Um…like three hours. You're thinking of going?" Abby said, her voice raising a perky octave with excitement.

"I don't know. I'm pretty sure I'm not a mountain cabin person."

"One thing's for sure, it will be secluded and quiet. I know it's somewhat comfortable. It gets rented quite a bit." Abby refilled her glass and watched her friend glance around the packed bar and restaurant.

"There's probably dead animals everywhere," Leigh laughed.

"I doubt it. You know…Ron went hunting often, but never brought any kind of meat home. I don't think he ever killed anything. Hell, for all I know it's another place he took his whores."

Leigh squeezed her hand. She knew how much his adultery had hurt her friend.

"So…? Are you going?"

Leigh smiled and shrugged. "I guess."

"Yay!"

"I need to do something. I feel like I'm heading down a path I don't want to be on."

"I agree. I've been worried about you, my friend. I think this will be great for you."

"I'll be right back," Leigh said, standing and slipping her jacket back on.

"Where are you going?"

"Outside to call Patty before I change my mind," she said, taking a long sip from her glass before walking away.

*

The cool wind caused Leigh to shiver as she searched her contacts for her boss's number. Patty Williamson, the head of the ER nurses, answered on the second ring.

"Patty, it's Leigh Myer. Listen, some personal stuff has come up and I was wondering if I could take my vacation time?"

"Funny you called, Leigh. I was going to talk with you on your next shift. I heard you've been a little short lately with a few of the doctors. Is everything okay?"

"Yes and no. However, I feel like taking a little time off to clear my head will do me a world of good."

"I don't see a problem with that. I'd rather have you at a hundred percent. You're the best at what you do, and we need you at your best." She paused for a second. "I believe you have both of your weeks still available. Our fiscal year doesn't roll over until early March, and I don't believe you've taken any time off."

"You are correct. I was hoping to take both weeks…starting tomorrow."

"That's a little short notice, but I should be able to make the schedule work. Take your time off and come back refreshed."

"Thank you, Patty."

"No problem. Have a nice time doing whatever you plan to do."

Leigh ended the call and rushed back inside.

"Well…" Abby asked, waiting in suspense.

"She gave me my full two weeks."

"Sweet!"

"I'm honestly surprised she went for it with no notice or anything."

"Maybe she's halfway through a bottle of wine, too!"

Leigh laughed. "Maybe. I'm sure that's why I let you talk me into this craziness."

Abby smiled and grabbed her phone. "I'm texting the property manager to get the address and lockbox code. I'll forward it to you."

"Are you sure no one is staying there right now? I know you rent it out to vacationers."

"When it's rented she sends me the information for approval. It's not booked at the moment. I'll have her block it off for the next two weeks."

"Sounds good. I should probably go home and pack."

"When do you plan on driving up?"

"In the morning. Otherwise, I may sober up and change my damn mind," Leigh chuckled.

"Here is the information. She just messaged me back. I'm forwarding it to you now. The town is Chester, but the cabin is up on Chester Mountain."

"I have no idea where that is."

"I sent you the address. Just put it in your GPS."

"Sounds good. I'm going to head out. Thank you so much. You're the best, you know that?"

"Call me when you get there. I'm sure the roads stay plowed, so you shouldn't have any problems," Abby replied, hugging her friend.

Chapter 2

Leigh programmed the GPS on her phone before tossing her suitcase into the backseat of her car. She headed out on the road with a fresh cup of coffee in the console and Aretha Franklin singing *Freeway of Love* loudly through the speakers.

"No turning back now," she mumbled to herself as she mashed the gas pedal.

"Drop the pedal and go!" she sang as she got onto the highway. "We're going riding on the freeway!"

*

Traffic getting out of the city wasn't too bad. She'd slept in, waiting for the morning rush to go by before leaving. That way, she'd arrive around lunchtime and have plenty of time to grocery shop and get situated.

She'd never driven north of the city she lived in, so the twists and turns were fascinating as she wound her way through the mountains. The roads were clean, but blankets of white snow were off in the distance, making their way towards the road's edge the closer she came to her destination.

With a little over thirty minutes left, she got off the interstate and onto the back roads. She noticed her phone had lost signal, but thankfully, the GPS was still tracking her progress. There was a lot more snow on the ground, literally covering everything in sight when she finally reached the Town of Chester, Vermont. As she drove through the storybook town, she was reminded of a Hallmark movie she'd once seen. There was a local post office about the size of a UPS store, a gas station with two pumps, a mom and pop style restaurant literally called Ma and Pa's, a general store no bigger than a CVS, a town hall, and a malt shop. All of the buildings were either historical structures from the turn of the twentieth century, or made to look as such; painted white, and crammed together on various corners of the four-way stop. The entire road at the intersection was made of brick, and each storefront was directly on the sidewalk. Designated parking lots with five to eight spaces were tucked behind the buildings here and there. She could see a few more buildings were further down the road, but the GPS was telling her to turn left to head up the mountain.

Unsure of what she'd find at the cabin, and with slim restaurant choices, she needed to be able to prepare some meals for herself. She followed the sign for parking and turned the corner, pulling into a small lot behind the general store.

As soon as Leigh parked the car, she pulled her leather jacket on and rushed inside. The dash of her car indicated that the temperature was a balmy twenty degrees, in the middle of a sunny day. *I'm going to freeze my ass off up here.*

"Good afternoon," a man said, tipping his head in her direction as she passed him in the entranceway.

"Hi," she replied with a smile, grabbing a small cart on wheels that was about a quarter size of a regular shopping cart. Then, she proceeded up and down each aisle, adding things to her basket here and there.

The store was small, and like any small-town general store, there was food, a bit of clothing, hardware and tools, and other odds and ends one might need.

After filling her cart to the top, she headed to the register, mentally going over the items in her head as the cashier rang them up.

"How long are you in town for?" he asked.

"Oh, about two weeks. I'm staying in my friend's cabin."

"That's nice. Are you going skiing while you're here?"

Leigh shook her head. "I've never skied. I've actually never been in heavy snow. We only get about two feet where I'm from and the city has the streets plowed and sidewalks cleared before anyone is up and about."

"Really? Well, you'll definitely be in a lot more snow in Chester, and especially up on Chester Mountain. The skiers tend to take over this time of year."

"Good to know." Leigh nodded.

"Enjoy your stay. If there is anything you need, we should have it. If we don't, you won't find it in town. They don't allow corporations or chain stores in our county."

"Also, good to know." *That means no Starbucks. Damn you, Abby.* Leigh smiled and headed out with her bags. As soon as she got into the car, her phone's GPS was complaining about recalculating because it hadn't moved since she'd left it on. She couldn't risk losing her signal and not being able to find the cabin.

*

Leigh was cruising along, halfway up the mountain to the cabin when she saw lights flashing in her rearview mirror. Unsure of where to pull over on the barely two-lane wide mountain road, she looked at the GPS. She had two miles to go until the cabin.

"You're going to have to go around me, or follow me to my destination. I can't risk getting my car stuck in that deep snow," she said aloud as she kept driving. She glanced in her mirror again, noticing that it was a green, full size pick up following her.

Chapter 3

Camden Gorely's day started as usual. She was a U.S. Fish and Wildlife Officer in the state of Vermont, as well as a team leader for Vermont Search and Rescue. Her days could go from writing tickets to hunters or off-roaders who broke the law, to combing the mountain for lost hikers and skiers. She loved her job and was damn good at it. She also loved the small town she'd grown up in, and generally cared for the people and animals around her.

With ski season in full swing, she worked a nine-hour shift patrolling the mountain for illegal hunting and taking calls for injured or pest animals, but she was on call twenty-four hours a day, seven days a week for SAR.

She'd just finished lunch and was heading back out to patrol the mountain roads, when she wound up behind a car going a little too fast up the mountain. The roads were freshly plowed, and no snow had come in the last twenty-four hours, but there were still icy conditions.

"Dispatch, this is Gorely. Be advised, I'm following a car North on Bear Road, going about ten over the limit. I've been lit up for about two miles now. Driver hasn't stopped," Camden radioed from the cab of her green truck with U.S. Fish and Wildlife Conservation and the Vermont FWC seal on the doors.

"Copy. Do you want me to call Crawford for backup?"

"Where the hell are you going? I know you have to see me in your mirror. Pull over," she mumbled, grabbing her radio again. “Negative. It looks like a vacationer. We’re pulling up at a rental cabin on Goose Neck Trail,” she replied, slamming the truck in park.

It was cold, but not like at night when it would be in the low teens with the wind chill below zero. Camden had on her regular, dark green uniform with a base layer under her pants and long-sleeved shirt, and her green tactical-style vest over it. Her uniform pants were somewhat water-resistant and had cargo pockets, similar to military fatigue pants. Her last name was stitched on a Velcro patch on her right chest area and a gold U.S. Fish and Wildlife badge was stitched on the opposite side. The Vermont FWC seal patch was sewn on the upper arm of both of her sleeves. Her gun was on her left hip and her radio and taser were on the right, with the radio mic attached to her vest. She also wore black, insulated boots with a rubber snow tread on the bottom, a pair of green gloves, and a green ski cap with the Vermont FWC seal on the front. The heavy jacket that matched her uniform was lying in the passenger seat.

Camden was too agitated to put on her jacket, hat or gloves, so she’d jumped out without them, marching directly up to the car to tap on the driver’s side window.

*

Leigh pulled into the narrow driveway as the GPS announced she had arrived at her destination. However, she was puzzled as to why the truck had followed...until the officer dressed in a green uniform, tapped loudly on the window.

She quickly pressed the button to lower it. “Is everything okay, officer?” she asked, looking around cautiously.

"I don't know, you tell me," Camden growled. "I've been trying to pull you over since you turned onto Bear Road. Are you aware the speed limit on a good day is only thirty-five? It's suggested that you travel at a safer speed, below twenty-five, during winter conditions. There are signs posted everywhere. You had to have passed at least three of them, yet you maintained a higher rate of speed. Is there an emergency I need to know about?"

Leigh blinked a few times as she took in the not-so-obvious woman standing at her window. From a distance, her close cropped, pixie cut, short hair looked more like salt and pepper gray, but up close, Leigh could tell it was more of a brown, with a lot of gray mixed in, obviously a sign of early graying since her face didn't have the age lines of someone who would be going almost completely gray. Thin lips formed a creased line as she waited impatiently for an answer.

Leigh was uncertain of her height since she was in the car, but she looked trim and fit under the bulky uniform. *In another time*...her mind trailed off as the officer's voice got her attention, pulling her from the fog.

"How about you give me your license and registration while you figure out why you were speeding on an icy mountain road, and neglected to pull over?"

*

Camden stood, stretching her back with her cold hands in her pockets while she waited for the woman to dig through her purse and glove box. She didn't mess with speeders too often, except up on the mountain. She'd seen too many people get into serious accidents on the ice and snowy terrain. Chester had a small police department with officers patrolling the streets, but the only people patrolling the mountain was FWC. Therefore, it was her duty as a federal law enforcement officer to take care of traffic accidents and other police type duties on the mountain roads. After being an officer with FWC for the last sixteen years, it was second nature, and simply another duty on her list.

When the woman finally handed her information out the window, Camden stepped over.

"I'm going to run this. You can roll your window back up to keep the heat in."

"Can I go inside? I'm staying here."

"No. This will just take a minute."

Camden got back into her truck, thankful the heater had kept it nice and warm. The low temperature wasn't too much of a problem with the layers of clothing she had on, it was the bone-chilling wind that blew out of nowhere that made her cold down to her bones. She quickly typed the woman's name *Leigh Myer* into the computer, noticing they were the same age, and she lived in one of the major cities a few hours away.

After a brief minute, the report came back with a clean driving record, no warrants for her arrest, and her car insurance was up to date. Camden grabbed her radio. "Dispatch, this Gorely. I'll be 10-8 from my location on Goose Neck in two minutes," she said, letting them know she was finished and about to leave. Then, she got out and walked back up to the car. A wave of light, floral scented, hot air blew at her when the woman rolled her window down.

Camden stepped back a second, surprised at how high she'd had the heater on and nice her perfume smelled. She took a longer look at her to make sure she matched the picture on the license. She was beautiful with a mixture of dirty blonde hair with natural highlights and light-colored eyes that seemed to shift from blue to gray depending on the reflection of the sunlight. Nevertheless, she was a vacationer who needed to slow down before she killed herself.

"Here you go," she said, handing her the documents. "By the looks of the bags in the backseat, you're just arriving, so I'm not going to write you a ticket. But if I see you speeding again, I'll double the fine. These roads are no joke, especially this time of year. You could easily hit a patch of ice and slam into a tree…or worse, go over the side of a cliff," she said sternly.

"I apologize, officer…"

"Gorely."

"Officer Gorely," Leigh said, finally seeing the name stitched on her uniform. "I've never been here before. In fact, this is my first time in the mountains. I'm more of a city girl. I honestly wasn't paying attention. I was just hoping my GPS didn't lose signal again and leave me stranded."

"Well, I suggest you pay more attention to the roads next time. It's quite easy to get around. Bear Road, which you just turned off of, is one of the main roads that takes you up and down the mountain, and is mostly used by residents. Trail Ridge Drive is the other main road and that one takes you up to the ski resort. People wind up on the wrong road often, so Bear Road sees a lot more traffic than usual during ski season. It's fairly narrow, so accidents do occur."

"Thank you for letting me know. I'll definitely slow down. It certainly wasn't my intention to speed. I was concentrating more on trying to find this place. I've never been in this much snow, to be honest."

Camden's radio crackled, so she turned the volume up slightly.

"A moose is circling on Eagle Landing Drive," the dispatcher said.

Camden grabbed the radio mic attached to her vest. "This is Gorely, I'm nearby. I'll be there in about five minutes."

"Copy."

Camden looked back at the woman in the car. Her thin lips curved briefly into a smile. "Have a good day…and welcome to Chester Mountain," she said before walking back to her truck.

Chapter 4

"That went well," Leigh muttered as she turned the car off and got out. The log cabin was an A-frame with a small porch at the front door, and a deck along the length of the back. Thick fir trees were scattered all around and a heavy blanket of white snow covered everything except the driveway and walkway. A bucket full of rock salt was beside the door to keep the porch and walkway free of ice. "Let's hope this goes better," she added to herself as she put in the code for the lockbox and retrieved a silver colored key.

The cabin was nothing like she'd expected. Abby said it had been a hunting cabin, but she was pretty sure that had been another lie. No dead animals were hanging on the walls. In fact, there was no hunting memorabilia at all. The open space seemed much larger than it was because of the high ceiling and large, A-shaped windows on one end over a set of French doors. Two more windows were on either side of the doors, making it look like the entire wall was made of glass. The rest of the walls, floor, and staircase were all made of pine and stained in a high gloss, golden finish. The ceramic sink and counter top in the L-shaped kitchen were white, matching the appliances, and the oak cabinets were stained the same as the walls.

A soft, whisky brown leather couch and matching recliner were in front of a stone fireplace, and a TV was on a stand beside it in the corner. The dining table, staircase rail, TV stand, coffee table and end tables were all handcrafted from the same type of wood, and stained to match the rest of the cabin. A ceiling fan hung over the couch area from a long pole attached to one of the two beams running the length of the cabin along the ceiling.

A short hallway was just off the kitchen and led to a decent sized bathroom with a double sink, and tub/shower combo, and a small bedroom. The double bed frame and matching dresser were both handmade and stained a darker walnut color, and the comforter set on the mattress was bright red.

Upstairs, she found the loft, which was the master bedroom. The rail overlooked the living room and kitchen space below and had a beautiful view through the massive windows across from it. The queen bed and matching dresser were nearly identical to the set in the other bedroom, but with a dark blue comforter.

Leigh went back downstairs and stood in the middle of the room, taking it all in. The square footage was only around a thousand, but it was laid out perfectly and felt much larger. Remembering the bags in the car, she rushed outside, slipping on a piece of ice under the snow and landing directly on her butt.

"Son of a bitch!" she spat, then began laughing hysterically as she carefully got back up and slowly retrieved her bags.

*

Camden went about the rest of her day without giving the speeding vacationer another thought, other than remembering how striking she was. She'd made a note to check her name on Google to see if she was one of the celebrities that snuck into town now and then for peace and quiet, and a lot of skiing. She didn't have a lot of time for TV, and certainly wasn't up to date on the latest Hollywood news.

She pulled into the plowed space in front of her small cabin and got out of the truck. It had been a long day and she was tired. She stepped inside, kicking her thick boots off at the door, then hung her uniform jacket on one of the pegs before walking over to her recliner to sit down for a minute. She still had two hours left on her shift and had planned to take her snowmobile out to check some of the trails, but she wanted to make a cup of coffee to warm up and eat a homemade granola bar for energy.

"Gorely, you around?" her radio crackled to life.

"Yeah, 10-7 at the moment. I'm about to take my sled out to Grizzly Pass to check the trails. There's been a few complaints of joy riders on private property around this time of day."

"Want some company?" Baker Crawford asked. He was as close to a partner as she had. All of the FWC officers were on their own on the mountain, but he was her backup if she ever needed it. They also worked SAR together, so they'd gotten close over the years.

"Sure, if you're out this way," she radioed back.

"I'm about to pull up," he said.

She stepped over to the door, opening it for him to come in. "What are you doing with your sled in your truck?"

"I just picked it up from the shop. It was an exhaust leak causing the loss of power. Anyway, I should've taken the trailer. You wouldn't believe how long it took me to get that damn animal cage out of there," he replied, slipping his boots off and hanging his jacket next to hers.

Baker was five years younger than Camden and only a few of inches taller than her five-foot seven frame. He had receding brown hair that he kept shaved down to the lowest guard and a matching jaw line beard that attached to his sideburns.

"I figured I'd stop by and see if you were going out. I need to run it anyway to make sure everything is fine."

"I'm ready when you are," she said, sipping her coffee.

"I'm good to go."

They both walked over, slipping their boots back on and lacing them up.

"See anything crazy today?" he asked.

"Nothing out of the normal."

"What happened with that speeder on Bear Road?"

Camden shook her head. "A vacationer scared of getting lost apparently. Never noticed me behind her. I followed her all the way to her rental cabin."

Baker laughed.

"Come on, we're burning daylight."

"Was she cute?"

"I'm too old for cute…besides, I'm also getting too old for hook ups with vacationers. That was fun in my twenties."

"I meant for me," he teased as they began setting up the ramps so he could back his sled out of the truck.

"I thought you were seeing that girl over in Black Creek?"

"*Was* being the keyword," he replied, climbing up into the truck and onto the seat of the sled. With a quick turn of the key, the machine rumbled to life. He put it in reverse, then slowly backed down the ramps.

Camden trudged through the thick snow over to the shed where she kept her snowmobile and UTV, while he filled his sled with gas. The double doors swung open, revealing her machines. She put her helmet on and quickly turned the key, making sure it was full of gas, then bumped it over to start the engine. It rumbled just as Baker's had, however, hers was a couple of years newer and slightly larger. She used it quite a bit for SAR in the winter, so she'd splurged when buying it a few years back. The state allotted a certain amount of money for equipment, and Camden added her own money to upgrade slightly from the barebones the state could afford.

As soon as the engine was warm, she pressed the throttle with her right thumb, waiting for the clutch to wind up and engage, lurching her forward and out of the shed. She left it running while she closed and locked the doors. Then, she sped over to where Baker was waiting for her.

"Click over to channel six," she said to him, then radioed dispatch to let them know where they would be and what channel. After that, she waved for him to follow and took off across her property at around twenty miles per hour, careful not to hit any large rocks or tree branches.

The snowmobile engines whined, echoing off the trees as they rode along, cutting a new trail in the snow. Baker followed as they left her property and cut across state owned land heading towards a few mapped trails a couple of miles away.

Once they hit the groomed trails, Camden squeezed the throttle a little harder, increasing her speed as she raced over tracks other sleds had made during the day. After about a half mile, she took a switchback and left the trail. They slowed down to a crawl, going around downed trees and patches of snow-covered ice as they wound higher and higher in the backcountry.

"Is this a black diamond snowmobile trail," Baker laughed into his radio.

"Funny," she replied. "We're almost to the area the illegal riders have been in. I simply took a short cut."

A few minutes later, Camden came to a stop and cut her engine. She motioned for him to do the same. Then, she got off her machine and walked over to him with her visor up.

"I've been all over this mountain for the last five years, and I'm pretty sure I've never been through that area you just took me through," he said.

"Made your ass pucker, didn't it?" she laughed.

"I'm not gonna lie."

"Listen," she said, removing her helmet to hear better. "They're over that way," she pointed. "I guarantee they're either on private property or unmapped state land."

"Let's go bust their asses."

Camden nodded and put her helmet back on. She had a feeling where they might be riding. She started her sled and pulled away quickly. Baker took off behind her, leaving about fifteen to twenty feet between them. Camden made sure to stay on state land and never crossover private property as she wound along the side of the mountain.

She was about to stop again to listen, when she spotted the red snowmobile shooting across fifty yards in front of her. She sped to the spot where the sled cut through the trees and saw it again up ahead.

"Crawford, you stay on him. I'm going to take a switchback up here and see if I can cut him off."

"Roger," he replied as she turned left. He maintained his speed, keeping the red machine in his line of sight as it wound around curves littered with trees.

*

Camden knew the rider would have to make a left hand turn soon and she was ready. As soon as the red sled appeared she shot out of the woods, coming up next to it. She made a motion for the driver to stop and kill the engine.

She turned her key and removed her helmet before getting off the sled and walking over to the young man. "Get off the snowmobile," she said.

Baker had also removed his helmet before stepping up next to her.

"License and registration."

"Ugh…I don't have that. My license is at the cabin."

"Where is the cabin?" she asked while Baker ran the numbers from the registration sticker.

"On the other side of that house," he said, pointing to a bungalow in the distance through the woods.

She nodded. "I had a feeling you were the one riding back here. First of all, this is state land that is not marked with trails that you're on right now. Second, to get here, you have to cut across private property. Neither of which are you permitted to be on."

"Really? You can't just ride all around?" he said, dumbfounded.

"No," Camden said sternly, shaking her head.

"There are hazards all over the land, which is why you are required to either stay on the groomed or clearly marked trails, or on your own property."

"Sled belongs to William Howard," Baker said, getting the information from dispatch. "Clear title, insurance is on file."

"It came with the rental cabin for the week," the guy said. "I honestly thought it was like skiing."

"Unless you're a professional skier or some kind of daredevil, you ski on groomed or clearly marked trails. So, I don't see what you mean," she replied sarcastically.

"So…do I get a ticket or…"

"The owners of the private property you've been riding all over can press charges against you and in that case, you'll go to jail. The same with the unmarked state land. Lucky for you, the property owners just want you stopped. One of them has a small pond on his land that is covered with snow this time of year. If you'd run over it, you would've fallen through and froze to death. I don't have to tell you about all the things that could happen to you while riding the backcountry in an area you're unfamiliar with, not to mention illegal to snowmobile in." Camden shook her head.

"If we write you a ticket, we write one for the owner as well. I don't think Mr. Howard would be too happy to know you blatantly disobeyed the snowmobile rules he left for you," Baker said.

"Listen, the sun is going down soon. You need to get back to your cabin…carefully, and park that sled before you wind up in bigger trouble or worse. I'll let the property owners know you won't be out on their land again."

He nodded.

"How long are you here?"

"We leave in the morning."

"Even better," Baker stated.

"Do you need us to show you how to get back where you're supposed to be?"

"Nah. I've been riding around for a few days. I know where to go."

"Don't let me hear you back out here riding around."

"I swear, we are leaving in the morning. I have no reason to lie to you. I apologize for all of this."

"Have a good night," Camden said, walking back to her sled.

"Why didn't you write him a ticket?"

"Because William Howard would've gotten one too. He and his wife are up in the city where she is getting treatment for cancer. They're renting their place out at top dollar with all of the bells and whistles to help pay for it."

"Damn. I didn't know that." Baker shook his head.

"Small town gossip," she replied, putting her helmet on.

Chapter 5

"Abby, I'm serious. This place is nothing like you think it is. I feel like I should pay you. You're obviously missing out on money for the next two weeks with me being here," Leigh said. She was sitting on the couch, leaning against the arm with her legs tucked under her.

"Honestly, Leigh, I've been thinking of selling it. I don't have to see how nice it is to know what Ron was doing there. He lied about so much, I'm not even sure he was really flying the routes he told me. He could've been anywhere. The airline was always moving him around from this flight to that one, and he had women everywhere."

"You'll get a pretty penny for it, that's for sure. I'm sorry he was such a piece of shit."

"It's not even the money. I was awarded half of his pension and he paid me off upfront so I wouldn't get more when he retires. I paid my house and car off, and I still have some left over, plus that cabin has been making money as well. Anyway, how are things?"

"Well, the town is the size of a postage stamp and set in some Christmas Hallmark movie. The cabin is cozy and twice the size of my apartment, so that's a plus. I slipped on the ice and busted my ass, but that was after a good-looking wildlife officer pulled me over for speeding on one of the mountain roads."

"No way. First of all, I hate the ice and snow. Second, I'm not surprised. You drive like a bat out of hell."

"Not on a mountain! I thought I was going slow. I wasn't paying attention because the damn GPS kept losing signal. I didn't want to be lost or stranded on this stupid mountain. The crazy thing is, she followed me all the way to the cabin because I had no idea she was behind me!"

"Oh, Leigh, that's hilarious!"

"She didn't find it funny."

"You said she was good-looking?"

"Yeah, in a rugged sort of way."

"See, the trip was a good idea after all."

"I did tell you I fell on the ice, right?" Leigh snickered.

"Maybe she can take a look at your bruised butt."

"You're funny. I'm not a damn animal. She's a wildlife officer."

"Exactly."

"I need to go so I can cook dinner."

"Wait, you drove all the way up there to relax and you're cooking?"

"I'm pretty sure there is only one restaurant in town and it's dark. If I went down the mountain…and made it to the bottom, I'd never find my way back up."

"Oh lord," Abby chuckled.

"I plan on venturing out tomorrow. I'll let you know how it goes."

"Can't wait," Abby laughed as she hung up.

Leigh set her phone down on the table and went out on the back deck in search of wood for the fire. She hadn't made a fire in years since her apartment didn't have a fireplace, but she was pretty sure she remembered how to do it.

Finding the dry pile of wood stacked nicely on a covered shelf, she chose a few larger pieces and walked back inside, shivering from the bone-chilling cold.

"I don't know how people live up here," she mumbled, setting the wood on the grate inside the fireplace. She searched around, finally locating the long matches on the mantel, and lit two. Both went out as soon as she touched the wood. She struck another one and held it close, but not touching the wood. Nothing happened and it went out. *What the hell?* She struck a couple more and the same thing happened.

She shook her head and tried a few more times with no luck. "Oh, the hell with it!" Pissed, she tossed the matchbox down on the table and went to turn the heat up.

*

Leigh wasn't much of a night owl, but she found it hard to stay awake after the quick dinner she'd thrown together. After her eyes slammed shut on the couch for the third time, she turned the TV off, forgetting what she'd even been watching, and headed up the stairs to the master bedroom loft. The only windows with curtains were the couple on the front of the house. The massive windows and doors on the end across from the loft were wide open and slightly scary. She wasn't accustomed to being able to see in and out so easily, and wondered if she should've brought some sort of protection with her. No one knew she was there, except the rental manager and even then, she didn't even know who that person was. It wasn't like she actually owned a gun or anything like that, but being there alone in the middle of nowhere, made her contemplate the idea of owning one.

By the time her head finally hit the pillow, all thoughts of the open windows were gone. She'd fallen asleep quickly from pure exhaustion. That and the extremely comfortable pillow top mattress.

Chapter 6

A tiny trail of steam rose from the mug in Camden's hand, filling her nostrils with the scent of freshly brewed coffee as she held the black ceramic in her hand. She stood near the window beside the dining table, peering out at the glistening white snow as the sun lifted above the trees. Her shift started at eight a.m., but she was always up and ready to go with the sun. Unless, of course, she'd been out all night working with SAR, which happened often this time of year. Then, trying to get up and out the door on time was like pulling a bear's teeth.

She checked her watch and grabbed her jacket, slipping it on over her tactical vest and uniform since it was a little colder than the day before. After finishing the last sip of her coffee, she poured the remainder of the pot into her travel mug and pulled her boots on at the door.

*

Leigh awoke as soon as the bright sunlight filled the cabin. It was like someone flipped a switch on a one-hundred-watt bulb. She stretched her arms over her head, allowing the sheet to slip down around her waist, revealing the thin tank top she'd slept in. She felt refreshed and energetic for the first time in months, and wasn't sure if it was the mountain air, or the fact that she wasn't going anywhere near the hospital for several days. Either way, she enjoyed the feeling. She tossed the heavy comforter aside and slid out of bed, shivering slightly from the chill in the air. The heater was on, but she'd gotten hot during the night and turned it down...apparently a little too far. The tiny tank top and shorts with nothing under them were no match for the fifty-eight-degree temperature in the cabin.

She padded down the stairs quickly and turned it back to sixty-five, which was what she'd had it on when she'd gone to bed. After that, she went into the kitchen and started the coffee pot, thankful it was user friendly since most of her coffee experience came from the Starbuck's drive-thru and the ratty old machine they used in the hospital, which she purposely steered clear of.

While she waited for it to brew, she grabbed the throw blanket from the back of the couch, wrapping it around herself as she walked over to the French doors to look out.

"Oh my..." she started, moving closer to the door. A large doe was standing on the other side of the deck, next to a tree, watching her fawn playing in the snow. Leigh wished she had her phone to take a picture, but knew she could spook them if she moved, so she stood completely still, watching in awe.

The coffeemaker beeped, indicating her brew was finished, but she didn't budge. She'd never seen anything so precious in all of her life. The mother walked around, sniffing the ground periodically, yet never straying far from her baby while he frolicked around, kicking snow up as he ran in one direction, then sped off in another.

By the time the doe had had enough and forced her little one to walk further into the woods, out of sight, Leigh's coffee was cold. However, the heater had finally warmed the cabin enough to toss the blanket back onto the couch. She filled a generic white mug from the cabinet and put it in the microwave to heat it back up. It was probably going to taste horrible, but it was well worth it.

Leigh grabbed her phone and sent a text to Abby while she waited for the microwave.

OMG saw a momma and baby deer right in the backyard...maybe 10 ft from the house at most! So amazing! Thanks again! Hope the shit hole isn't too bad today!

A few minutes later, she was sitting on the couch, forcing herself to drink the coffee, when her phone went off.

Wow! Did you get a pic? I would've peed my pants! Shit hole is in full swing as usual!

Leigh texted back and explained how she was stuck at the window for what felt like an hour, but she'd planned to take a little hike around the property later, hoping to see them again.

*

"Listen, you can backtrack all you want, but a witness saw you hunting earlier today," Camden said, shifting her weight from one foot to the other in agitation. She despised liars, but people with blatant disregard for other people's safety drove her mad. "You do realize you were within fifty yards of a groomed ski trail? You could've killed someone."

"It wasn't me. I was…I was home," the man said, stumbling over his words.

"Do I need to go check the ski trail cameras? I'm sure they will show whoever was hunting. A deer darted across the ski trail, thankfully no one hit it. Deer are smart. They usually stay away from the ski trails, so someone was obviously chasing it. If you come clean, you'll save yourself a lot of trouble and heavier fines. However, if I have to go up to the resort and pull the camera footage and see you chasing that deer with a rifle in your hand, you can bet you will be going to jail."

The man scratched his beard, sighing as he shook his head. "I was just trying to feed my family," he said in defeat.

Always the same damn excuse. "I understand that, but there are laws and regulations that you must follow. This time of year, hunting is closed on the face of the mountain. Anyone with a license to hunt in Willow County knows it's only permitted on the backside of the mountain."

The man hung his head and nodded.

"You admit to hunting on the face of Chester Mountain, causing a deer to impede the groom ski trails, correct?"

"Yeah," he muttered.

"I'm going to write you three citations. The first is for hunting illegally, meaning in the wrong area; the second is for carrying a loaded gun on ski resort property, and; the third is for impeding the ski trails. You will lose your hunting license for one year, and you must appear before a judge for adjudication wherein you will be given the chance to enter testimony. Signing these does not admit guilt. It simply means you understand that you must obtain a court date and appear before a judge. Do you understand everything I have said to you?"

"Yeah," he replied, reaching for the pen to sign the paperwork. "Holy shit! These fines are over two-thousand dollars!"

"Holy shit, you could've killed someone with your illegal hunting activity and should be thankful you're not going to jail!" she retorted, taking the papers back after he signed them.

"You're right. I was clearly in the wrong. My wife is going to shoot me herself."

"Good luck with that," Camden said as she turned and walked back to her truck. It was three-thirty, which meant it would be dark in an hour, and in an hour and a half, she'd be able to call it a day.

As soon as she pulled out of the man's driveway, a call came over the radio activating Search and Rescue. She turned her lights and siren on and sped off in the direction of the address listed, which was back up on the mountain.

*

"What do you mean you're lost?" Abby squeaked. "What's going on?"

"In the woods. I left the cabin to go for a little hike and wound up following animal prints. The next thing I know, I turn around and the cabin is out of sight."

"How would I know what to do? I've never even been there. Why in the world are you out hiking, anyway? I didn't know you hiked."

"I need help, Abby. Not a bunch of questions. I only have one bar on my phone and the GPS isn't getting a signal," Leigh said, trying to calm the panic rising inside of her. "I had to go even further to get the one bar to call you! My battery is only at twenty-five percent because it was roaming the whole time I was trying to find a signal."

"Stay calm. I'm going to call 9-1-1. Are there any landmarks you can see?" Abby said.

"No, just trees and woods. Everything is covered in white snow. It all blends together."

"Okay. It'll be okay. I'm going to hang up with you to call for help. Stay off your phone in case they need to call it to track you. Keep your GPS on."

"There's no signal."

"It doesn't matter, just do it."

*

The cabin looked vaguely familiar when Camden pulled up behind two other FWC trucks and a Chester Police Department SUV, but she'd been around nearly every residence on the mountain at one time or another.

"What's going on?" she asked as she got out and opened the extended cab door to get her SAR equipment which was stored behind the driver's seat.

"A woman is lost. She went hiking about two hours ago from this cabin. She's a vacationer with no snow experience, and according to her friend, who owns the cabin, she's not a hiker cither," Baker said.

"So, no snowshoes, I assume."

"I doubt it."

Camden looked around. "We've had some snowfall in the last two hours, so finding her tracks is going to be difficult." She placed her green FWC jacket on her seat and slipped into her bright red SAR jacket with gray stripes across the shoulders. It was a heavy jacket, capable of keeping someone warm in temperatures below zero, or for extended hours in the teens. It had several pockets, which were pre-packed with gear, and a lanyard hung off the front chest area for a handheld GPS. She pulled on a pair of gray, insulated gloves with the same temperature rating as the jacket and clipped her radio mic to a loop on the upper chest. She was already wearing a thick base layer under her uniform pants, which were more like heavy-duty military ACU pants that are used for combat and have several pockets, plus thick wool socks inside her insulated boots. She pulled a red, insulated ski cap onto her head, covering her ears, then closed the door and locked her truck.

"Listen up," she said, pulling the group of five together. "We have no idea which way she went, or how she is dressed. She's already been out here for two hours, and the temperature is steadily dropping. It'll be dark in an hour. She won't survive the night, especially with this storm coming in, so this is do or die."

Everyone nodded in agreement.

"Let's split up, each taking a different direction. The 9-1-1 report stated she'd seen a deer in the backyard that morning. More than likely, she went for a walk to see more wildlife and got turned around. She can't be too far away. Let's go to channel six. I don't need to tell you to mark this position on your GPS or check in on the radio every fifteen minutes, you've all done this enough times. Someone does need to stay behind in case she somehow returns."

"I'll stay back," the Chester Police Officer said.

"Roger. Have EMS on standby," she said. "Let's go."

Everyone headed off in a different direction, starting from the back of the cabin. Baker took off with search and rescue dog, Otis in tow. He'd picked up a faint scent from the car in the driveway, but it wasn't long before he'd lost it. Camden headed northwest, trudging through the snow at a brisk pace while scanning all around for any sign of color against the white snow covering the ground and trees. She kept looking at the terrain, changing her path several times to accommodate someone with no experience on the mountain or with the conditions.

Chapter 7

"God, please let someone find me," Leigh whispered, shoving her hands further into her jacket. Thankfully, she'd gone into the town at the base of the mountain earlier in the day and purchased a slightly longer than waist-length, heavy coat, a ski cap, gloves, and snow boots. She was still shivering from the cold because she only had one layer of clothing under her coat and was wearing jeans with a pair of long underwear beneath them, and regular socks instead of thick wool ones. Her phone battery had finally died, leaving her completely alone. "Damn it, this was so stupid of me. Why did I even come up here?"

She shook her head to keep from crying. She was strong-willed, and breaking down wasn't going to help her situation. She needed to think. She'd been wandering for what seemed like hours with no signs of life, or the animals she'd been in search of to begin with.

She wasn't sure if she should keep walking, or stand and wait to be rescued, but she wasn't the kind to wait around, so she trudged on. The snow was close to the top of her boots in some areas.

When she came to somewhat of a clearing, she noticed smoke in the distance. "Oh, please let that be someone's fireplace!" She quickly began heading in the direction, but she was tired and hungry, having burned all of her energy walking around for over two hours while trying to keep warm. So, her strides were slow and close together.

*

Camden continued along her chosen path, looking for any sign of boot prints, when the second fifteen-minute radio check came and went. She'd been walking for over half an hour and the sun was gradually starting it's decent. "Come on, let one of us find her," she whispered, then looked up to see a very faint trail of gray in the air. *Smoke.* She grabbed the radio mic clipped to her jacket and pressed the button. "This is Gorely. I have smoke in the air about two hundred yards away. I'll need to take a switchback to get down there. I'm above the tree line."

"Do you think it's her?" Baker replied.

"If she was an experienced hiker, she would've started a fire, but I don't know. If it's another cabin, I'm hoping she saw the smoke and headed in that direction. I'm about fifty yards from the switchback," she said.

As soon as she was on the other side of the switchback, which took her down the mountain slightly without the steep decline, Camden pulled her binoculars out and began looking around in the general direction the smoke was coming from. Finally, she spotted something dark moving through the trees. It was either a bear or the lost hiker some thirty yards away. One of the last rays of sun shone through the trees at just the right angle for her to see it was someone in a blue jacket and jeans.

"This is Gorely," she radioed. "I have a visual, thirty yards ahead of me and heading west." She gave her position and picked up her pace. She couldn't run through the snow to begin with, and burning all of her energy would be a bad idea. Instead, she moved as quickly as she could, and put her hands to her mouth, calling out to the person.

"Hello! Vermont Search and Rescue!"

*

Leigh was tired. The cold and hunger were starting to take their toll on her. *I saw the smoke over these trees. It has to be up ahead. Just hold on. You've been through worse. You'll make it.* She kept mentally reassuring herself over and over as she continued walking at a snail's pace. After what felt like ten minutes of going nowhere, she swore she'd heard a voice. She paused, thinking it was her mind playing tricks on her, then kept going.

A minute later, she heard it again. This time she recognized the words: search and rescue. She immediately turned around, scanning through the trees until her eyes landed on something red, heading her way.

"Oh, thank God!" she cried and began moving as quickly as her cold legs and feet would allow.

It didn't take long for her to reach the rescuer, who was walking with a strong, steady gait that was close to a light jog. "Oh, my God. I'm so glad you found me," she said, coming face to face with…the wildlife officer? *What the hell?*

*

Camden rushed as quickly as she could towards the woman as she radioed her final position.

"Standby for an extraction point," the Chester officer radioed back as he checked the map spread across the hood of his SUV, looking for the closest place for them to exit the woods and be picked up. Two of the FWC officers on the SAR crew had already returned once they'd heard she'd been found, and were waiting to go retrieve them.

As she grew near, Camden had a feeling she recognized the woman. It wasn't until she was face to face with her, two feet apart that it dawned on her. She shook her head. "I didn't see this coming," she said.

"You?" Leigh mumbled. "I thought…"

"Surprised to see me?" Camden asked.

"Yes. No. I don't know."

"How about we start with you. Can you feel your fingers and toes?"

"Yes, but I'm freezing."

"You don't have enough layers on," Camden replied, pulling a couple of small packets from one of her pockets. She tore into them and pulled out something that she began shaking vigorously. "Open your boots."

"What for?" Leigh squeaked.

"These are foot warmers. They'll warm your feet before you get frostbite. I have a pair to put inside your jacket pockets as well. Shove your hands in and they'll warm your torso and your hands at the same time."

Leigh did as she was instructed and immediately noticed the warmth slowly spreading through her body.

"Here," Camden said, holding some kind of granola energy bar and a small bottle of water that she'd mysteriously pulled from her jacket. She also drank a water and ate a bar of her own. "This will give you the energy you'll need to get out of here."

"How did you find me?" Leigh asked, sipping the water and munching on the bar full of nuts, grains, mini chocolate chips, honey, and peanut butter, surprised at how good it actually tasted. Either that or she was so hungry a shoe would taste delicious. She wasn't completely sure.

"I hoped you'd seen the smoke and headed this way."

"I did. How did you know?"

"I've been doing this a long time," Camden replied.

"I thought you were with Fish and Wildlife?"

"I am. Most of us are certified to do both. I'm actually a search and rescue team leader, so I do this quite often."

"Wow."

"Gorely, head west, southwest and you should come to a creek. Follow it and you'll come out onto Bear Road. Here are the coordinates," Baker radioed. "I will be there waiting for you. EMS is en route."

"How are you feeling? Are you hurt anywhere?" Camden asked her.

"No. I'm okay. Much warmer now, thank you…for everything."

"Cancel EMS. She's okay. We'll meet you at extraction," she radioed back.

"Roger."

"I'm sorry I don't remember your name."

"Leigh…Myer."

"Camden Gorely," she replied, sticking her hand out.

Leigh felt a slight squeeze when their gloved hands touched.

"Are you ready to get out of here? We have about a thirty-minute walk…unfortunately, in the dark," Camden said, as the last of the sun faded away. She pulled her headlamp from her jacket pocket, slipped it on over her ski cap, and switched it on.

"I was ready two hours ago, trust me," Leigh said.

"You're lucky I found you. There is a snowstorm coming in tonight," Camden said as they began walking. "Don't be shy. The terrain is a mess and it's dark. If you need help, grab my arm or my hand. If you need to slow down, say so."

"Okay," Leigh replied as they began walking. "This isn't me. I don't hike."

"You picked an odd time to start."

Leigh couldn't see her expression in the dark, but she felt the need to explain herself anyhow. "I saw two deer this morning right in the back behind the deck of my cabin. I got excited and took a walk to see what else I could find. It's so beautiful up here."

"Good thing you didn't find a bear," Camden stated seriously. "Deer will just run from you, but a bear might've given you a sniff."

"Oh, great." Leigh swallowed the lump in her throat. "I never thought about that. I was actually hoping to see a moose. I've lived in Vermont my whole life, albeit in the city, but I've always wanted to see one."

"You have a better chance of seeing a bear."

"Seriously, you're scaring me with this bear talk." Leigh nonchalantly looked around.

"It's true. Moose tend to hide. You were pretty far into the woods, so you could've seen one, but if it spotted you first, it would've gone the other direction. They're pretty skittish."

"I'm sure you've seen one."

"I saw one yesterday. Right after I left you, in fact. I had to put him down."

"Oh, no. Why?"

"They can get brain worm. It makes them sort of go crazy. They walk in circles over and over. Putting them down actually is the humane way of putting them out of their misery before they hurt someone accidentally."

"Does that happen often?"

"No. I see it maybe twice a year."

"That's so sad."

Camden nodded, causing the light emitting from her head to bounce up and down. Suddenly, Leigh screeched, grabbing her hand as she slipped on a patch of icy snow. Camden pulled her hard to keep Leigh from going to the ground and accidentally tugged Leigh against her in the process. "It's slippery. We're close to the creek edge."

"These boots are supposed to keep me from slipping on ice," Leigh grumbled, taking a step back to put some space between them

"Snow boots handle the snow well, but nothing really works on ice except spikes. But, if you walk carefully and don't pull your foot as you walk, you won't slip. It takes some practice to learn how to walk on ice."

"Tell me about it. I busted my ass in the driveway yesterday…right after you left, actually. Which is why I bought these new boots this morning."

"Throw some salt rock down. It'll melt away."

"I did," Leigh replied, letting go of the hand she was still holding.

Camden checked the GPS. "It's not too much further. Maybe fifty or sixty yards. Are you warm enough?"

"Yes," Leigh answered.

"See those lights up ahead? That's my partner, Baker Crawford. He's waiting to pick us up."

"Wonderful. I can't wait to get the hell out of these woods."

Camden smiled.

*

"I'm glad you're okay," Baker said as they walked over to his truck. It was running with the heat blasting inside. "It's going to get bad out there later tonight."

"Thank you. I'd still be there if Officer Gorely hadn't found me."

"She's the best," he said with a smile. "I hope you don't mind a little dog hair. Otis was out with me, helping to find you," he added, opening the door to the truck. He had a crew cab with four full doors. The large German Sheppard was sitting on the back seat, waiting patiently.

"He's adorable," Leigh said.

"I'll ride with Otis. You take the front seat," Camden said.

"It's okay. I don't mind."

"We're old friends," Camden added, getting in beside the dog. He waited for her to extend her hand. Then, he sniffed it and licked her face before lying down on the seat.

Leigh smiled and got into the front passenger seat.

Baker put the truck in drive and headed towards the cabin. The rest of the crew had been dismissed once Baker radioed that he could see them, so the only vehicles in the driveway were Leigh's car and Camden's truck.

"I don't know how to thank you," Leigh said, getting a little choked up when she got out of the truck.

"It's fine. This is my job…our job."

Leigh nodded.

"What are your plans for tomorrow?" Camden asked.

“Uh…” Leigh stumbled.

“I pulled you over for speeding yesterday and rescued you in the woods today. I just wanted to know what I was in for tomorrow since we keep running into each other,” she said with a cheeky grin.

“Oh.” Leigh laughed and shook her head. “I’m not leaving this cabin, so you’re safe to go about your day.”

“I appreciate that. Have a good night.”

“You too.” Leigh waved and headed into the cabin.

Baker stood in front of his truck. His hands were in his jacket pockets and a puzzled expression on his face. “Care to explain?”

“What?”

“Nothing.” He shrugged.

“Uh-huh. Get out of here. I’m tired, hungry, slightly cold, and I want to go home,” she grumbled. “Great work tonight,” she added, shaking his hand before going to get into her truck.

Chapter 8

Leigh stared out the window across the cabin at what looked like a real-life Bob Ross painting of beautiful spruce and fir trees covered with white snow, and bare trees jutting out of the ground like white stick figures. “I could lie here all day,” she murmured, snuggling the heavy comforter.

Her ordeal the day before had shaken her more than she’d realized, but the attractive wildlife officer coming to her rescue had stirred her in a completely different way…one she wasn’t interested in exploring, not physically, and certainly not mentally. She’d gone up to Chester Mountain to clear her head and slow down, not complicate her life even more.

A light dusting of snow began falling as she reached over to grab her ringing cell phone. “I’m certainly not going anywhere now,” she mumbled.

“What? Hello? Leigh?”

“Hey,” she replied, clearing her throat.

“Thank God you’re okay. I was pacing the floor until you finally texted me.”

“I had to wait for my phone to find life again. I’m sorry it took so long. I would’ve asked the wildlife officer to use her phone, but I couldn’t remember your number. Hell, I don’t think I actually know your number.”

“Don’t you just love technology? I think it’s made us all dumber, to be honest.”

“I agree.”

"So, wait…the good-looking wildlife officer from yesterday? She was with you?"

"She rescued me."

"Get out of here! Are you serious?"

"Yep," Leigh sighed. "She also works with search and rescue."

"Snap a picture next time you see her."

"What?! No. And I don't plan on seeing her again."

"You weren't planning on getting lost in the woods either," Abby chided.

"Yeah, well, you can bet your ass I won't do it again," Leigh declared.

"How the hell did it happen, anyway? I've known you for five years. You've never gone hiking."

"Looking back on it now, I was stupid. I don't know what the hell I was thinking. After seeing those deer, I wondered if I'd see a moose, so I took a walk. The next thing I know, I turned around and there was nothing but trees behind me. I tried walking back in the direction I thought I came from, but I must've turned and didn't remember."

"Wait…you got lost walking around looking for a moose? Who are you? And what have you done with Leigh Myer?"

"Funny." Leigh rolled her eyes as she got out of the bed. She'd waited long enough for a cup of coffee. She noticed a lot more snow had fallen during the night, adding nearly six inches to the ground. "It was actually quite relaxing…until I realized I was lost. It's really beautiful up here, Abby. It reminds me of a Christmas Hallmark movie."

"So, you've said."

"The view from my bed is like a life-sized Bob Ross painting. You should really see this place, Abby."

"No thanks. I'm good right here in the city. Hey, Doctor Parnell asked where you were yesterday."

"What did he want?"

"Probably to get you to do his bitch work like usual."

"Asshole," Leigh grumbled.

"Ah…there's my friend," Abby chuckled. "So, what are your plans for today, Miss Adventurer?"

"It's snowing pretty heavy at the moment; therefore, I'm staying right here in this cabin."

"Good idea. Listen, I gotta go. My shift starts in half an hour. Thankfully, I'm off for the next two days."

"Tell Parnell to kiss my ass."

"I honestly think he likes you and knows he can't have you, so he's being a dick."

"Why are men so stupid?"

Abby laughed. "Girl, if I knew, I wouldn't have married an asshole cheater who put me through hell."

"Yeah," Leigh sighed softly.

*

Camden was happy to have a day off and was planning on replacing the kitchen faucet, until she noticed the conditions outside. She was usually called in to help cover the roads when it was snowing heavily.

She put her hand on the wall next to the window, leaning slightly towards it while she looked out. Steam from the mug of coffee she was holding fogged one of the square panels. Stepping away, she glanced at the faucet boxes sitting on the dining table.

"I know as soon as I shut the water off and start this, they'll call," she muttered, shaking her head and walking away to gather her white-out gear and place it on the futon couch by the door. She'd kept everything she needed for fish and wildlife and search and rescue in the truck. White-out conditions weren't rare up on the mountain, but they weren't often enough to carry the extra equipment with her on a daily basis.

*

Two hours later, Camden hadn't heard from anyone, so she shut off the water to her cabin and squeezed herself into the cabinet under the sink. The nut on the old faucet took a little extra strength to get it loose with the pipe wrench in the tight space, but once she broke it free, she unhooked the water lines and removed it easily.

Camden's barefoot tapped the floor to the beat of the Dion song playing on the radio. It only picked up two stations; one was the eighties and the other was the oldies. They both drove her crazy at first, but she'd slowly grown accustomed to them over the years.

"Oh, I'm the type of guy who will never settle down. Where pretty girls are, you know that I'm around," she sang as she got the new faucet out of the box. "They call me the wanderer, yeah the wanderer. I roam around, around, around," she continued, crawling back under the sink.

When she reached up to tighten the new faucet nut, her phone began ringing. On instinct, Camden sat up, banging her forehead on the cabinet she was lying in. "Son of a bitch!" she yelped, immediately putting her hand up to see if she'd broken the skin. Thankfully, she'd just have a nasty bruise.

By the time the throbbing pain subsided enough for her to slide herself out, the ringing had stopped and the voicemail notification chimed. She ignored the missed call log and went straight to the message.

"Hey, just checking to see if you were called. Apparently, I was given a real day off. Otis and I are making chili. You're welcome to stop by. Otherwise, I'll bring you some tomorrow. Be safe if you're out in this mess. Tomorrow should be loads of fun with all of this fresh powder."

"Damn you, Baker," she growled, tossing the phone onto her recliner a few feet away as she turned to go back to the sink. On a whim, she spun around and picked it up.

Didn't get called. Working on the sink. Chili will be great for lunch tomorrow! she texted. Then, she went down the hall to the bathroom to look at the knot already forming on her forehead near her hairline.

Fire by the Pointer Sisters was playing when she walked back into the room. Camden grabbed the pipe wrench from the counter, singing into it, "I say I don't love you, but you know I'm a liar," as she got back down on the floor under the sink. "Cause when we kiss…ohhh, fire!" she continued, tightening the water lines while both feet tapped to the music.

Once she was finished, she carefully extricated herself, turned the water back on, and flipped the handle up. The new faucet was bronze like the old one, but much taller, giving her more room in the sink. The spout was also retractable which was an added bonus and a feature she hadn't had before.

"Piece of cake," she gloated.

*

Unable to find anything interesting on the TV, Leigh turned to the radio. The first two stations were country, which she'd moved past, before coming to a stop on a station playing The Pointer Sisters. She turned up the volume, then danced and sung her way into the kitchen to make herself something for lunch.

"You had a hold on me right from the start. A grip so tight I couldn't tear it apart," she sang into the fork she was holding.

The microwave beeped, indicating her leftovers were nuked and ready to eat. She pulled the bowl out and sat down on the couch with her body turned so she could see out the French doors and massive windows surrounding them. The heavy snowfall looked like it had slowed down, but she had no plans to go outside and check it out. Her mind drifted to the wildlife officer *Camden Gorely*, wondering if she was out working in the harsh conditions.

"She probably thinks I'm crazy," she mumbled through bites of pasta.

*

"Did you get that faucet put in?" an old man asked.

Camden smiled even though she was on the phone. "Yes, Uncle Pa. I finished a couple of hours ago, actually."

"I said I'd come help you."

"It wasn't a big deal. How was business today?"

"Oh, pretty slow. Not many people out and about town with that heavy snow. The plows could barely keep up."

"I'm sure the roads were horrible," Camden agreed.

"You weren't out in it, were you?"

"No, surprisingly."

"Good. We were worried you'd be called in."

"The trails and mountain access roads were closed. Anyone on the mountain was pretty much stuck inside. Tomorrow will be a mess I'm sure. Everyone will be out in the fresh powder."

"Yeah. You be careful out there."

"Always. My love to you and Aunt Ma," she said before hanging up and walking outside onto the small, open front porch. A couple of inches of snow had blown in, up against her door, but the heavy dusting of snow had completely stopped. She slipped her boots on and grabbed the shovel to go clear it from her door.

Chapter 9

Leigh held her breath as she slowly followed the road down the mountain. The plow had come and cleaned the snow away, but there was still ice on the ground. She wanted to explore the town, and her stomach was growling. She remembered the small mom and pop restaurant she'd seen when she'd first arrived, except there were no open parking spaces nearby, and more than a handful of people were standing outside, obviously waiting on a table. She was about to circle back around when a space opened up. She quickly whipped into it and walked the short distance down the sidewalk to the restaurant entrance.

"Welcome to Ma and Pa's," said an older lady with white hair pulled up in a loose bun. She smiled and pushed her dark-blue framed glasses up a little higher on her nose. "It's about a thirty-minute wait for a table right now."

Leigh looked around, noticing there were only about ten tables in the whole place and a diner-style bar in the back with a few open stools.

"Is it okay to go to the bar?"

"Sure." The woman smiled, waving her hand towards that area.

As she walked away, Leigh noticed someone in a green uniform near one end. She couldn't tell if the person was male or female until she heard laughter. *It's her!* She headed over to the open seat next to her as soon as an older man walked away.

*

"Lou, that's hilarious," Camden said with a smile. "How in the hell did you get it out of your house?"

"I haven't." The old man shook his head. "Damn thing's still in there!"

"Oh, shit," she laughed. "Did you call it in?"

"Yes. They told me someone would be out today."

"I'm headed up the mountain in a little while, I'll come by on my way and get it out of there. Will you be around?"

"Yeah," he said, patting her on the shoulder as he stood and pulled a ski cap onto his nearly bald head before walking away.

"This seat taken?" a female voice asked.

Camden turned her head slightly, noticing the vacationer, *Leigh*. "It is now," she replied with a smile.

"What's good here?" Leigh asked, pulling a menu from the stack nearby.

"What isn't?"

"That good, huh?"

"Breakfast, lunch, and dinner."

Leigh nodded, perusing the menu. "If you're not heading out right away, I was hoping to buy you a cup of coffee or something to say thank you."

"That's not necessary. I was just doing my job. Besides, any more coffee and I'm going to be floating."

Leigh chuckled.

"Although, a blueberry muffin would be good for the road."

"Deal," Leigh said, looking up to get the server's attention. She quickly ordered her breakfast and added the muffin.

"My phone didn't ring yesterday, and seeing as how you're here now, you must've made it through the day with no issues," Camden said.

"It's a miracle," Leigh replied with a cheeky grin. "I honestly never went outside."

"I'm sure no one else did either. The entire mountain was closed."

"Wow. How often does that happen?"

"Only a few times during the winter season, when we get white-out conditions." Camden checked her watch.

"Are you about to leave?"

"In a few minutes." Camden nodded. "I'm heading up to the snowmobile trails, but I have to go get a weasel out of a guy's house first."

Leigh laughed. "Seriously?"

"Yep."

"Do they bite?"

"I hope not."

"That's crazy," Leigh exclaimed. She shook her head when she watched Camden's thin lips curl into a grin. "Now, I hope it does bite you."

Camden laughed.

The older woman at the hostess stand when Leigh had arrived, walked over with the blueberry muffin. "I had a feeling this was for you," she said, patting Camden on the forearm.

"Thanks. You know me so well," Camden replied with a smile.

"Since you were knee-high to a grasshopper." The older lady called over her shoulder as she walked away to take care of a table.

"So, you're obviously not a skier. What brought you to Chester Mountain?" Camden questioned, turning her attention back to the beautiful woman beside her. Lou's weasel could wait. There was something about this woman that she couldn't quite put her finger on.

"I don't know. Life I guess." Leigh sipped her coffee.

"That's…interesting."

"Not really. My friend owns the cabin I'm staying in. It was her idea to come up here actually."

Camden nodded. "What do you do?"

"I'm a nurse practitioner in the ER of a very busy, dilapidated old hospital."

"Don't let Doctor John find out you're here. He'll be recruiting you to stay."

"Who is he?"

"The only doctor within thirty miles of here. His office is right down the street."

"Wow. I bet he's busy."

"Yeah. He's about to retire and hand the reins to his son. He's wanted to add a nurse practitioner forever."

"I'm only here for two weeks…max. He'll have to look elsewhere." Leigh smiled.

"Yeah," Camden trailed off as Leigh's breakfast plate was placed in front of her. "I should probably go deal with that weasel and let you eat breakfast. If I don't see you again, enjoy your time in Chester."

Leigh placed her hand on Camden's, stopping her from getting up.

Camden froze, looking from the hand touching hers, warming her skin like an insulated glove, to the gorgeous bluish-gray eyes staring back at her.

"Thank you for finding me yesterday. You saved my life," Leigh said sincerely.

"You're welcome," Camden murmured.

Leigh removed her hand and Camden disappeared into the crowd of people still waiting for a table.

*

Lou's place was a two-story farmhouse that sat just above the base of the mountain. He'd owned several acres and a working dairy farm before retiring twenty years earlier and selling everything off. His wife had passed away three years ago, so he was alone in the old house.

"Alright," Camden said, pulling on thick, arm length protective sleeves. "Where is it?"

"I trapped it in the spare room downstairs," Lou replied, showing her the way.

Camden walked inside and Lou closed the door. The last thing they needed was the thing getting loose in the rest of the house. There were way too many hiding places.

As she walked around the bed, the small animal darted past her. Camden dove on the ground, grabbing the long, skinny mammal with one hand around its torso and the other near its hind legs. It squealed and began biting at her covered hands, but its sharp teeth were too tiny to penetrate the thick material.

She quickly got up off the floor, holding the squirmy animal out at arm's length. "I got it!" she yelled.

Lou pulled the door open and slid in the small, cat carrier style cage that she'd brought along with her. Camden let go of its hind legs, still gripping its torso with her other hand as she shoved it inside and slammed the door shut. It started flailing around, scratching at the plastic.

"Man, that thing is pissed!" Lou exclaimed.

"Yeah," Camden chuckled. "I'm going to take it to a wooded area a few miles away and let it go."

"Hopefully, it doesn't return."

She shook her head. "Nah, it'll probably avoid the area."

"Great."

"Have a good day," she said, walking out of the house with the carrier.

"I will now, thanks, Camden."

She stowed the cage on the front floorboard of her truck, then slipped into the driver's seat. "You behave and I won't leave you in bear territory, you got it?" she said, glancing down at the animal staring back at her as she backed out of the driveway.

*

Leigh finished her breakfast, leaving a good portion on the plate. It was most definitely a country breakfast, and a lot more than she was used to eating. However, it had been the best breakfast she'd ever had.

Afterward, she walked around for a few hours, snapping pictures and taking in the beauty of the small, postcard town. She'd stopped in various places and talked to a few locals and other vacationers. One particular store was very small and full of locally made jams, jelly, butter, maple syrup, which was the state staple, and a few other foods. She'd purchased a handful of items to try during her stay. On the way out, she passed by the century-old church and stopped on the sidewalk out front.

"You're welcome to come inside," a male voice said as she peeked through the open doors.

"Oh, no thanks. I'm just walking around."

"Are you sure?" the pastor said, walking outside to greet her. "There's a lot of history in this little building."

"I don't doubt it."

"We only have services on Sundays, but the church is open seven days a week to anyone seeking salvation, or simply needing a reminder."

"What is it you think I'm after?" she asked, meeting his eyes.

"You're running from something," he replied softly.

Slightly taken aback, she cleared her throat and shifted her weight.

"You'll know when it's time to stop," he added, offering a gentle smile.

"Thank you." Leigh nodded and walked away. She wasn't a religious person, not the least bit, but somehow that clergyman had seen right through her, and it rattled her. She headed back to her car and started the engine.

Chapter 10

Camden sat in her UTV, thankful she'd worn extra layers to protect her from the temperature in the teens and wind chill down to the high single digits. She was parked between two large trees where she could see down the trail in front of her in both directions, but no one would see her until they were right on her and passing by.

In the past two hours, she'd busted five people for speeding, and one for not wearing a helmet. The 35 MPH trail speed limit was posted in several places, and was also on the trail maps available for anyone new to the area and heading out for a ride.

Hearing another sled approaching, she held her radar gun up, zeroing in on the blue machine racing towards her from the left. The number 47 lit in bright red LED lights. Camden shook her head and started the UTV. She put it in gear and pulled out to the edge of the trail and got out. The thin light bar on the front and back had tiny blue strobes flashing.

"Don't you run…" she mumbled, walking further into the trail as the sled slow down. The last she thing wanted to do was chase the damn thing all over the mountain. There was no way she'd be able to keep up in the UTV.

She was standing close to the middle of the trail as the driver approached and cut the engine. "Where are you coming from?" Camden asked.

"Timber Pass," he replied, removing his helmet.

"You have your ID and registration?"

He nodded and got his wallet out of his jacket pocket. "Did I do something wrong?"

"Are you aware of the speed limit on this trail?"

He shook his head. "I wasn't paying attention. I just bought this sled from my buddy. I was out riding around to see how good it ran."

"Between here and the pass, you went by at least four posted signs."

"Damn," he mumbled.

"Sit tight for a second."

Camden walked over to her UTV and sat down on the seat while she radioed dispatch to run his license and registration. At the same time, she wrote out the speeding ticket. By the time she'd finished, she got word that he was clear, and headed back over to him. He was leaning against the sled, smoking a cigarette, which he tossed down as she walked up.

"It's a $5000 fine for tossing lit cigarettes down on state-owned land," she scolded.

"Seriously?" he squeaked and dove down, looking for it in the snow.

"You're lucky there is heavy snow on the ground to put it out. How do you think forest fires are started? Bears and deer don't smoke!"

He gulped down the lump in his throat. "I…I'm sorry. I didn't—"

"Exactly. You didn't think about the consequences of tossing that lit cigarette down, or driving twelve miles per hour over the limit, which is set for a reason. It's not a guesstimate or suggestion," she lectured. "First of all, there are hazards that you will not see while operating that machine at a high rate of speed. Second, there are other riders, including children, all over these trails."

"I really am sorry. I wasn't paying attention."

She handed him the ticket. "This is a citation for speeding on a marked, public trail. Sign on the line. This is not an admission of guilt. It simply means you agree to either pay the fine by the date on the back, or set an adjudication to go in front of a judge."

He nodded, signing his name.

Camden kept the top copy and gave him the yellow one. Then, she went back to her UTV as he donned his helmet and started the machine. She grinned as he drove away at a much safer speed.

Satisfied that she'd put somewhat of a dent in the speeders, she started the UTV and headed back towards her cabin to get her truck. Since her UTV was tagged for the street, she turned off the trail to save some time, cutting her own path to the main road nearby, which would take her further down to pick up a different trail.

She was barely a half mile away from where she'd been sitting, deep inside the trails, when she spotted a car off the road. It was facing the wrong direction after having obviously spun on the ice. "Shit," she muttered, flipping her lights and siren on. Thankfully, the car was out of the way of traffic passing by. As she got closer, she could tell the back corner was up against a snowbank and the tires were in snow too deep to drive out of on their own.

*

"Come on," Leigh grumbled, pressing the gas pedal, but the tires just spun in the wet snow. "This isn't happening to me," she cried, pounding the steering wheel with the ball of her fist. Nearly in tears and clenching her jaw, she begged herself to hold it together. *Please, please, please.*

The pastor had spooked her, seemingly looking right into her soul. Wanting to get as far away as possible, she'd headed back up to the cabin. Albeit, a little faster than she should have, which was why her car had spun around on the patch of ice and was currently stuck in the snow.

A light tap on the window got her attention. Leigh turned her head, seeing an FWC officer, dressed in their signature green uniform with a ski cap pulled down low, and sunglasses. *Oh, thank God.*

"I am so glad to see you," she said, opening her door.

"We have to stop meeting like this," Camden said, pulling her sunglasses off. "People will start talking," she teased, surprised to see that it was Leigh's car stuck in the snow.

"What…I..." Leigh mumbled nervously.

"I'm only kidding. But, it looks like you didn't heed my advice on following the speed limit."

"It wasn't intentional," she sighed.

"It never is." Camden shrugged. "At least you're okay. You *are* okay, right?" she questioned, looking her up and down as Leigh got out of the car wearing the same tight jeans, boots, and coat she'd seen her in earlier that morning, except a scarf was wrapped around her neck this time. The natural highlights in her wheat-blonde hair were even lighter in the sunlight as it hung down over her shoulders. *God, you're beautiful.*

"What? Yes. I'm fine, but my car is stuck."

"I see that. I can pull it out with my truck, but it's at my cabin, a few miles away. I can't advise you to stay here.

Even though the car is off the road, someone else could come along and hit the same ice and crash into it."

"You mean I have to ride with you in that thing?" Leigh grimaced, looking at the UTV.

Camden nodded.

"It looks cold. You…look cold."

"It is, if you're not dressed properly. Do you have a hat and gloves?"

"They're in the car," she replied, opening the door to get them out.

"Good. Bundle up as best you can," Camden said, walking over to the UTV. It had a windshield and doors, but no windows and certainly no heater.

Leigh climbed in and Camden helped her buckle the safety harness that went over her shoulders, before placing a helmet over her head that resembled something a cyclist or skateboarder would wear.

"Dispatch, Gorely. Be advised, there is a vehicle stuck in a snowbank on Bear Road about a mile south of Goose Neck. I'm with the driver now in my UTV, heading to get my truck," she radioed as she got into the opposite side, pulled her matching helmet on over her ski cap, and buckled herself in.

"Roger," the dispatcher replied. "Do you need EMS or a tow truck?"

"Negative. I'll pull it out with my truck. It doesn't appear to be damaged and the driver has no injuries," she radioed back as she started the machine and took off.

Leigh lurched back, grabbing onto the dash handle for dear life.

"I'm barely doing the speed limit," Camden laughed.

"Uh-huh."

"Hold on," Camden said, turning off the road and cutting her own path through the woods.

"Holy shit!" Leigh exclaimed over the noise of the engine.

"I thought you liked to go fast," Camden laughed.

Leigh cut her eyes at the woman next to her, almost daring her to make her mad. She wasn't a speeder, per se, but she did go over the limit from time to time. Never anything excessive, of course. But, the mild crash had startled her, and the idea of racing around the mountain where anything could happen with very little protection around her, wasn't appealing at the moment.

Camden kept her eyes on the terrain, though she was sure the woman next to her was staring in her direction. She grinned and kept driving…until they came up on a groomed trail that was a lot smoother ride. A few snowmobiles passed by before they cut off the trail again, onto untouched snow with trees all around.

Leigh gripped the handle so hard, her knuckles were going numb. *Where the hell are we going? She said her cabin? Right?*

"It's not too much further, about a half-mile," Camden said.

Finally, the trees opened up to the backside of a small cabin, nearly half the size of the one she was staying in. A bench made of tree limbs was off the side of the open front porch, with a handmade, stone fire pit in front of it. Camden brought the UTV to a stop at the double doors of a nearby shed. Leigh noticed the green FWC truck in the driveway.

Camden got out and pulled the doors open, revealing a bright green snowmobile with a wide empty space next to it, and a toolbox with a wide bench in the back. She quickly got back in and drove the UTV inside, parking it in the space beside the sled.

When she cut the engine, she grabbed her ticket book, and got out again, while Leigh remained in the UTV. Realizing she didn't know how to undo the safety harness, Camden went over to help her. "You just pull this tab," she said, grabbing a red strap. The harness loosened easily. Then, she pressed the button to unbuckle it. "There you go." She grinned, opening the door.

"Thanks," Leigh uttered, getting out. "Is this where you live?"

"Yep," Camden nodded, unlocking the truck's doors with the key fob. She'd already hit the electric start to get it going. "You can go get in. I just need to lock this up."

The distinct smell of mahogany and cedarwood, mixed with magnolia flowers, permeated the air inside the truck, catching Leigh's attention right away. It was rugged, but soft, and tickled her senses. She looked around for an air freshener of some sort when she realized it was probably Camden's cologne. She closed her eyes, inhaling the exotic scent.

*

Camden grabbed an extra snatch rope from her toolbox, then closed and locked the doors. She tossed the rope into the back of her truck next to the metal animal cage.

"We'll have your car out in a few minutes," she informed, climbing into the truck and buckling her seatbelt.

Leigh looked at her and smiled. *Why do you have to be so charming and smell so damn good?*

They were a little ways down the road when her radio went off. “Gorely, dispatch. We have a baby bear reported in a home on Snowshoe Lane. Are you still in the area?”

“Roger. Responding now,” she replied into her radio mic. “This is an emergency call. I have to go to it.”

“It’s okay. I understand.”

“I can have another officer meet me and take you to get your car out.”

Leigh shrugged. “It’s not like I have anything else going on. It’s fine.” She didn’t want to admit that she was a little intrigued about possibly seeing a real bear.

Camden turned the truck around and headed in the opposite direction with her lights and siren going. She was traveling a little faster than the speed limit.

“Gorely, you need an assist?” Baker radioed.

“Standby,” she replied, turning on a street a mile away, and eventually coming to a stop outside of a cabin that looked more like a house than the more traditional log structures found around the mountain. “Stay here,” she said, looking at Leigh as she put the truck in park. “I’ll leave it running so the heat is blowing.”

“Are you really going to go in there alone and get a bear out?” she questioned nervously.

“Yep. It’s my job,” Camden answered before getting out and opening the animal cage. She pulled out the smaller, plastic cat-carrier style cage, setting it aside. Then, she opened her toolbox and grabbed the thick protective sleeves she’d donned earlier in the day to remove the weasel.

*

"It's in the kitchen," a woman said from inside her car as Camden walked up. She'd rolled the window halfway down to talk to her. "I'm staying in here."

Camden smiled and nodded. "I understand. How big is it?"

"I don't know. I didn't hang out to see."

"Okay. I'm going to go check things out. Stay in here."

"Don't worry. I'm not going anywhere."

Camden walked up the couple of stairs and opened the door cautiously. Stepping inside, she kept one hand on her gun as she slowly peered around. Finally, she found a little black bear cub, no bigger than a small dog, sitting on the kitchen floor eating cheese crackers from a box he'd torn open. She walked closer, careful not to scare him. As soon as he saw her, he rolled over to his back, exposing his belly.

"Hi, little buddy," she whispered.

She bent down, coercing him to come closer. When he did, she lightly pet him. Seeing him relax even further, she sat down on the floor beside him and grabbed a handful of crackers. He made some cute squeaky noises and began eating them from her hand while she continued to pet his fur.

"Come on, I won't hurt you," she murmured.

As soon as she had complete control, she picked him up, cradling him with his paws out away from her body so he couldn't claw her as she walked out of the house. If he tried to bite, his tiny baby teeth wouldn't penetrate the protective sleeves.

*

Leigh gasped when she saw Camden come out of the house carrying a black ball of fur. “What the heck?”

Camden passed by her window, holding the baby bear up for her to see it.

“Oh, my gosh!” She quickly turned in her seat, trying to see what was happening, but the top of the toolbox was blocking her view as Camden placed the bear in the cage. She watched her go back in the house quickly, then she seemed to put something else in there with the animal. Leigh wanted to get out of the truck to take a better look at the cuddly little creature but knew it was best for her to stay put.

A minute later, Camden opened the driver door of the truck and slid into the seat, dusting the snow off her boots before shutting it. “All set?” she asked.

“Is that a bear you carried out?”

“Yeah. He’s just a baby, probably ten or twelve weeks old at most. His mother most likely went into hibernation after we got our first massive snowfall, and left him. I’m actually surprised he has survived this long.”

“What are you going to do with him?”

“I’ll take him to the animal conservation where veterinarians and animal keepers will care for him until the spring, then let him go back into the wild. It’s a place about a half-hour outside of Chester, where people can go year-round and see the animals that have been rescued. It’s kind of like a special zoo. It’s a nonprofit, so the money people pay to get in goes to helping the animals. I actually volunteered there to get community service hours for high school, and credits for college,” she replied, backing out of the driveway and heading down the road.

“Wow. I’d love to see it if you don’t mind.”

Camden shrugged. “I need to go pull your car out first.”

“Yes, that would be good,” Leigh chuckled. “I still can’t believe there is a bear in the back of this truck. What did you give him? I thought I saw you go back into the house.”

“The box of cheese crackers he was in there eating.”

“Seriously?” Leigh laughed, looking over at her.

“Yeah.” Camden grinned. “He’s hungry.”

Leigh smiled and shook her head. This woman was unlike anyone she’d ever met. The more time she’d spent around her, the more Camden Gorely intrigued her. *Don’t make me regret coming here.*

Chapter 11

"So, what happened with the weasel this morning?" Leigh asked as they drove along the county roads between Chester and Granville, where the conservatory was located. "I don't see any bandages."

Camden shrugged. "He was a mean little shit, but I got him out of the house without getting bitten."

"What did you do with him?"

"Tossed him back into the woods a few miles away."

"Does that happen often? Animals in people's houses, I mean."

"Nah…it's a fluke dealing with two in one day, but it does happen a few times a month."

"Wow. I couldn't imagine some wild animal in my kitchen. I'd probably faint and the damn thing would eat me," Leigh laughed.

Camden chuckled. "I've never encountered anything larger than a small bear in someone's house, and they aren't big enough to eat you…yet. It's going to hurt like hell if it bites you though. Same with a weasel or possum. They all have a nasty bite with sharp teeth."

"Wonderful," she muttered. "So, what else do you do besides get animals out of houses and catch speeders?"

"I basically enforce the law on the mountain from top to bottom. Mostly, dealing with hunters who can't follow simple rules. I also police the streams and creek for illegal fishing."

Leigh nodded.

"It's probably not as exciting as working in an emergency room," she added, pulling into the parking lot. "We shouldn't be here long."

Leigh got out and waited by the truck while Camden went inside. She couldn't help peering over the side at the little ball of dark fur in the metal cage. His snout was light brown, but the rest of his coat was shiny and black. He was sitting in the corner, looking around. The cardboard cracker box was destroyed with no evidence of the contents anywhere. "You're certainly cute," she said.

"Thank you," Camden replied from a few feet away, startling her.

Leigh jumped out of her skin." Oh, my God, you scared me," she exclaimed, shaking her head. "And I was talking to the bear, so…"

"Do you want to pet him?" Camden asked, lowering the tailgate as she prepared to remove the bear.

"Seriously?"

Camden shrugged. "He likes you."

Leigh furrowed her brow. "How do you know that?"

"Did he growl at you?"

"No."

Camden grinned.

Leigh rolled her eyes.

"Camden, we can put him in here to get him inside," a young woman said.

Leigh turned to see the brunette coming towards them with a small metal cage on a cart. She turned her chocolate-colored eyes to Leigh for a brief second, seemingly sizing her up as she maneuvered to the back of the truck, right beside Camden. *Slow down, honey,* Leigh thought, biting her tongue.

"That'll work." Camden opened the cage and pulled the fury mammal out. He made a tiny growling sound when she grabbed him, but he settled as soon as she began petting him.

"He's adorable," the young woman cooed. "You're so good with him."

Leigh rolled her eyes.

Camden slid him into the cage on the cart and closed the door. "He's all yours," she said, removing the protective sleeves. "Is Doctor Sullivan busy?"

"She was making rounds when you came in. I'm sure she's going to check him out right away."

"Okay." Camden saw Leigh out of the corner of her eye. "I'm sorry. Kelsey, this is Leigh Myer."

The young girl turned, acting like she had no idea Leigh had been standing there. "Oh, hi."

"Kelsey is one of the animal handlers here," Camden said, finishing her introduction. "Anyway, if it's okay, I'm going to take her around a little bit."

The young girl shrugged, then looked at Camden and smiled like a schoolgirl with a crush. "I'll tell the doc you're here," she said before pushing the cart towards the door.

"Well…you want to see some animals?" Camden asked as she pushed her sunglasses up and turned her pretty hazel eyes in Leigh's direction.

"Uh…yeah…sure."

"We can head back if you want—"

"No…I'm fine."

"Great." Camden hit the button to lock her truck and nodded for Leigh to come along as they headed towards the door. She grabbed the handle, ushering her in first.

*

The conservation center took care of sick or injured animals, but it was also a wildlife park for animals who could no longer be put back in the wild, or ones that needed to be rehabilitated. They also cared for baby animals who had been abandoned, preparing them for release once they were large enough to go into the wild. All of the schools in surrounding towns visited on field trips, and it was also open to the public like a zoo, with all of the proceeds going to help the animals. The building Leigh and Camden had entered was the vet facility with indoor cages that housed the animals with various sicknesses or injuries. They currently had few bears, a couple of deer, and a number of other locally found species, meandering about in different sized cages. The rest of the animals were in large outdoor cages in the park for people to see and learn about as they walked around.

"Over here, they have a little deer," Camden said excitedly. "She was found wandering around down in Chester last week with a serious limp. We thought she'd been shot at first, but there was no wound anywhere."

Leigh's heart melted when she saw the tiny deer, curled up in a ball in the corner with her legs tucked under her. Her head was turned around so she was facing the cage entrance. Her fur was light brown. "Awe," Leigh murmured.

Camden moved closer and held a carrot through one of the fence holes and the little animal got up. Both women watched like giddy kids as she walked over, sniffing the offering before taking a bite.

"Stick your fingers through and pet her," Camden whispered.

Leigh was mixed with anticipation and apprehension as she reached out, softly grazing the warm, slightly coarse fur of the deer as it gnawed on the carrot Camden was holding. Her racing heart slowly calmed as she continued petting the animal in soft, slow strokes.

"How old is she?" Leigh asked when she finished the snack and walked back over to sit down in the haystack.

"About six or seven months," a woman answered.

Leigh turned to see a woman standing nearby, wearing light blue scrubs. Her brown hair was pulled back in a bun.

"That little bear is a handful," she laughed, shaking her head.

"I should've brought you the weasel from this morning. Now, he was a handful," Camden chuckled, stepping over to hug the woman.

"No thanks," the woman laughed again, shaking her head.

"Leigh, this is Heather Sullivan. She's the head veterinarian here, and my cousin."

"Oh, wow," Leigh mumbled, shaking her hand.

"I see why Kelsey had her feathers all in a ruffle." Heather smiled. "It's nice to meet you."

Camden met her cousin's eyes and shook her head.

"So, what do you think of Misty?"

"Who's Misty?" Leigh asked, raising a brow.

Heather nodded towards the cage behind them where the deer was lying down.

"She's beautiful."

"Leigh got lost hiking recently because of a deer in her yard. She went in search of it," Camden stated.

"No. I saw the deer and her baby, and decided to go see if I could spot a moose."

"They hide in the thicket," Heather said.

"Yeah, I figured once I realized I was lost."

"I came to her rescue," Camden boasted.

Heather laughed. "Come on, let me show you around."

*

Leigh got to see half a dozen different animals, and pet a few more as well, including the little bear, which they'd saved for last. She was surprised at how coarse his hair felt as she'd brushed her hand over his back. The sun was already going down by the time they got back to Leigh's cabin. Camden pulled into the driveway and put the truck in park.

"Do you want me to go inside and check for animals?" she teased.

"I think I'm good. Thank you for taking me with you."

"Sure. It was my pleasure. Have a good evening."

"You too," Leigh said, smiling as her eyes found Camden's. She pulled away from the intense gaze and got out of the truck.

Camden watched her walk to the door and go inside before driving away.

*

"How were the trails today?" Baker asked as he sipped his beer.

"I'd almost forgotten about working them earlier," she replied, eating a bite of stew. "I had a pretty crazy day that actually started with a damn weasel in Louis Hainsworth's house."

He laughed. "Oh, they have a nasty bite."

"No kidding. This was one pretty pissed when I got there, but I was able to get it into the small cage without it chewing one of my fingers off. Anyway, I went to the trails after that." She ate a bite of stew and drank a sip of beer to wash it down before continuing. "I sat around for about two and a half hours. I got a handful of speeders and one guy with no helmet."

"That's not bad."

"I ran into Leigh Myer, stuck in a snowbank after spinning off the road on a patch of ice."

"Leigh Myer?"

"The hiker…"

"Oh… yeah. I remember her."

"We rode back to my house to change from the UTV to my truck, then before I could pull her car out, I got called to get a bear cub out of a house."

"You didn't take her with you…"

"Yeah." She nodded. "It was an emergency call and I was only a few minutes away, as opposed to going to her car in the opposite direction first."

"I heard you went out to the conservatory. I assume you got the bear."

"Yeah, he was maybe twelve weeks old at most. I hate to see them separated from their mother as babies, but he was fine when we got there."

"Wait. She went with you?"

Camden sipped her beer and nodded. "She asked."

Baker raised a brow.

"I took her around to see the animals. I'm pretty sure it opened her eyes. I don't think she wanted to leave."

"Uh-huh," he uttered.

"What was your day like?"

"It certainly wasn't as exciting as yours. So, when are you seeing her again?"

"I haven't planned to see her at all. It just keeps happening."

"Like fate," he implied.

"Not likely."

He shrugged. "I've known you for about five years, and I've never seen you date anyone."

"We live in a small town. The pickings are slim to none."

"She's pretty."

"She's a vacationer."

"Aren't those your favorite?"

"Not anymore. I'm too old for that shit."

"All I'm saying is, maybe she keeps falling into your lap for a reason."

"She *is* beautiful," she sighed, her mind drifting to Leigh's bluish-gray eyes as she nonchalantly peeled the label from her bottle. "Damn it, I'm not going there," she muttered, clearing her thoughts.

Baker checked his watch. "I should probably head out. Thanks for the stew."

"It's the least I could do to repay you for the chili," she shrugged.

"Maybe we should start a restaurant," he joked.

"Definitely not. My family certainly doesn't do it for the money."

He nodded. "What are you doing tomorrow?"

"Relaxing. I might take the snowmobile out or something. I didn't make any plans. I hate taking extra days off, but if I don't use these vacation days, I'll lose them."

"That's because you never take time off."

"I wouldn't know what to do with it."

He laughed. "Give them to me. I can find plenty of things to do."

Camden shook her head and smiled. "Get out of here."

*

"Oh, my God, Leigh! Are you okay?" Abby gasped.

"Yeah. I just bumped the snowbank, but I'd spun around and was stuck in the snow."

"Girl, I'm beginning to think you need to come back to the city," Abby laughed.

'I know right," Leigh chuckled. "If it wasn't for Camden coming by in her UTV, I have no idea how long I would've sat there."

"Camden?" Abby questioned. "Who is that?"

"She's the wildlife officer I keep running into."

"So, she came to your rescue again?"

"Pretty much," Leigh mumbled, sipping her wine. "I rode with her to her cabin to get her truck so she could pull my car out of the snow, then she got a call about a bear in someone's house."

"Did you go with her?"

"I had to because it was an emergency. I'm so glad I did. Abby, that baby bear was the cutest thing I have ever seen," she cooed. "I expected his fur to be soft, but it was coarse and really thick."

"Wait a second. You touched a bear?"

"Yeah. Camden and I took him to this place that rehabs injured or sick animals. They also take in babies who are taken from their mothers and prepare them to go out into the wild when they are old enough. It's a really neat place. I saw a baby deer too. Now, she was really soft, and so warm."

"Okay…who are you? And what have you done with my friend?"

Leigh laughed. "I just texted you a picture of the bear."

"Oh, how cute!"

"The other picture is a red fox that lives at the conservatory-like a family dog. Someone declawed him like a house cat and domesticated him, so he can't ever live in the wild. His name is Sly."

"Who's that holding him?"

"Camden."

"I see why you keep needing rescuing. I'm not gay, but if I were, I'd be up there with you. She looks like a snack, and girl, you are hungry!"

Leigh laughed. "Um…nothing is happening, or going to happen between us."

"Uh-huh."

"She *is* charming, and she wears the sexist smelling cologne. It's like a mixture of mahogany and cedar, similar to a man's cologne, but has a hint of magnolia. It's rugged, yet light and slightly sweet. I don't know how else to describe it, but it's divine."

"Uh-huh. And nothing is happening," Abby muttered.

"I'm serious." Leigh finished her wine and set the glass on the table as she curled her legs under her.

"You're there, she's there. She's hot, you're gorgeous. It sounds like fate to me. What more do you need? She's obviously not straight. Is she married?"

"I don't know. I don't know anything about her."

"Does she wear a ring?"

"She's been in gloves the whole time." Leigh thought back to seeing her at the restaurant and in the conservatory. "Wait, no ring. I saw her hands this morning at breakfast and then when she was petting the animals."

"So, you had breakfast with her, too?"

"No, she was there when I went in."

"You obviously keep running into each other for a reason."

"We only spoke for a few minutes, then she left to go get a weasel out of a house. It's not like I actually had breakfast with her."

"What's with the animals in people's houses? They don't shut their doors up there?"

"I have no idea. She says it happens a few times a month."

"Oh, hell no. I'll stay in the city."

Leigh giggled. "I need to go to bed. It's been a long day."

"I can't wait to see what your sexy officer has in store for you tomorrow. Perhaps a tour around her cabin…"

"On that note, I'm hanging up," Leigh guffawed.

Chapter 12

Leigh ran her hands over the soft sheets, feeling the coolness of the empty space next to her. The sun was just beginning to rise, casting an orange glow over the snow-covered trees and ground. Camden's hazel eyes filled her thoughts, reminding her of a wild animal. *I should be running from you.*

Before she knew it, she was out of the bed, dressed, and heading down the mountain towards the restaurant she'd eaten at the day before. She circled around several times, looking for Camden's green truck in one of the parking lots, but never found it. Eventually, she parked and went inside to eat, but the place was packed. She headed back out, deciding to shop around at some of the local stores for a gift to take back to Abby, all the while, watching for the green truck, and avoiding the old church.

"How much is this?" she asked, holding a statue of a moose on skis. "It looks like the sticker might have fallen off."

An older lady stepped out from behind the counter and walked over to her. "I believe they are all twenty-five."

"I'll take it," Leigh said, going into her purse for the cash. She hadn't found anything for Abby, but the statue would be a wonderful reminder of her trip once she returned home.

As soon as she walked out of the store, she saw an elderly woman slip and fall on the ice. Leigh immediately rushed over to her. "Ma'am, are you okay?"

The woman had a bleeding gash on the back of her head. Leigh quickly packed her hand with snow and stuck it on the wound. "You need EMS."

"It'll take them forever. The clinic's just down the street. Call Dr. John," she said.

"Do your back or hips hurt?"

"No. Just my head and my arm."

Leigh looked around. A couple of people had rushed over. "Can someone please call 9-1-1?"

"It'll be quicker if you take her down to Dr. John," a man said.

Leigh sighed in frustration. "Are you on blood thinners, ma'am?"

"Yes. Are you a doctor?" the woman asked, noticing Leigh assess her from top to bottom.

"No, ma'am. I'm a nurse practitioner. My car is over there. I'm going to go get it. Can you sit with her, sir?"

"Sure, but I don't know what to do."

"Just keep fresh snow on that cut. I'll be back in a minute," Leigh said before jogging across the street. She hopped in her car and sped out of the parking lot, pulling up alongside the curb. She threw it in park, and rushed around to help the man get her loaded into the front seat. Leigh grabbed a sweatshirt from the backseat that she kept for cold days in the hospital and used it to hold the snow against the woman's bleeding head. Once she was back in the driver's seat, she stepped on the gas, careful not to speed too fast through the middle of town. "Where is this clinic?"

"Right up here on the left. You can't miss it. Dr. John's been here for over thirty years."

"I'm new in town, so don't let me pass it," Leigh replied, looking ahead. She finally saw the sign for Chester

Clinic and Local Emergency. Dr. David John and Dr. Eric John were the names underneath. She pulled up to the door and rushed inside. "I need a wheelchair. I have an elderly woman in my car who needs emergency assistance."

A man wearing khaki pants, a white button-down shirt under a maroon sweater, and a white lab coat rushed around the check-in counter where he'd been standing. For a brief second, he reminded Leigh of Dermot Mulroney with his thick dark hair falling over his forehead and square jaw. He was definitely handsome. He grabbed a nearby wheelchair and rushed outside behind her.

"She fell on some ice and has an occipital laceration with a possible contusion. She's hemorrhaging due to blood thinners," Leigh said. "She wasn't knocked out, but I'd do a CT scan just to be safe. I tried to get someone to call 9-1-1, but everyone said to bring her here."

The man looked oddly at her.

"Sorry. I'm a trauma nurse practitioner. I'm here on vacation and happened to see her fall," she said as she opened the car door.

"Oh, Dr. John, I'm afraid it's a bad one this time," the older woman said.

"Heavens, Mrs. Whitmore…how in the world did you do this?"

"These darn new boots. I slipped on the ice."

"You're right," he murmured to Leigh after looking at her head. "Let's get you inside and take a better look at this."

Leigh helped him get her into the wheelchair, then rushed inside behind them. That's when she noticed the packed waiting room. "Oh my, it's busy in here."

"It's just me and my father. He's older and a little slower than he used to be. "I'm Eric John, by the way."

"Leigh Myer," she replied. "What are they all here for?"

"Oh, anything from a slip on the ice to a nasty cold," he replied, pushing Mrs. Whitmore into a room. "I'm going to get you up on this bed and we'll take a good look at that cut. You're going to need some stitches and we're going to do a CT scan to make sure there are no fractures or hematomas, okay?"

"I trust you." She smiled.

"I'm also going to have someone call Bud."

"Thank you."

"So, you're a nurse practitioner?" he asked once they stepped out of the room.

"Yes. I'm licensed in Vermont. I work at County General Hospital."

He nodded.

"I could take care of some of those patients for you while you tend to Mrs. Whitmore, if you'd like."

"Are you sure? You're here on vacation."

"It's nothing. Show me where you keep your scrubs. I'll get changed and be ready to go."

"We don't wear them. Dad says that makes the place feel too stuffy," he laughed.

She pursed her lips. "Okay, I guess I can go with what I've got on. How about a stethoscope?"

"In the top drawer at the check-in desk. Are you sure you're okay doing this?"

"I wouldn't have offered if I wasn't. Please…tend to her. I'll be fine." She walked up front, searching the drawers until she found the stethoscope, which she hung around her neck. "Okay," she whispered under her breath as she grabbed the first clipboard. Everything in the clinic was old school pen and paper. Even her old raggedy hospital wasn't that far behind the times.

"I'm working on changing everything to a new computer system with handheld tablets once dad retires next month," he said, stepping around her. "Can I have your attention, please? Due to an emergency, we're a little behind schedule. This is Leigh, she's a city hospital nurse practitioner, meaning she can do just about everything a doctor can do. She's offered to help us out by seeing some patients. Of course, if you'd rather wait for myself or my father, it may be a couple of hours."

"I'm just going to go down the list here," Leigh said. "Harriet Belcher?"

"That's me," an older woman stood up and set the magazine she'd been reading back onto the pile.

"Wonderful." Leigh shook hands with her before walking her back to a room. "What brings you in today? It says here you have a sore throat."

"Yes. It's been hurting like the dickens for two days now. I can barely eat anything."

"Have a seat up on the table and I'll take a look at it. Are you on any medications?"

"Yes. They're all listed on the second page," she replied, nodding towards the paperwork on the clipboard.

"Great." Leigh took her temperature and checked her ears. Everything was normal. "Open your mouth for me." The woman did as she was told and Leigh saw the culprit right away. Her throat and mouth were covered with white puffy bumps. "Are you on any new medication?"

The woman nodded. "I have two new inhalers, actually. They're for my emphysema. Do you smoke?"

"No, ma'am."

"Good girl. Don't ever start," she said, shaking her head. "I feel okay with my meds, and don't need an oxygen tank. I'm lucky. They caught it early."

"Well, Mrs. Belcher, it looks like you have a nasty case of thrush. Have you ever had that before?"

"No. I don't recall. Is it contagious?"

Leigh chuckled. "No, ma'am. It's sort of like a yeast infection in your mouth. It's caused by the inhaled medicine. I'm going to write you a prescription for an antibiotic. That should clear it up in a few days. Also, eat some plain yogurt. That'll help as well, and always gargle with water and rinse your mouth after you take your medicine. That'll keep it from reoccurring."

"Thank you," the older woman said.

Leigh showed her out and handed her the prescription. Then, she grabbed the next chart. "Harold Pearce?"

"I'll wait for Doc John," he rasped, coughing.

"Okay, but that sounds like a nasty cold. I could have you out of here and home in your bed."

"Fine. I've had two heart attacks," he said, walking up to her.

"Well, I've had none, so I think we're good," she replied with a smile as she showed him into the room. "How long have you had that cough?"

"About two weeks. My nose is all snotty and I'm coughing up green shit."

Leigh grinned and nodded. She quickly went to work checking his temperature, looking in his nose and throat, then listening to his lungs. "Your lungs sound clear, so no pneumonia. It sounds like an upper respiratory infection. I'm going to write you a prescription for an antibiotic. I want you to also get Mucinex. It's over the counter. It's an expectorant that will make your coughing more productive, and it also controls the cough. If this hasn't cleared up in a couple of weeks or gets worse, come back in, but I think you'll be fine."

"I'm going to take your word for it," he said.

"Sounds good." She winked.

*

After seeing another half dozen patients, the waiting room was beginning to thin out. There were only three more people waiting. Mrs. Whitmore thankfully did not have a skull fracture, so Dr. John had sewn up her head and sent her home with her husband an hour earlier.

"Thank you so much for doing this. Can we pay you anything?" the senior Dr. John said.

"Oh, no. It was my pleasure. I love interacting with patients and solving their problems. I don't get to do much of that in the hospital."

"At least let me buy you lunch," the younger Dr. John said.

"Go on. I've got these last three."

"It can't be lunchtime already," she replied, checking her watch.

"How about a cup of coffee and a muffin instead?"

"Sure." She smiled, feeling her stomach growl from skipping breakfast.

*

Ma and Pa's restaurant was packed, but they were shown to a table within a couple of minutes. "If you haven't eaten here, everything is good," he said.

"I've only had breakfast," she replied, perusing the menu.

"So, what brings you to Chester? Are you and your husband skiing?"

"No husband, and I'm not a skier. Actually, I came up to my friend's cabin for a little R&R."

"And I put you to work," he laughed.

"Nah, I put myself to work. I can't resist helping people. It's what makes me good at my job."

"You're definitely good, that's for sure. Say, you're not looking to hang around in Chester are you? Maybe thinking of getting away from the city for longer than a vacation?"

"No. Why?"

"My father is retiring in a month. After that, it'll just be me. We have a part-time nurse, but a nurse practitioner with trauma experience who can see patients would be a dream come true around here. I don't have a huge budget, but there's some wiggle room…if you're interested."

"Oh, wow. Thank you for the offer, but I have to decline. I'm only here for two weeks, and then I have to get back to the hospital and my normal life in the city."

The older lady running the restaurant came over to take their orders.

"Get whatever you want. It's on me," he said. "This is Leigh. She's a nurse practitioner who is here on vacation and would you believe she just spent the last two hours helping us with patients down at the clinic?"

"Did you really? That's very kind of you," the older lady said.

"It was nothing. However, I am hungry after all of that," Leigh replied, ordering a cup of coffee and a fresh muffin.

Once the lady had both orders, she disappeared to the kitchen.

"Since you won't let me give you a job, how about dinner one night before you go?"

"Oh, lunch is more than enough, Doctor John."

"Please…call me, Eric."

"Thank you for the offer, Eric…but I have a full schedule for the rest of my time here," she lied.

"Well, definitely don't let me keep you from enjoying our town and our mountain," he said with a smile.

*

A white, snowy rooster tail shot out from behind the snowmobile as Camden cut her own trail across state-owned land. She made a quick turn, heading down the mountain on a switchback. She loved the rush of riding her snowmobile fast through the snow, between the trees, and near the edge that dropped off hundreds of feet.

She'd passed by a couple of other fast riders, but she wasn't working and didn't have her ticket book with her. Since they weren't doing anything stupid, and not racing through the groomed trails, she didn't have a reason to mess with them. Instead, she made another turn to go in the opposite direction, which led to the road Leigh's cabin was on. She spotted her car turning in the driveway and crossed the road, coming to a stop behind her.

*

Leigh bobbed her head to the Beatles *Hard Day's Night* as she turned off the main road, heading back to the cabin after spending close to half the day in town. She was happy the plow company had finally come to clear the light snow from the driveway. Sliding around in it when she was leaving that morning, was certainly no fun. The city she lived in was plowed constantly, so she never bothered with actual snow tires, although she did keep all-weather tires on her car.

As soon as she turned the car off and swung the door open, she heard the whine of a snowmobile. She got out in time to see the green machine pull into the driveway behind her car. The driver was unrecognizable in a bright blue jacket, black bib pants, and a black and blue, full-faced helmet. Leigh stiffened with fear. No one knew where she was except Abby. She contemplated getting back into her car, but the anxiety building inside of her faded as soon as the driver's helmet was removed. Camden's smiling face greeted her like a ray of sunshine.

"Hey," Camden said, climbing off the machine and walking towards her.

"You scared the hell out of me. I had no idea who you were."

"Sorry. Safety first," Camden replied, nodding towards the helmet she'd placed on her seat.

"Where's your uniform?"

"I *do* get days off every now and then." Camden grinned. "I stopped by to see if you wanted to go for a ride."

"What? On that thing?"

"There are some beautiful places on this mountain that are only accessible by snowmobile. I'll give you a tour if you want."

Leigh looked at the menacing-looking machine, then back at Camden patiently waiting for an answer. She bit her lower lip between her teeth and sighed.

"I won't let you get hurt," Camden murmured, sensing her apprehension.

"Alright," she said, grinning. "I don't have any ski clothes though."

"I probably have something that will fit you. I need to gas up anyway. Make sure you're wearing a base layer under your jeans and jacket, and have thick, wool socks on inside your boots. My cabin is only about two miles away. Once we get there, you can change into snowboard pants and a jacket. They'll keep you warm."

"Let me put this stuff in the cabin really quick. I'm already wearing layers under my clothes, so I should be good to go."

Camden watched her walk away, before going back to the sled to retrieve the goggles she kept in a pouch above the handlebars. She had them in case she ever needed to give up her helmet. That way, she'd be able to see to drive.

*

"This is crazy," Leigh mumbled to herself as she set her purse and bags down on the couch. She looked out the window at Camden leaning against the seat of the sled like the cool kid with the best bicycle in the neighborhood. *Damn you for being so charismatic.*

"Abby would die if she knew what I was about to do," she laughed to herself as she pulled the door closed and locked it, storing the key in her coat pocket. "All ready," she exclaimed with a big smile.

Camden handed Leigh her helmet.

"Isn't this yours?"

"Yes, but I trust myself. You've never been on one of these, correct?"

Leigh nodded.

"Besides, if you think it's cold now, wait until we're moving. It'll keep you warm. And, I promised to keep you safe." She shrugged. "My snowmobile is mostly used for work, so it's not a traditional two-seater, per se. Instead of a passenger behind the driver, there is a cargo box that sits there. It's easy to take off, so I remove it when I'm not working. Anyway, the seat is plenty big enough for two people, but there are no handles for a passenger." Camden turned, facing her. "What I'm trying to say is, you'll have to hold onto me the whole time. Is that okay?"

Leigh nodded, afraid her voice would fail her if she tried to speak.

"Okay. Let me help you with that, and we'll get going." Camden pointed to the helmet. "Slide it on and I'll help you get it buckled."

As soon as she pulled the helmet down over her head Leigh smelled Camden's cologne. *Oh, good lord. I'm not going to survive this.*

Camden buckled the straps, then climbed onto the sled. She held her hand out to assist Leigh as she swung her leg over the seat, placing her boot on the foot rail along the side. "Whatever you do, keep your feet on this rail at all times, and don't let go of me. You can't squeeze me to death, so don't be afraid to hold on tight. Also, you want to keep that visor open about half an inch to allow some air to come on. Otherwise, it'll be fogged up. If you need to talk to me or stop for any reason, just tap me like this…" Camden patted her on the top of her shoulder. "It doesn't matter where, as long as it's hard enough to get my attention. Any questions?"

"No," Leigh muttered, shaking her head. *I must be going crazy to willingly get on the back of this thing.*

"Here we go!" Camden bumped the key and the machine came to life, vibrating underneath them as it idled. She slid the goggles down over her eyes, then pulled up her jacket's hood. She tightened the drawstrings to keep it tight around her so she'd be warm.

Leigh slid closer, wrapping her arms around Camden's waist. *I've lost my damn mind.*

Camden pressed the thumb lever about halfway, allowing the clutch to engage. Then, the sled took off with the teeth of the drive belt making a loud chattering sound on the ground as they crossed the street. Once they were in the snow, the noise disappeared. She quickly cut between two trees and over a low snowbank, before picking her speed up slightly as she motored along the untouched terrain. She stayed around 15MPH so it wouldn't be too cold for Leigh since she wasn't wearing the proper clothing. She avoided the groomed trails because she was breaking the law by not wearing a helmet. Instead, she rode through the fresh powder of the backcountry, careful to avoid rocks and logs.

*

Leigh knew they weren't going very fast, but she still held on for dear life. Her legs were freezing. Her upper body was tucked behind Camden and mostly against her, so she was fairly warm. The sled rocked around, rolling from side to side and up and down with the terrain beneath it. When they came up on a tight turn for a switchback that would climb them a little higher, Camden threw her hips to the side, nearly hanging her butt off the sled to help it turn as she gassed the engine. Leigh had no idea what to do, so she moved with her, just not as far off the seat. The snowmobile raced around the turn and began climbing through the heavy snow. The front skis came off the ground as the belt dug in, pulling them up the hill. Leigh was scared to look left. She was sure they were near the edge of the mountain and she didn't want to see how far down the fall would be.

Camden seemed at ease, driving the machine like she'd been doing this all of her life, which made Leigh feel a little less anxious.

Before long, they came to a small clearing full of white snow. Leigh remembered seeing it when they were in the UTV, so she knew Camden's cabin was close by. *Finally.* She hoped the blood in her legs wasn't frozen.

*

Camden slid to a stop near her driveway, but still in the snow so she wasn't riding across the pavement. She turned the key to stop the engine and pulled the goggles off. "Everything okay?" she asked, feeling Leigh slide back away from her before climbing off.

"My legs are ice cold," Leigh said, trying to get the helmet loose.

Camden stepped over to her and unbuckled it. "Come on," she said, nodding towards her cabin as she carried the helmet over and unlocked the door.

Leigh looked around as she walked in behind her. The cabin was definitely smaller than the one she was in, but it felt cozy, and certainly lived in. It reminded her of a rustic bachelor pad. The main room had a gray recliner in the middle, facing a small TV on a wooden stand. A blue and black flannel blanket was hung off the back, and a handmade end table sat next to it. A wood-burning stove was beside the TV stand, and a futon couch was against the wall by the door, adjacent to the chair. A small, four-person dining table sat near the wall on the opposite side of the room, a few feet from the chair. A small, open storage loft was above the front door and futon couch, and extended about four feet into the room. The kitchen was basically the strip of wall behind the recliner. The refrigerator and stove were beside the ladder accessing the loft, near the door. Upper and lower cabinets ran the short length of the countertop across to the far wall where the pantry was located. It was similar to a studio apartment, except there was a bathroom and bedroom down a small hallway off the main room. The floors and walls throughout the cabin were all pine with a light-colored stain, similar to what was in the cabin she was staying in. Multi-colored throw rugs were on the floor in various areas.

"This probably doesn't compare to the place you're staying in," Camden said, watching her take in her surroundings.

"It's bigger than it looks." Leigh smiled. "I like it."

"Thanks. It's just me, so I don't need anything extravagant." Camden shrugged. "The bathroom is down the hall, if you need to go. Let me grab that snow gear for you to wear."

*

Curious, Leigh checked out the bathroom. She looked in the mirror, running her fingers through her hair to shake it out a bit. The room was small. The single sink had a toilet on one side with a double cabinet above it, and a tub with a dark blue shower curtain on the other side. A matching, larger double cabinet was below the sink.

When she walked out, Leigh peered into the open doorway of Camden's bedroom. She had a queen bed with a single nightstand beside it. The walk-in closet extended from the wall in the corner and had a bi-fold door. A heavy quilt made of various shades of blue covered the bed.

"I'm not a neat freak," Camden murmured playfully, catching her peeking into her room. "It's just easier to keep things clean. Then, I don't have to use what little time off I get, cleaning."

"I'm sorry," Leigh uttered, turning away from the doorway, nearly running into her in the short hallway. Camden had removed her jacket, revealing the overall style top to her bib pants and the light blue shirt that she wore as her base layer. It was long-sleeved with a raised collar, similar to a turtle neck, and form-fitting to keep her warm. She looked sort of like a stylish, snow lumberjack. Leigh found this look just as eye-catching as the FWC uniform, but she knew it wasn't the clothing. It was the striking woman underneath that had her attention.

"There's no reason to be sorry for curiosity." Camden smiled. "However, I should be the one apologizing. I seem to have forgotten my hospitality manners. The only house guests I ever have are my family, or Baker, and they all help themselves. Would you like something to drink? Maybe a cup of coffee or hot cocoa to warm you up?"

"No, I'm fine." Leigh smiled. "So, your family lives here?"

"Yes. You met Heather, she lives up in Granville where the conservatory is. My parents are down in Chester. They moved off the mountain about five or six years ago."

Leigh nodded, meeting her eyes for a split second.

Camden cleared her throat and reached for the black bib pants and white and blue jacket that were lying on the futon. “These should fit you. They’re a little tight on me. Anyway, keep your base layer on and put these over it. You should be plenty warm enough.”

Leigh grabbed the clothing, remembering how small the bathroom was. “Do you mind if I change in your room?”

“Sure. I’ll be outside gassing up the sled. Come out when you’re ready to go,” Camden said, pulling on her jacket.

Chapter 13

The jacket and bib pants were a little big, maybe a size above what Leigh would buy for herself. The bulky material made her feel like a balloon. Nevertheless, she was glad she had it on once they were racing through the woods on the snowmobile. She was wearing the same helmet she'd had on before, while Camden wore a similar one. They only butted heads once, before she learned to keep her head slightly to left, looking over Camden's shoulder.

The snowmobile sped through the snow throwing a rooster tail behind it. They bounced over rocks, and tilted sideways in tight turns, going much faster than they had earlier. The front skis came off the ground several times as they climbed switchbacks.

The entire trip was completely out of the box for Leigh, but being on the back of that sled was unlike anything she could've imagined doing. She gripped Camden a little tighter as the sled wobbled over an icy patch of snow.

A few minutes later, the sled came to a stop. Leigh slid back when she felt the engine shut off. She had no idea where they were. The evergreen trees were white with snow, blending everything together.

Camden got off the machine and removed her helmet, hanging it from the handlebars before helping Leigh out of hers. "This is White Tail Gorge," she said, grabbing Leigh's hand and pulling her over to a cliff that dropped off to a raging river below.

"Wow," Leigh murmured.

"It's a class two and three whitewater rapids section of the White Tail River."

"It's beautiful. So, powerful."

"The gorge isn't near the groomed snowmobile or ski trails, but it used to be on the map system. The state had it removed after three people jumped off in one year."

"Oh my…"

"It's sort of a hidden gem now."

Leigh nodded, peering over once more at the rushing water.

"Have you been to the ski resort?"

Leigh shook her head.

"There's a lot of hustle and bustle around there. They have a snow tube park with eight lanes, a snowmobile course for kids, and they also do snowmobile tours on the groomed trails. There are three different lifts to take you to different parts of the mountain from green trails, which are the easiest, all the way to black diamonds." She grabbed her helmet from the bar. "Ready to keep going?"

"Sure. Where are we headed to next?"

"The top of the mountain," Camden said, putting her helmet back on.

Leigh stared at her for a second, waiting for some indication she was kidding. She never got one as Camden tightened her helmet and got onto the sled, bumping the key to start it up. *Oh, Dear God…*She got on behind her, wrapping her arms tightly around Camden's waist before they took off once again.

*

Camden wasn't going as fast as she would be if she were alone, but she kept her speed up, maneuvering the sled easily over the uneven terrain, coming nearly to a stop as she threw her weight to the side to help the skis go around a tight turn for a switchback that took them up even higher, before gunning the throttle once again. Racing up the mountain was exhilarating. There was more of a direct path, but it was sketchy at times. The last thing she'd wanted to do was scare Leigh. Instead, she took the scenic route, sticking to the switchbacks that allowed her to climb a little at a time along the side of the mountain.

Leigh watched the woods literally open before her eyes as they reached the top. The ski lift moved at a steady pace, dropping skiers and snowboarders off a little less than a hundred yards away. Each person hopped off the seat and headed down the mountain, followed by the person behind them and so on. Some people got off and skied to the side before going down. She was too busy watching them to see the log cabin situated maybe thirty yards from the ski lift.

Suddenly, the sled came to a stop and the engine cut off. Leigh turned her head, seeing the cabin beside them. A large wooden sign with *Hill Top* painted on it, was in front of the building.

"It's not a five-star restaurant, but it has a pretty good view," Camden said with a smile, hanging her helmet on the handlebars. "I thought you might be hungry."

"I'm starving, and this is amazing!" Leigh exclaimed, getting a better view of the open area once her helmet was off. "Damn. I forgot to grab my wallet when we left my cabin."

"It's on me." Camden smiled and held her arm out, nodding for Leigh to walk in front of her.

*

The restaurant was small, with several picnic tables spread all around, and a cafeteria-style line in the back. They quickly found a seat with a view of the lift and placed their jackets on it before getting in line.

Leigh read over the chalkboard menu, deciding on a bowl of chicken noodle soup and half a turkey sandwich, along with a cup of coffee. She grinned when she heard Camden order a grilled cheese with tomato bisque. That had been her second choice.

"They change the menu every day," Camden said, paying for the order and grabbing the tray.

"Really? That's interesting." Leigh took the seat across from her at the small table.

"They never know how busy a day will be. They ride up on the snow cat before the sun comes up and decide based on what they have in stock. I've been coming here for years. That's the main lift. From here you can access many of the trails. There is a separate lift that takes you to the black diamond runs for the extremely advanced skiers, and one that goes to the green trails for the beginners. Obviously, this one is the most popular, which is why the restaurant is here."

"Do you ski?"

"Oh, yeah. We have to be able to ski to work search and rescue. I grew up skiing and snowboarding on this mountain. I stuck with skiing and gave up snowboarding several years ago. I've been down every trail many times over the years. The blue lines are a bit of a challenge and can be super fast if you take the right line. The green ones are usually packed with kids and parents, so I don't go down them often. The black diamonds are the most dangerous. You really have to know what you're doing. We have to help locate missing skiers on those runs every year."

"This is amazing by the way," Leigh cooed between bites of food.

"Yeah, everything is pretty good. You can't beat warm soup and a dip-able sandwich when it's twenty degrees outside."

"Is that what it is? I didn't look at my phone before we left."

"It's in the teens up here and probably mid-twenties at the bottom," Camden answered. "So, you've never skied or snowboarded?"

"Nope. Actually, the hike the other day was the most hair-raising thing I'd ever done. At least until I got on the back of that snowmobile. That definitely takes the cake."

Camden laughed. "You're just getting it all out in one shot, huh?"

"Something like that," Leigh chuckled softly.

Camden watched the way her mouth turned up at the corners while her grayish-blue eyes blinked softly. She knew the stirring in the pit of her stomach all too well, and another useless fling with a vacationer wasn't what she wanted.

"So, how long have you been a wildlife officer?"

"A little over sixteen years."

Leigh nearly got lost in her hazel green eyes, zeroing in on the golden-brown specs inside them as she spoke. "Sixteen years?" she mumbled.

"Yep. I started as a volunteer with SAR for a year when I first got out of college, while I was going through the lengthy process to get accepted to the federal law enforcement academy." Camden pushed her empty bowl and plate aside. "You think I'm older, don't you?"

Leigh shook her head. "No. I figured you were probably four or five years younger than me and just had premature graying. It happens."

"It started when I was twenty-five and by the time I was thirty-five, I had this." Camden shrugged. "I turned forty a few months ago. I guess it's starting to fit."

Leigh smiled. "I like it."

"Thanks."

"We're the same age, by the way."

"I don't see any gray on you." Camden raised a brow.

"Oh, they're in there, trust me. I don't dye it. This mix of blonde shades is all-natural. You wouldn't believe how many times I get stopped by women wanting to know who does my hair."

"I can see why. It's beautiful."

"Thanks." Leigh smiled shyly.

Camden returned the smile with one of her own before dumping their trash. When she returned to the table, Leigh had already put her jacket on. She quickly grabbed her coat and slipped it on.

*

Once again, the snowmobile raced through the woods, except this time, they were at a different part of the mountain top. Leigh wasn't sure how far they were from the clearing where the lift and restaurant were, but they were completely out of sight, lost behind the curtain of white, evergreen trees. She hadn't asked where they were going and Camden hadn't offered. She didn't care. She couldn't think of the last time she'd had so much fun. Riding on the snowmobile was scary and exhilarating at the same time.

Camden felt Leigh tighten her hold and was thankful they had thick bulky layers between them. *If I were able to feel your warm body against me, I'd be gone. What am I saying? I'm already down that road, and I have no idea how to turn around.* She shook the thoughts from her head, forcing herself to concentrate on driving.

Before she knew it, they were at their next destination. Camden softly squeezed the brake lever over and over, carefully bringing the sled to a stop without skidding out of control. She killed the engine and got off once Leigh slid back away from her. She'd finally figured out her helmet straps, so Camden didn't need to help her.

"Where are we?" Leigh asked, hanging her helmet on the handlebar. They were surrounded by forest.

"Turn around," Camden replied, placing her helmet on thc opposite side.

Leigh spun around, taken aback when she saw a wide opening in the mountain.

"This is a natural cave. There are carvings inside that indicate it could be hundreds of years old. We can look around, but this time of year, you don't want to venture too far inside. Bears tend to hibernate in there." Camden winked and grinned.

"This is…unbelievable," Leigh mumbled, taking in the site before locking eyes with Camden. "Thank you."

Camden smiled brightly.

"You're…" Leigh bit her lower lip.

Camden stepped closer.

"I can't find the words," Leigh murmured.

"Then don't," Camden whispered, removing her glove. She placed her warm hand on the side of Leigh's face as she closed the distance between them, pressing their lips together softly.

Leigh allowed the kiss for a split second longer than she should have. Her body said yes, but her head screamed no. She pulled away, closing her eyes before opening them to Camden. Her lips tingled and her chest tightened.

"I'm sorry," Camden sighed.

"Don't be. I wanted that as much as you did. It's just…"

"Bad timing?"

"Yeah. I came here to get away from reality for a bit and sort of find myself…meeting you certainly wasn't in the cards. It's going to be hard enough to leave with you being just a friend."

"I know. I feel the same way, which is why I never meant for that to happen." Camden checked her watch. "We should probably head back down. It's going to take a little bit, and it'll start getting dark in a couple of hours."

Leigh took a deep breath, letting it out slowly as she looked back at the cave. "It really is neat. Thank you for showing this to me."

"You're welcome."

*

The ride back down the mountain was filled with the same switchbacks, twists, and turns, and uneven terrain as the ride up, except this time, they took the turns slower, careful with the weight going downhill. Camden controlled the machine with precision movement, despite beating herself up over the kiss. She knew it was a bad idea before it even happened, but she couldn't stop herself. She'd noticed the way Leigh had looked at her in the restaurant, and when she saw it again in front of the cave…her body reacted, leaving her with a simple kiss that had lasted only a few seconds, and a belly full of regret.

Leigh tried to force the kiss from her thoughts, concentrating on looking over Camden's shoulder instead, but the softness of Camden's lips still lingered on her mouth. *Damn you for making me want you.* She was too busy in her own head to realize they were pulling up to Camden's cabin.

*

Camden let out a deep breath as the sled came to a stop outside of the shed beside her cabin. She turned the key, shutting the machine off. "I'll open the cabin so you can change while I get the snowmobile put away," she said, removing her helmet.

"That's fine," Leigh replied, noticing a difference in her demeanor.

Camden stayed silent as she unlocked the door, swinging it open. As soon as Leigh stepped inside, she walked away.

Leigh quickly changed back into her jeans and jacket, leaving the snow gear neatly on the futon by the door. She took one last look around the cabin before pulling the door shut behind her.

*

The sun was beginning to set in the distance, casting a shadow over the mountain. Leigh hated the silence in the truck as they rode along. She glanced at Camden a few times, hoping to catch her eyes, but she was concentrating on the road.

"I had a great time today. I can't thank you enough," she finally blurted.

"I enjoyed it," Camden replied, smiling at her as she pulled into the driveway behind Leigh's car.

"You bought my lunch and everything. Please let me make you dinner."

Camden put the truck in park and turned slightly in her seat, about to answer her when a loud beeping noise echoed through the truck. Camden quickly turned the volume up on the CB radio attached to the computer.

"Search and rescue, we have a twenty-two-year-old male snowmobile rider missing on the mountain approximately four hours, and unfamiliar with the terrain. Report to 14 Deer Bend Road," the dispatcher said.

Camden shook her head as the call repeated.

"Are you going?"

"Yeah," she nodded. "We always have to go, no matter what."

"Are you tired? Will you be out there all night, or do you work in shifts?"

"We'll be there until we find him. It's almost dark. If we don't, and he's hurt or improperly dressed, he'll die. We're trained for this. Sometimes I have to be awake and alert for twenty-plus hours."

"Give me your phone," Leigh said as Camden reached for the radio mic to call in. "Why?"

"Because I'm giving you my number."

Camden handed it to her.

"Call me when you are home safe. I don't care what time it is. Otherwise, I'll worry about you all night."

"Leigh—"

"Please, just do it. I know it's your job, but I'm new to all of this." *And to you.*

"Alright," Camden nodded, taking her phone back. "Dispatch, this is Gorely. Do we know what trail he took?"

"Elk."

"Roger. I'm about twenty minutes out. I need to load my UTV."

"Copy," the dispatcher replied.

"Gorely, you can double up with me. I'm loaded and rolling."

"10-4," she replied. "I gotta go." Camden turned her eyes up to meet Leigh's. "But, I'll take a rain check on that dinner invitation."

"Be safe." Leigh smiled, squeezing her hand before opening the door and getting out.

Chapter 14

"Hopefully, he hasn't gone off-trail. Keep your eyes peeled," Camden said, addressing the SAR officers. "Do we know if there was GPS tracking on the sled?"

"We're still waiting for the rental company to give us the last known waypoint," another officer replied. "He had the sled rented for three days yesterday, so no one was expecting it back. His girlfriend said he left around noon and told her was going to take a ride on Elk Trail."

"Why did she wait four hours to report him missing?"

"She's not into snowmobiling, so she went up to the resort spa. When she returned, she figured he'd come back and left again. When he still wasn't back an hour later, she called it in," the same officer answered.

"Okay. Let's get out there and find him. Radio those coordinates as soon as you have them," she said, folding the trail map they'd all been looking at. Then, she climbed into the passenger seat of Baker's UTV. He started the engine and followed everyone towards the trail. They all dispersed, going in different directions along the trail, as well as off the trail into the backcountry.

"I hope he just ran out of gas somewhere, or is still out riding and just forgot which trail to take to get back. I heard he'd forgotten to take his phone with him," he said, his voice carrying over the two-way radio headsets connected to their helmets so they could communicate when they were working together.

"Yeah," she agreed. "You know the sign for Evergreen Trail is up here. What if he took the switchback?"

"You want to check it out?"

Camden's eyes were glued to the binoculars, searching through the trees until the sun was gone. "We might as well. I'm going to tell the guys behind us to keep going further up Elk." She grabbed the radio mic attached to her chest, and told the two UTV's behind her to keep climbing up the mountain along the trail. Then, she pulled her night vision binoculars out. "Davidson, you have those coordinates yet?"

"Negative."

"Damn," she muttered, scanning through the trees as they turned to take the other trail. The infrared on the night binos picked up a deer over a hundred yards away, along with a moose about fifty yards to the left of it. "If he's bundled and the ski isn't on, I may not see anything with these."

"Yeah, I was thinking that too."

"Gorely, just texted you the coordinates. It looks like Buck Trail, not Elk," the officer radioed.

"We're on Evergreen," she replied before putting the coordinates into her handheld GPS. She waited for the waypoint to pop up on the screen, showing the relevance to their position. Finally, it popped up, showing the point over a mile away from their position. She secured the GPS on the dash.

"We're about two minutes away," Davidson radioed. "It looks like he might've gone off the trail."

"Roger," she replied. "Stop here," she said to Baker. "If they need an assist, we'll need to turn around and go back down."

"Yeah," he agreed, pulling to a stop.

"Gorely, we have the sled, but no rider. It's mangled pretty good," Davidson radioed. "I just sent you a picture."

Camden took her glove off to check the message on her phone. "Oh God," she mumbled.

"Holy shit," Baker exclaimed, seeing the photo of the wrecked snowmobile.

"He went over the edge. That's damaged from a tumble," she sighed, grabbing her radio. "Davidson, he took a tumble. Depending on where he went over, he could be anywhere."

"I agree," he replied.

"We're on the way back down. Park the UTV's and get out on foot. You can't chance running him over. ETA, two minutes," she radioed. "Haul ass, Baker."

*

Camden's senses were already heightened from the rush of being out on a call, but her adrenaline went into overdrive when she saw the wrecked sled up close. She and Baker joined the rest of the small group, scanning the ground with flashlights and calling his name, until he was found some thirty yards from the snowmobile.

"He's alive and alert," one of the officer's radioed, popping up a flare so the rest of the group could find him.

Camden and Baker were the closest. She held her medical bag tightly as she ran as much as she could in the heavy snow. The rider was on his back with his helmet still on. His jacket was torn, and both of his legs were twisted at odd angles.

She dropped down in the snow next to him, taking a pulse. Then, she put a cervical collar on his neck and held him still while Baker and the other officer removed his helmet.

"I'm so cold," he whispered.

"We'll get you warmed up in just a minute. Can you tell me what hurts?"

"Everything," he whimpered. "I'm afraid to move."

"Definitely do not move. Your legs are both broken." She grabbed her radio. "We need a backboard now! And, a UTV with a bed for transport." She switched to the main channel. "Dispatch, this is Gorely. We have him. We're going to need EMS."

"What's your location?"

"We're about fifty yards off Buck Trail. It looks like the rider went over the side at Evergreen Trail. It's about a sixty-foot drop."

"EMS is standing by on Bear Road. What's your rendezvous?" Dispatch replied.

Camden thought about it for a second. "We can get him to Eagle Point. I'll send an escort ahead with road flares."

"Roger," Dispatch said.

"Alright. We're going to put you on this board so we can carry you out to the UTV. I want you to focus on maintaining even, steady breathing," Camden informed, sliding the backboard next to him. "On three, let's roll him to the right side."

He screamed in pain as the team worked together getting him secured. Then, she went into the medical bag and gave him a shot of morphine before pulling out a thermal blanket to cover him, wrapping it around the backboard. Then, they each grabbed a handle and lifted him off the ground, holding the backboard at waist height.

"Am I going to die?" he mumbled as the drugs kicked in.

"Not while you're with me. I promise you that," she replied.

The terrain off the trail in that area was uneven, with downed logs and rocks. It took longer than anyone thought to get him from the spot they'd found him, to the waiting UTV. Once they had him strapped down, she hopped in the back next to him to maintain his vitals as they road down the trail to exit near the closest street. She kept listening to his breathing with the stethoscope. As long as he was inhaling and exhaling, he was alive. That was all that mattered to her.

It took about ten minutes for the UTV to reach the awaiting EMS vehicle. Bright flares lit everything up around them, coloring the snow reddish-orange. The two teams worked together to transfer the injured rider from the SAR backboard to the EMS one. Then, EMS went to work getting him secured, and hooked to an IV line, before taking off down the mountain as carefully and quickly as possible.

Camden breathed out a sigh of relief as she watched the flashing lights fade until they were no longer visible. "Let's call it a night, guys. I'll write up the report in the morning," she said to the search and rescue officers standing nearby.

"Gorely, we loaded the sled on a UTV bed. We'll meet you back at zero," Baker radioed.

"Roger," she said, climbing back into the bed of the UTV so she could ride back to her truck.

*

Camden was exhausted by the time she pulled up at her cabin. She walked inside, kicking her boots off at the door while removing her bright red SAR jacket. She laid it on the futon beside the snow gear Leigh had worn, reminding her she'd promised to call. In all of her years working with search and rescue, she'd never come home and called someone to say she was home safely. Not even her parents. They worried, of course, but they knew she was very good at her job. Otherwise, she wouldn't be doing it. Still, it felt odd as she sat in the recliner, waiting for the ringing line to be answered.

*

"Hello?" Leigh answered tentatively, seeing the unknown number.

"It's Camden. I'm home. I promised to call."

Oh. Thank God. "Did you find the snowmobiler?"

"Yeah. He wrecked and broke some bones."

"Wow. Good thing you guys found him. Were they open fractures or closed?"

"Closed."

"Was he unconscious?" she questioned. "I'm sorry. I immediately go into trauma nurse mode. I'm sure you did your job correctly."

"He was actually alert and in a hell of a lot of pain. I secured him to the backboard with the c-collar and shot him up with morphine. That's about all we can do unless he isn't breathing."

"How did he wreck?"

"He went over the side of a sixty-foot cliff," Camden sighed.

"Oh, dear God!" she gasped. "He's lucky to be alive!"

"Yeah, no kidding. I think the heavy snow cushioned his fall somewhat. Plus, I think he may have landed on his legs, which is way better than his head."

"For sure. He might not have survived with a fractured skull. Do you see a lot of accidents like this?"

"I guess we have our fair share. Some are minor, but others have been quite tragic, especially in the summer months with people out on four-wheelers. We had an avalanche my second year with search and rescue, and a group of four skiers were trapped. It took over an hour just to get to them. Two wound up together and were able to dig enough around themselves to create an air pocket. The other two were separated and didn't survive."

"That's terrible."

"They were locals, which made it worse. The town did a big memorial for them."

"This place really is like a movie," Leigh uttered to herself.

"What was that? I didn't hear you."

"I said it's crazy how much your day can change in an instant."

"Yeah. No two are ever the same, that's for sure," Camden laughed quietly.

The soft sound of her voice through the phone made Leigh want to be near her. She closed her eyes, listening to her talk about different calls she'd had over the years.

"I'm sorry. I'm probably boring you to tears. It's late," Camden said, clearing her throat.

"It *is* late, and you should get some sleep. I'm sure you're working tomorrow."

Camden checked her watch. "In a few hours, actually."

"Oh my gosh. Go get in bed. I'm glad you called, and you were not boring me, by the way. I like listening to you."

"Thanks."

"Hey, before I hang up. Do you want to cash in that rain check for dinner tomorrow night? Or tonight? Whatever the hell it is?"

"Sure," Camden laughed. "I'm off around four-thirty or five, depending on how the day goes. I'll call you."

"Sounds good."

Camden hung up the phone and stared at the dark screen for a minute. She shook the thoughts from her head before they could form, and stood up.

*

"Oh…what are you doing, Leigh?" she sighed, setting her phone on the nightstand before pulling the covers up higher. The cabin was dark except for the nightlight that stayed on in the kitchen below the loft. "Dinner to thank her for everything. That's all it is," she told herself. *But, if she kisses me again…*she trailed off in her head as she fell asleep.

Chapter 15

Camden was on her third cup of coffee after having drunk the first two at home, as she rode through the woods in Baker's UTV. She held her arm up, doing her best not to spill the drink through the sipping hole when the machine bounced over the icy snow.

"Are you sure we're going the right way?" she asked.

"Yes." He looked at his GPS again to make sure.

They were on their way to stake out a hunting blind to try and catch the owner in the act. It was positioned too close to the ski trails to begin with, but they'd also received word that the owner was not tagging deer and had killed at least three bucks with antlers using bait, all of which were illegal. They'd found the blind the week before, along with evidence of baiting with apple cores, scattered corn, and salt lick blocks.

"We're close. Let's stop here and hide the UTV," he said, pulling the machine between two massive evergreen trees.

Camden set her coffee down and picked up her binoculars. This was the third time they'd staked out the blind, hoping to catch him in the act.

"How are things going with the vacationer?"

"Huh?" Camden mumbled.

"Weren't you with her all day yesterday?"

She shrugged. "It's not what you think."

He nodded.

"I guess we've kind of become friends…sort of. I barely know her. We keep running into each other, really."

"Maybe it's fate," he said nonchalantly.

"Ha!" Camden laughed.

"I'm just say…" he muttered.

"Saying what, exactly?"

"You're different around her. She's certainly nothing like the ski bunnies who are looking to hookup."

"They're damn near half my age. I don't have time for that mess."

"That's my point. She may be the one."

"The one to do what?"

"Bring you out of bachelorhood."

Camden shook her head as she guffawed. "Since when are you so concerned with my love life? You're the one who is in love with my cousin, but won't make a damn move."

"What?" he squeaked.

"I know you have a thing for Heather."

"How have you noticed anything with that puppy-dog-eyed teenager falling all over you every time you're there?" he deadpanned.

"Oh, please. She's not a teenager, but she is a kid…to me anyway. I'm certainly not going there."

"Was she there when you took the vacationer with you to drop off the bear?"

"The vacationer's name is Leigh. And yes, she was there."

"Oh, boy."

Camden gave him a sideways glance before taking a sip of her coffee. "She has a crush. She'll get over it, no matter who is with me," she replied, peering back through her binoculars.

"Uh-huh." He shook his head. "You have any plans for tonight? I was thinking of making spaghetti."

"With deer meat?"

"Yeah, probably. I'm trying to get rid of what's in the freezer. Joe gave me a shit ton of it when he got that buck early in the season."

Camden shook her head. "You know Heather's a vegetarian, right?"

"What? Seriously?"

"Yes. She's a veterinarian for a wild animal conservation. Her job is to save them. Not eat them!"

"I'm not a hunter. The meat was given to me."

She shrugged. "Probably all the same to her. She does eat seafood or chicken here and there, but she will not eat anything that is wild on this mountain. I guarantee that."

"Well, you eat it, and I invited you, not her."

"I eat it because I don't want a sacrificed animal to be wasted. I don't hunt either. To each his own and everything, it's just not something I'm interested in doing. Now, I'll fish like it's nobody's business."

"Yeah, but you throw them back," he laughed.

"It's called fishing for sport," she chided. "Anyway, I can't do anything tonight. I have plans."

"With Leigh?"

"As a matter of fact, yes. She wanted to make dinner to say thank you for everything, but I'm thinking of taking her to the restaurant."

"Ohhhhh…meeting the family. She must've passed Heather's inspection. I don't think you've ever taken anyone to meet your parents."

"You're funny."

"I'm serious."

"I took *you*."

"I live here. They already knew me. They know everyone in town."

"Uh-huh." She was about to say something else when she saw something moving near the blind. "He's here," she whispered.

"I see him. He's heading to the blind."

"Son of a bitch," she muttered, seeing him toss apple cores and corn on the snow-covered ground. "Let's go bust his ass."

"Hold on," Baker said, starting the UTV and roaring out of the tress with the throttle wide open. The machine made so much noise suddenly, the entire blind fell over and ripped apart as the man tried to get out of it. The UTV skidded to a stop and both officers jumped out.

"Stand up!" Camden yelled with her hand on her gun. "Don't even think of running."

"I'm not," he said, standing with his hands up.

"We know who you are, and we also know you've shot at least three bucks from right here—"

"I.." He began to talk, cutting Baker off.

Camden moved closer to him. "First, you have to be 500 yards from the ski runs, hiking trails, off-road trails, or residents. You're maybe 200 at best, which is why there is no hunting on this side of the mountain. Anyone with a license or tags knows this. Second, you haven't tagged any of the deer you've killed. Any deer that is killed must be tagged immediately and reported to our station in town within 48 hours. Third, we watched you spread bait. The use of bait is prohibited in the state of Vermont."

He just stared at them.

"Deer got your tongue?" Baker said.

"I haven't killed any deer. This is my first time coming here."

"That's a lie," Baker said, pulling up the screenshots of the man's social media pages of him out in this spot with each dead buck after he killed it.

"I'm in those pictures, but I wasn't the one who killed the deer. Three different friends shot them on separate occasions."

"I'm not buying any of the deer shit you're selling," Camden said, shaking her head. "Let me see your hunting license."

He went into his back pocket, retrieving his wallet. He opened the bi-fold and handed her the paper license. She stepped over to the UTV to call it in for validation and write the tickets while Baker took photos of the bait to go with the video he'd made on his phone.

"Alright, Mr. Burgess. You're getting cited today for hunting within 500 yards of an open ski run, hiking trail, off-road trail, or residence. As well as, killing more than one deer with points, not tagging any deer you have killed, and baiting. You need to sign the bottom of each of these and contact the judge for arbitration. This is not an admission of guilt. It means you understand that you must appear in front of a judge in regard to these claims. Your state of Vermont hunting license will be revoked for a minimum period of one year from today's date. However, the judge has the final discretion," Camden said, handing him over three-thousand dollars in fines.

"Son of a bitch," he mumbled, signing his name on each one.

"Where is the meat from the three-pointed bucks?" Baker asked. "We need to confiscate any carcass or meat in your possession."

"It's in the deep freezer at my house and the taxidermy guy over in Collier has the heads. He's mounting them for me."

"Is the address on your license correct?"

"Yeah."

"Okay. We'll meet you at your house to collect the meat. We'll need the name of the company or individual doing the taxidermy work, as well."

"Alright," he sighed.

"Do you need a ride to your vehicle?"

"My quad is parked up on that switchback," he said.

"We'll meet you at your house, then," Camden replied, walking back to the passenger seat of the UTV. Her coffee was still warm enough to drink thanks to the high dollar thermal container she used. She took a long swallow before putting her seatbelt on.

"Talk about an idiot," Baker said, shaking his head as he started the UTV.

"Yep. These guys act like the law doesn't apply to them."

"Well, his bank account and his pride will prove otherwise," Baker said as he put the machine in gear and drove away.

*

Camden knocked on the door and shoved her hands into the pockets of her jeans. *Why am I so nervous? This is stupid. Thank you for getting in my head Baker. You ass.* She took a deep breath and cleared her throat as she waited. *Is she bathing the cat? What the hell. It's cold out here.*

Suddenly, the door swung open and Leigh stepped into the door frame. Camden's mouth watered as she ran her eyes over the beautiful woman in front of her. She was dressed in jeans and a crème colored cable knit sweater that hugged her breasts and slim torso. Her dirty blonde hair cascaded over her shoulders, stopping at the top of her breasts.

Leigh was surprised to see the wildlife officer in jeans, a black Henley shirt, and a black down jacket. She looked refreshed and definitely younger out of the uniform. Her woodsy, floral-scented cologne lingered in the air.

Camden's lips curled into a smile as their eyes met.

"You look different," Leigh muttered.

"I clean up every now and then," Camden teased.

"I like it."

Camden grinned, causing Leigh to shift her focus from the hazel green eyes staring back at her, to the slightly parted lips beckoning her to come closer. She swallowed the lump in her throat and backed up.

"I wasn't sure what you'd want to eat—"

"Actually, I was hoping you'd join me for dinner in town," Camden blurted.

"Oh." Leigh nodded. "Yeah, sure."

Camden walked inside to wait for Leigh to slip into her snow boots and heavy coat. Once she was ready, they walked out of the cabin. "I'm sorry I'm in the work truck. It's my only transportation."

"I don't mind." *You could be driving the Beverly Hillbillies car and I'd still go anywhere with you.*

Camden opened her door first, then went around and got in on the driver's side.

The short drive down the mountain only took a few minutes since the roads weren't bad. She pulled into the parking lot behind Ma and Pa's, thankful there was an open space.

"I know you were here for breakfast the other day, but have you been back?" Camden asked as they walked along the sidewalk to the front of the small building.

"Yes, but I've only had breakfast. It's been fantastic. I'm sure their dinner menu is great too."

Camden pulled the door open, nodding for Leigh to go inside first. All of the tables were full, except one, and there were no open stools at the bar.

"I held you a table by the fireplace," the older woman said, smiling at Camden, and looking oddly at the woman walking with her. "It's nice to see you again, Leigh."

"Thank you. She loves your breakfast. I told her dinner is even better," Camden replied as they walked over to the table.

"Wonderful," the older lady said.

Leigh noticed the older man with a head full of grayish-white hair and age lines creasing his face. He was always waiting tables just like the older woman. She figured he was probably her husband. She also noticed Dr. Eric John sitting alone at a nearby table.

"Evening, Camden," Dr. John said, wiping his face on his napkin.

"Doctor John." She smiled and nodded.

The older lady turned to him. "Can I get you anything else, Doctor John?"

"Oh, no thank you. It was excellent as always." He put the cash on the table for his bill and stood. "Leigh, it's nice to see you. Thank you again for yesterday. I enjoyed our time together."

"You're welcome. I'm glad I was able to help out." She smiled.

"My offer still stands." He winked before walking away.

Camden eyed her suspiciously. "An older lady fell on the ice yesterday in front of me. I rushed her there because she had a head laceration and the place was packed with patients. I stayed for a couple of hours and helped them clear it out."

"Wow. That's amazing. How come you didn't mention it?"

"Someone appeared out of nowhere and whisked me off, racing around the mountain on a snowmobile!" she teased.

The older lady returned with two glasses of water. "I hope Camden has remembered her manners," she said.

"Well, she did pull me over my first day here…"

"You were speeding," Camden chided with a smile.

"She also came to my rescue when I got lost hiking. And, she took me on a snowmobile tour around the mountain. So, I guess she redeemed herself," Leigh teased.

"You be nice to this sweet girl. I heard what she did yesterday," the older lady said, patting Camden on the hand. "And she's pretty," she whispered to her as she stepped away to let them look over the menu.

The older man patted Camden on the shoulder. "We're about out of dumplings. I put a bowl to the side," he said, smiling and nodding at Leigh as he continued walking by.

"You must come here a lot," Leigh muttered, noticing the sentiment shared between both of the owners and Camden. "They seem to know you well."

"They're my parents."

"What?!"

"Technically, they are my aunt and uncle, but they adopted me when I was about two. My birth mother got pregnant by someone she barely knew and never saw him again. She is Aunt Ma's little sister from her father's middle-aged love affair. Anyway, we lived in the city. One day she left with her trucker boyfriend and never returned to pick me up at daycare, or at all for that matter. Aunt Ma and Uncle Pa were her only next of kin, so they quickly came down and got me when child services called them. They finally found her in Canada and she signed the papers right away to allow them to adopt me. She'd had no business having a kid to begin with."

"Wow," Leigh gasped.

"I know it sounds like a sad sob story, but I've had a great life. Uncle Pa worked for fish and wildlife and search and rescue too. He retired when I was in high school. Aunt Ma worked for the school district until they decided to buy this old place as a retirement investment. They've been working here together ever since. They are the most genuine, loving people I've ever met."

"Are you two ready to order?" the older lady asked, walking back over to them.

Camden waved for the older man to come over to the table. "Aunt Ma, I know you've met her, but Uncle Pa, this is Leigh Myer. She's visiting from the city. I've been showing her around a bit."

"After Camden found her when she was lost in the woods," Aunt Ma said, nodding to the older man.

"That's my girl." He winked.

"Anyway," Camden continued, "Leigh, these are my parents."

"It's nice to meet you both. You have a lovely restaurant and an amazing daughter," she said, smiling at Camden.

"I need to go check the kitchen. Ms. Myer, it is nice meeting you as well. You couldn't be in better company," Uncle Pa replied before walking away.

Camden and Leigh quickly gave their order and Aunt Ma left the table.

"They seem like genuinely sweet people."

"Thanks."

"So, I have to ask. Why Aunt Ma and Uncle Pa?"

"Well…they weren't sure what to have me call them in the beginning while they were searching for my mother. They never were able to have children and had always wanted to be called Ma and Pa. They were my aunt and uncle, so they just put it together. When they bought this place, it had been called the Bear's Den. I knew they'd wanted to rename it, so when I mentioned Ma and Pa's, they loved it."

Leigh sat across from her with her hands clasped together, and her lips parted slightly in a smile. *People like you don't exist in real life.*

"What?" Camden smiled back at her.

"Nothing. I was just thinking about how this place had reminded me of a Hallmark movie when I'd first arrived. I honestly feel like I'm in a movie. Genuine people don't exist anymore outside of the TV."

"I promise, I'm not an actor and this isn't a movie set." Camden winked.

Aunt Ma appeared at that moment with their food. "Enjoy it. Let me know if there is anything I can get for you." She patted both of them on the hand before walking away.

"So, what about your parents? Are you close?"

"Yes. They are both retired and live in the city. I talk to them quite often."

Camden nodded.

"They'd probably keel over if I told them where I was and what I'd been doing for the past few days."

"Wait…they don't know you're here?"

Leigh shook her head. "It was a spur of the moment decision."

"I see."

Leigh sensed a shift in Camden, almost immediately. "My best friend knows I'm here. She owns the cabin," she said, easing her.

"That's good. It's not necessarily Deliverance or anything like that up here, but a single woman staying in a vacation home is pretty rare."

"What makes you think I'm single?" Leigh raised a brow.

"I..uh…meant single as in alone. There's no one staying there with you…am I right?"

"You are correct."

"So?"

"Here is the check. There's no rush, and if you'd like dessert, Ms. Myer, please let me know. This one will only eat apple pie with vanilla ice cream and maple syrup," Aunt Ma said, shaking her head. "He's the same way," she added, nodding toward her husband. "However, tonight we have strawberry cheesecake."

"That sounds delicious, but I'm afraid I'm full from dinner. The food is excellent," Leigh replied.

"Wonderful. Thank you. I'll leave you be then."

Chapter 16

After hugs from both of Camden's parents, they left the restaurant and headed back up the mountain. Camden pulled into Leigh's driveway behind her car and turned off the engine. Leigh got out and Camden walked her to the door.

"I'm just checking to see if there are any bears inside," Camden teased with a playful smile.

"Come in," Leigh laughed, opening the door. "Would you like a glass of wine while you look around?"

"Sure."

"Red or white?" Leigh asked, walking into the kitchen.

"I'm good with whatever you're having."

"Would you mind throwing some logs together for a fire? I can't ever seem to get it right. That's probably why I don't have a fireplace in my apartment," Leigh called from across the room.

Camden grab four split logs from the short stack near the fireplace and arranged them perfectly. "You know, you never answered me earlier," she said over her shoulder as she put a couple of pieces of loose kindling underneath.

"About what?"

"Your being single," she replied, finding the long matches. She struck one against the side of the box and began lighting the kindling.

"I didn't realize you'd asked."

"It was sort of implied, I guess." Camden shrugged, returning the matches to the mantel while she watched the first orange flame begin to lick the edge of the log above it.

Leigh paused mid pour, holding the glass of wine tightly in her hand. She turned her head, looking at Camden's back. *I knew the moment I laid eyes on you...* "I'm…uh…not with anyone…no," she muttered. "It's not an easy subject for me. I'm sorry."

"I'm sorry for prying," Camden said, meeting her gaze from across the room as the fire began burning brightly, casting an orange glow behind her.

"It's fine." Leigh swallowed the nervous lump in her throat and went back to the wine.

Camden noticed the loft above the kitchen. "Is that the master?" she asked, changing the sensitive subject.

"Yes. I love it. I wake up to those picture windows every morning."

Camden turned her head, looking opposite from the loft at the French doors and massive windows around them. There wasn't much to see in the dark, but she could imagine the view. "Wow."

"It's breathtaking," Leigh said, handing her a glass of red wine.

"So are you," Camden whispered.

Leigh's mouth curled slowly into a smile as her eyes rose to meet Camden's.

"I'm sorry. I seem to keep—"

Leigh pressed her lips to Camden's, stopping her sentence with a gentle kiss. Her chest ached like someone was squeezing the breath out of her as her mouth lingered.

Taken by surprise, Camden nearly dropped the wine glass she was holding. Leigh's mouth was just as soft and inviting as it had been when they'd shared their first kiss.

After a few agonizingly long seconds, she pulled away, looking into the heavy-lidded eyes staring back at her. She grabbed Leigh's glass from her and set them both on the table.

Leigh held her breath, almost wincing as Camden's hand moved slowly towards her face. It landed so gently, she wasn't sure she felt it, until her thumb began to slide softly over her cheek. She closed her tear-filled eyes and allowed herself to feel the delicate touch.

Witnessing the emotions play across Leigh's face made Camden's jaw clench. She'd never been close to anyone who had experienced abuse, but it was written all over the woman in front of her. "I won't hurt you. I promise," she whispered, wiping away a loose tear with her thumb before pulling her hand back.

Leigh reached up, stopping her and pressing her hand back against her cheek.

Camden grabbed Leigh's other hand and brought it to her chest just above her breasts. Leigh's watery eyes fluttered open. Camden stared into them for what felt like minutes. She was lost, swimming among the sea of grayish-blue.

The trepidation began to lift from Leigh like a sluggish raincloud, fading away. She eased her hand up, feeling the warm, smooth skin of Camden's neck before her fingers slid over the short hair on the back of her head. She parted her own lips with her tongue, licking them as her heart raced. The gap between them closed automatically as her mouth inched towards Camden's.

The kiss was delicate at first. Camden wasn't sure their lips were touching at all until Leigh's tongue grazed hers. Her body yearned for more, urging her to take it further, but she held back, allowing Leigh to control their pace. She didn't have to wait long as Leigh let go of the hand she was holding against her cheek, running it over Camden's arm, all the way to her shoulder.

Camden put her hands on Leigh's waist, pulling their hips together, creating full body contact for the first time as the kiss deepened naturally. She felt Leigh move against her, fueling the desire burning in her belly.

Leigh slowly broke the kiss, pulling away breathlessly as her eyes met Camden's. The flickering flames of the fire failed in comparison to the heat spreading through her body. She knew the feeling of desire, but it had been so long since she'd felt it, she wasn't sure her timid self would allow her the pleasure she desperately wanted.

Camden watched her step away and remove the heavy throw blankets from the back of the couch before placing them on the floor in front of the fireplace. "We don't have to go any further," she said softly.

Leigh's chest tightened. Meeting her gaze, she whispered, "I don't want to stop."

Camden closed the gap between them, gently kissing her as her arms wrapped around her waist. Leigh ran her hands under Camden's shirt, feeling the warm, smooth skin of her torso as she pulled it up.

Delicate kisses were traded as they removed each other's clothes agonizingly slow. Each layer was placed aside until they were pressed against each other with nothing between them. The heavy logs in the fireplace burned hot, shrouding them in warmth. Camden took her time running her hands up Leigh's back from her waist, settling up under the hair cascading over her shoulders as their lips met once more.

Leigh moaned into her mouth as her hands slid up Camden's torso, cupping her breasts and running her thumbs over peaked nipples. It had been so long since she'd really *felt* another woman. She'd had sex, but it was quick and to the point, and she never saw them again. This was something she hadn't done in so long, she'd forgotten what it was like to make love.

Camden leaned back when the kiss came to an end, keeping their hips pressed together. The apprehension she'd first seen in the beautiful eyes staring back at her was long gone, having been replaced by a hunger that made her weak in the knees. She glanced down at the blankets, then back at her. Leigh nodded slightly, then stepped back, tugging Camden's hand as she went down to the floor.

They lay on their sides, trading tender, lingering kisses that gradually increased as they ran their hands over each other. Leigh paused Camden's hand in place when it passed over her lower abdomen.

Camden started pulling away from the kiss until Leigh reassured her by pushing her hand lower. Her fingers slid through the warm, silky wet folds, causing Leigh's body to tremble. She took her time exploring every detail with delicate passes back and forth.

Leigh slid her hand from Camden's breast down to her hip. Feeling her legs open, she continued, tracing a path all the way to the wetness awaiting her. She opened her mouth, teasing Camden with her tongue as her fingers circled the outside of her clit.

Camden struggled to concentrate with the unbearably slow pace. She was sure her body was going to fly apart long before she reached the orgasm building deep inside. She focused her attention on Leigh, matching her intoxicating kisses and arousing strokes, feeling her body grow more rigid by the second. Leigh moaned against her mouth as the orgasm tore through her, jerking her hips wildly. Camden let go at the same time, her tensed body pulsating everywhere Leigh touched her.

They lie together, wrapped in each other's arms until their racing hearts began to calm. The fire had reduced to orange, glowing embers. Camden reached for the edge of the blanket, looking to pull it up over them, but Leigh backed away from her and stood up, holding her hand out.

Taking the offered hand, Camden stood and followed her across the room to the narrow staircase leading up to the loft. At the top, Leigh guided her over to the bed and pulled the comforter aside. She wasn't sure if she should stay, or if they should even keep going for that matter. Leigh's fearful reaction to her first touch left her uneasy. The last thing she'd wanted to do was overstep. She tried searching her eyes, but the moonlight and soft glow of the fire were the only illumination.

Sensing Camden's hesitation, Leigh moved closer, placing her head on her shoulder, just under her chin, and her hand in the center of her chest. "Is this okay?"

Camden wrapped her arms around her. "Absolutely."

"There's so much I want to say…" Leigh whispered.

"I'm not asking for anything, but I *am* here if and when you're ready to talk," Camden replied softly.

"Thank you."

Chapter 17

Camden tried stretching her sore muscles, causing her eyes to flutter open. The realization that she wasn't at home, hit her like a bat to the chest as memories of the night filled her head. She glanced around. The sun was just starting to rise, filling the room with orange rays. Her eyes landed on the slumbering woman next to her and the aching in her body from lying on the floor for so long, faded away. She reached over, brushing the hair from her face with her finger.

Suddenly, Leigh jerked back, opening her eyes wildly. Her heart raced out of control. Seeing Camden's face and her caring eyes helped calm her.

"Are you okay?" Camden whispered, concerned with the fear she saw in Leigh's eyes when she'd first opened them.

"Yeah," she murmured, clearing her throat.

"I'm going to go," Camden said, pulling the covers back.

"Don't…" Leigh muttered, putting her hand on her arm. "I promise I didn't forget you were next to me."

"I know." Camden nodded. "I have to be on shift in less than an hour, but I'd like to have dinner again tonight… if you want."

"I'd like that." Leigh smiled. "I was supposed to cook for you before you whisked me away to meet your parents, who I think are wonderful, by the way."

The corners of Camden's mouth turned up in a grin.

"Will you be done around the same time?"

"Yes, barring unforeseen circumstances."

"Like a bear in someone's house?" Leigh teased.

"Yeah. Something like that." Camden smiled brightly.

Leigh reached out, placing her palm against Camden's cheek. *I can't fall for you. It's already going to break my heart when I leave.*

Camden grabbed her hand and kissed the center of it. Then she got out of the bed, giving Leigh a look at her lithe figure in the light. "You were right. The view really is amazing."

"Yeah," she mumbled, looking at Camden instead of the scenery through the large windows.

*

Leigh pulled into a parking space behind the general store and went inside in search of capers to go with the dinner she'd decided to make. After walking a few aisles, she went up front to ask the cashier and found several townspeople gathered around talking.

"What's going on?" she asked.

"There's a missing skier up on the mountain," one person said. "A nineteen-year-old male. Search and rescue has been looking for him for about an hour."

"Oh, my." Her heart sunk knowing Camden was out there.

"Did you need help finding anything?" the cashier asked.

"Uh…yeah." Leigh cleared her throat. "Capers."

"Check aisle four with the canned goods."

"Thanks," Leigh said, walking back down the aisle she'd just come from. Her mind was on Camden, making her unable to concentrate. She walked back up front and set her basket back in the bin. She didn't say anything else to the handful of gathered people as she walked out.

*

Camden skied down the edge of Timber Run, the ski trail the missing young man was on. Another SAR officer was coming down the opposite side at the same slow pace, checking the tree line, with Baker and another officer coming behind them.

"Are you sure we're on the right trail?" she radioed. "We've been down this run three times."

"Timber Run is what was reported," Baker replied.

"Ground control? Can we confirm the location?" she radioed to the SAR officer who was at the ski resort with the family, handling the logistics of everyone searching the mountain, while Camden led the search.

"Gorely, standby," he radioed.

She was three-quarters of the way down and once again hadn't seen anything other than skiers and snowboarders all around her, and a stray fox in the trees. Lying on the floor for a couple of hours had been a bad idea, especially with having to ski the mountain the next day over and over.

She hadn't heard back from ground control by the time she reached the bottom, so she skied over to the resort instead of getting back on the lift for the fourth time. "SAR crew, regroup at the resort," she radioed.

"I just spoke to the father," the ground controller said, seeing her walk into the lobby. "He said he had something to tell me…away from his family."

"Where is he?"

"He said he'd be right back."

"I'm going to have the crew come in and warm up with some coffee. Let's talk to him and find out what he has to say before we go back out," she said, checking her watch. It was close to three-thirty. They'd been on the mountain for over two hours. She walked over to the coffee stand, pouring herself a cup. Baker had come in behind her, as well as another SAR officer, and both were already sitting in chairs, drinking coffee.

"Alright. I'm sorry," the father said, stepping over to the crew. "Gavin might be somewhere else."

"What do you mean?" Camden asked, feeling the coffee begin to warm her from the inside.

"He always takes this lift, but he hikes over to other runs sometimes. He likes adventure. He's a good skier. He grew up on this mountain," he sighed.

"Is there a chance he's just been skiing down and riding back up and no one has seen him?" she asked.

He shook his head. "He told his mom he was only going for an hour because he had to go to work at noon. That was at nine this morning. He's never missed a day of work, nor has he been late in the three years he's worked there."

"Okay." Camden nodded. "We're going to find him," she reassured, patting his arm before walking back to her crew. "Here's the gist. This kid could be anywhere. Apparently, he hikes to other runs from this lift."

"Seriously?" Baker muttered. "They could've mentioned that two hours ago."

"I agree, but there's nothing we can do about it now. Travis, call the office and get the helo in the air immediately." She spread the trail map out against the wall. "We'll start with Kamikaze Run."

"That's a double black diamond," Baker squeaked.

"Are you capable of getting down it?" she asked.

He nodded.

She called out the rest of the trails that were accessible from the main lift, explaining how they'll go down each one as a team. Then, everyone put their gear back on and headed out to the lift. She and Baker hopped into the same chair and pulled the bar closed. It quickly rose off the ground, sending them up a hundred yards from the ground.

"You really think he's over there?" Baker asked, knowing that as the leader, she usually tried to place herself where she expected the person to be.

"I don't know."

"How do we know he's not just skiing down a different trail?"

"He was supposed to be at work a few hours ago. He's never missed a day, or been late."

"Damn," he muttered.

"If he's not on one of the diamonds, he's in the backcountry," she said, hearing the helicopter coming. "If he's off the trail, hopefully, they'll see him."

"Yeah."

"SAR crew, once we hike over, let's follow the same format, two ski wide, and two ski the interior of the trail, but make sure we're staggered…and go as slow as possible," she radioed, then adjusted her position to hop off the lift chair.

Baker went with her, skiing off the chair before it went around the half-circle to take it back down to the bottom of the run. Kamikaze was about a twenty-five-yard skiing hike through the woods using a cut trail.

Once they reached the head of the run, Camden gave a thumbs up to everyone and waited for them to return it. She checked her ski bindings to make sure they were locked in place, then pointed her skis down to get going. She stayed along the right-side edge, keeping mostly on the edge of her skis with them pointed inward to scrub her speed, unless she had to go around a tree or large rock. Being a black diamond, the trail had hazards, as well as jumps and extremely unlevel, steep and treacherous terrain. They were known for being the most challenging, but had also claimed a number of lives over the years.

"Gorely, this is Helo One. I'm headed over towards your position now. The other black diamond is a negative," the pilot radioed.

"Roger, Helo One," she replied, having stopped to listen to the transmission, before continuing on.

Halfway down the mountain, Camden spotted something lime green in the snow, just off the trail on the right side. "I have a visual!" she radioed, pointing her skis forward to go faster. Once she reached him, she clicked the buttons to remove her skis, then she threw her poles down next to them before jumping down on her knees next to the limp body. He was on his side, and by the drip of blood coming from his nose and corner of his mouth, she thought maybe he'd hit his head. He was wearing a black helmet, but it may not stop a hard-enough blow to the skull. She removed her glove and felt his neck for a pulse. His skin was ice cold and the vertebrae shifted eerily when she pushed in on his neck under his chin, indicating his neck was broken. He'd obviously crashed while skiing and flew off the trail, which was why no one had reported him. The rest of the group reached her location, skiing to a stop. She signaled for them to turn their radios off so she wouldn't be heard.

"He's gone. His cervical spine is fractured," she said solemnly as the helo worked its way towards them. Let's get the inflatable stretcher ready to go. We'll have to ski down with him."

Baker opened his backpack and the crew began the task of inflating the special stretcher they carried with them. It had a hard bottom that unfolded and snapped into place. Then, the rails all the way around inflated to keep the patient stable.

"Helo One, we have him. Thanks for giving us another set of eyes," she radioed, waving to the pilot. "Ground control, you copy?"

"Roger," the officer working at the base answered.

"10-45 Delta," she replied, indicating they had found him and he was deceased. She used the scanner code in case the family was nearby. That way, he could take them away from the mass of people and tell them.

"Copy," he said.

"Alright. Let's get him strapped in good and head down this damn mountain," she said.

Everyone took one of the tethers coming from the corner of the sleigh-style stretcher, then they began slowly skiing down the mountain together.

*

Leigh still hadn't heard from Camden by the time the sun went down. She turned on the TV, but with no local news channel, there was no report of the missing skier. She silently hoped Camden wasn't still out there. She thought of calling her, wondering if maybe she'd just gone home…but as soon as she picked up her phone, it began ringing.

"Hey," she answered.

"I'm sorry. I should've been there two hours ago," Camden sighed.

"Come over anyway," Leigh said.

"Are you sure?"

"I wouldn't ask if I wasn't."

"I'll be inside in a minute."

"Wait. What?" Leigh looked out the window, seeing headlights pull into the driveway. She rushed over, opening the door quickly.

Camden stepped out of the truck. She'd traded her uniform for jeans, and a thick flannel shirt under her jacket. She walked over to the open door, smiling softly at the beautiful woman waiting for her. She kicked her boots off on the mat inside and removed her jacket.

"I'm sorry for basically showing up…late," she said.

"Don't be. I'm glad you're here. I heard there was a missing skier. Did you find him?" Leigh asked.

Camden nodded. "He was gone."

"Oh, my God. I'm so sorry," Leigh gasped, wrapping her arms around Camden.

Camden had no idea what it was like to come home to someone and allow them to comfort her after a tough day on the job. However, Leigh's warm body felt good against her. "It never gets easier when we lose someone up there, but I think this one stung a little more. He was only nineteen."

"He had his whole life ahead of him," Leigh sighed.

They separated and walked over to the couch. Camden held her arm out and Leigh snuggled in next to her. "Yeah. I'm pretty sure his father had a feeling it was bad. It took him nearly two hours to tell us that he was probably on a different trail than what we were searching."

"What?! Why on Earth would he do that? Could you have saved him if you'd been there earlier?"

"We may have kept him alive, but his neck was snapped nearly in half. He would've been paralyzed for the rest of his life…or worse. I have a feeling he knew his son wouldn't want to live like that. He probably thought if it was bad, it was best to let him go peacefully doing what he loved. Otherwise, if he'd just broken a leg or something, he would've survived and been awaiting our arrival. The whole family was devastated. It was extremely sad."

"That must be some kind of parent's intuition or something. Still, I'm sure they were distraught."

"I agree."

"Did you ever want to be one?" Leigh asked.

"What? A parent?"

She nodded.

"I've never dated anyone long enough to live together, much less think of something long term," Camden said with a shrug. "I guess the thought never really crossed my mind. You?"

Leigh nodded. "At one time I did. Looking back on it now, I'm grateful it never happened."

Camden saw the shadow cross over her eyes and was sure it happened when she thought about a painful memory. "It smells good in here," she said, changing the subject.

"I can heat it up if you're hungry."

"I'd rather just do this…if you don't mind. I'm not really hungry. I'm sorry."

"No. It's fine. You had a rough day. I don't think I'd eat either."

"How was your day? What did you do?"

Leigh smiled. "I didn't have anyone whisk me away to some wild adventure, so I went into town to get a few things and came back and cooked."

"See, now I feel bad for not eating," Camden muttered.

"It really is fine."

Camden wished she'd started a fire when she'd arrived because at the moment she didn't have the energy to do so. She held Leigh a little tighter against her. The fact that they barely knew anything about each other never crossed her mind. There was something about Leigh Myer that drew her like a moth to a flame. If she became too close and got burned in the end, she had a feeling it was going to be well worth it.

"Are you on shift tomorrow?" Leigh asked.

When she didn't respond, Leigh lifted her head to see Camden's eyes closed. She smiled and pulled the throw blanket up over them before snuggling against the sleeping woman once more. "I think I could love you…and that scares me to death," she whispered. *I swore I'd never let anyone close again.*

Chapter 18

The room was dim with only a soft light glowing in the kitchen. Camden stared around the room. She certainly wasn't at home and the warm body curled against her meant she wasn't alone. *Leigh,* she thought, realizing where she was. Her back and shoulders ached from sleeping in a sitting position on the couch. She needed to move, but the slumbering woman beside her looked so peaceful. Camden gently pushed her away, towards the other side of the couch, so she could extract herself. Once she was free, she stood, stretching like a Cheshire cat causing her spine to cracked a couple of times. She put Leigh's legs up on the couch to help her stretch out, then she pulled the throw blanket up over her. She thought about kissing her cheek, and hesitated, hovering inches away. She settled for brushing her knuckles over her smooth skin instead, gasping when Leigh jerked away, awakening with a frightened look on her face.

"I'm sorry," Camden murmured, backing away. "I didn't mean to wake you, or startle you, for that matter."

"It's…fine," she softly sighed as she sat up. "I scare easily these days," she added, brushing her hair over her shoulder. "Where are you going? It's the middle of the night?"

"My back couldn't take that couch any longer, and you looked so serene in your sleep. I tried not to disturb you. I was about to head home."

"The bed upstairs is a lot more comfortable," Leigh stated.

"I remember." The corner of Camden's mouth turned up in a half-grin.

Leigh stood, allowing the blanket to fall away. She grabbed Camden's hand and led her towards the narrow staircase. Camden let go at the top, and Leigh turned to face her.

"What are we doing?' she whispered.

"Getting in bed."

"Leigh…"

"I don't know, Camden." Leigh shook her head. "It's been so long since I let anyone in. I don't…" she paused, wiping a single tear. "I don't know if I even know how to do that anymore."

"I don't expect anything from you, but I'm here if you want to talk about it," Camden said.

"I've never…talked about it," she sighed. "At least, not to anyone other than my parents and the therapist I used to see."

Camden grabbed her hand and ran her thumb over the back of it. "You don't have to now, either. I mean it, Leigh. I'm okay with whatever this is."

Leigh shook her head. "You shouldn't be. You're an amazing person. You deserve so much more than what I can give you." She pressed her free hand to Camden's mouth when she began to speak. "I never expected to fa…" She bit her lower lip. "I care for you, way more than I thought possible, and it happened so quickly. I wasn't planning for any of this. I came up here to clear my head and try to get rid of the darkness that keeps following me. You have no idea how much of a bright light you've been."

"You brought something into my life that I never knew was missing. Please don't push me away. I know you're leaving, and this isn't forever."

Leigh closed the gap between them, kissing her passionately. Camden's mouth opened against hers and probing tongues grazed one another. Both women growled as they struggled to remove the clothing separating them.

Once they'd freed themselves, Leigh tugged her towards the bed. She layed down, pulling Camden on top, silently urging her to take the lead as she spread her legs and pushed her hand down between them. Camden hesitated. She wasn't sure how far she could, or should go, and the last thing she'd wanted to do was go too far, or hurt her.

"It's okay," Leigh whispered. "I want you to touch me."

Camden bent her head, meeting her lips in a passionate kiss as her hand moved lower. She slid her fingers through the wetness, teasing her entrance before passing lightly over her clit several times.

Leigh dug her fingers into Camden's back and turned her head to break the searing kiss. "Go inside," she panted. "I need to feel you."

Camden's chest wall squeezed her lungs and her gut did a flip as her libido went into over-drive. She paused for a second, tamping down her own arousal, before sliding one finger inside of her. Leigh opened to her beautifully. Seeing she had a little more room, she pulled out and slid two back inside.

Leigh gasped as her back arched, and she pushed her hips down onto the fingers plunging in and out of her in a slow, steady motion. She refused to think about the last time she was this intimate with someone because it paled in comparison to the incredible sensation her body was experiencing at the moment. She ran her hand through Camden's short hair, pulling lightly as their lips came together once more. Their mouths quickly opened, allowing their tongues to dance the slow tango of a sensual kiss that left them breathless. Camden backed away slightly, biting and teasing her lower lip before going back for more.

Leigh's thighs began to close as her orgasm started building. Camden pushed her hips down, holding them open wide so she could peak even higher. Her fingers went in deep, then came three-quarters of the way out in unhurried, timely strokes.

"Oh, my God," Leigh rasped hungrily, digging the short nails of one hand into Camden's back while the other tugged at the sheets. Her legs quivered as the climax ripped through her body, leaving her gasping for air and limp in its wake.

Camden carefully pulled her fingers free and kissed her softly before sliding to the side, still lying halfway on her. She watched her face, hoping to see happiness in her beautiful eyes once they opened.

Leigh reached up, running her hand over Camden's cheek as her half-lidded eyes slowly came into focus and her mouth curled into a warm smile. She leaned over slightly, connecting their lips for a lingering kiss as she urged Camden onto her back. When the kiss ended, she brushed her hair over her shoulder and inched her way down Camden's body, dragging her tongue down the center of her torso. Her hair followed the same path, tickling Camden's sensitive skin.

Camden swallowed the lump in her throat as Leigh settled between her legs. She couldn't remember the last time she'd let someone get that intimate with her. Leigh's eyes met hers with a questioning gaze. Camden reached down, interlacing their fingers together on one hand. She watched Leigh's tongue snake out and flatten against her. She trembled as the first touch set her nerves on fire.

There was nothing languid or leisurely about Leigh's strokes as she ran her tongue along a direct path, circling Camden's sensitive clit and sucking it between her lips, before teasing her entrance. The sensation nearly drove Camden right over the edge. She quickly held her breath, hoping she could reboot her body before it betrayed her. However, the first wave of euphoria began to wash over her. She squeezed Leigh's hand and grasped the sheets as her hips bucked against her mouth. Her chest heaved and she was certain she'd growled like an animal, but she didn't care. She rode the orgasmic high until she couldn't take it any longer.

Leigh lifted her mouth and began kissing her way back up Camden's limp body, stopping at her lips. The erotic taste of herself on Leigh's tongue sent Camden's body right back into overdrive.

"We could probably keep at this all night," Leigh whispered, grinning as she pulled out of the kiss and settled against her side.

"Yeah." Camden smiled, wrapping her arms around her.

"You've got to be exhausted from today."

Camden nodded, meeting her with heavy-lidded eyes.

Leigh kissed her cheek and laid her head on her shoulder, tucking her forehead against Camden's chin. A tiny tear escaped one of her eyes and rolled down her cheek.

Chapter 19

The sun had barely climbed over the horizon when Camden had gone home to shower and put on a fresh uniform. The restaurant already had a line of customers outside when she rode by and pulled into the only open parking space.

"You look beat," Aunt Ma said, giving her a quick hug when she walked in.

"I'd be lying if I said I wasn't tired."

"There's an open spot at the bar. I'll be right over with coffee and breakfast. Do you want the usual?"

"That's fine. Thank you." Camden smiled and walked away. "Hey, old man," she teased, patting Uncle Pa on the shoulders as she passed by him.

"Hey, kiddo. How are you doing after yesterday?"

"I'm okay." She nodded. She wasn't exactly used to seeing death on the mountain, but she'd seen her fair share over the years. It never got easier, but she'd learned to let it go quickly before it consumed her.

"I'm here…anytime," he said, knowing what she was going through after spending thirty years on that mountain, doing the same job.

"Thanks."

"Go get something to eat, and take an extra cup of coffee to go when you leave. You'll need it."

She smiled and headed over to the open seat at the end of the bar. Aunt Ma appeared two minutes later with a plate of food and a steaming cup of coffee with creamer already in it. She immediately dug in, ignoring the conversations going on around her, until her radio went off.

"Gorely, are you rolling yet? We have an injured river otter reported south of the inlet near the bridge," dispatch said.

"Copy. I'm at Ma and Pa's. Leaving now," she replied before swallowing a couple of huge bites of food.

"Here you go," Aunt Ma said, handing her a fresh cup of coffee in a go-cup, as well as a fresh muffin from the oven.

"Thanks. Put the bill on my tab. I'll square up with you on my next day off."

"Oh, no you won't. You eat free here and you know it."

Camden shook her head. "Thanks. Love to you both." She grabbed her coffee and muffin bag and took off out of the restaurant.

*

It took all of ten minutes for Camden to get out of town towards the bridge that crossed the river. She parked and got out, searching along the bank. When she spotted the furry little creature, lying against some rocks, she went back to the truck and pulled her hip waders on.

"I'm coming for you, buddy. Don't claw me to death, and I'll save you. Do we have a deal?" she said as she got into the thigh-deep, icy water and walked towards his location. Reaching out with her gloved hands, she was able to free him from the rocks he was stuck on. He barely moved, which was completely unusual. There was no way he'd survive out there in his lethargic condition, so she carried him up to the truck and placed him in the cat-style carrier and put it on the floorboard of the truck to keep him warm.

"Gorely to dispatch. I have the otter. Heading out to the conservatory," she radioed after removing her waders.

"Copy," dispatch replied.

"Alright, bud. What kind of music do you like?" she muttered, looking down at the creature staring back at her. "You're lucky. I make the weasels ride in the back," she added, starting the truck and backing away from the river bank.

*

The drive out to the conservatory was uneventful, and extremely quiet. She'd hoped the little guy hadn't bit the dust on the way. She parked at the front and got out, carrying the cage inside with her.

"Is this the otter?" Kelsey asked, rushing up to her.

"Yeah. Is Dr. Sullivan around? I'm not sure if he's dead or alive."

"Come on, she's in the back," the young girl said, eager to be close to her in any way possible.

They walked down the hall and stopped in one of the exam rooms. Heather came from the other end of the hall, meeting them inside.

"I've got this. Kelsey, go help with the morning rounds," she said, disappointing the young tech. "That crush is going to get her in trouble one of these days," she muttered.

"I'd never go there," Camden said.

"I know *you* wouldn't…besides, I hear you and that pretty blonde are an item."

"What? Who told you that?"

"The family gossip mill, of course," Heather laughed.

"Seriously? They see me with her once and tell everyone?"

"Have you thought about it from their angle? How many women have you taken to dinner at the restaurant…and introduced them?"

Camden pursed her lips and sighed. "We're not dating."

"Ah…so you're just sleeping together."

"Is the otter dead, or what?" Camden grumbled, changing the subject.

Heather laughed. "He's in shock. I'll give him a sedative to calm him. I think he'll be fine, but I need to check him out thoroughly and make sure there are no injuries."

Camden nodded. "Let me know how it goes. I need to get back to town."

"Don't be too hard on them. They just want to see you happy…and settled with someone."

"I am happy. Whether or not I am in a relationship with someone isn't going to change that. What about you?"

"What about me?" Heather squeaked.

"You really have no idea, do you?"

"About what?" Heather injected the otter with the sedative and put him in an incubator type cage.

"Baker?"

"Huh? Baker…your partner?"

"We don't really have partners, but yes, he works with me a lot."

"Okay? What about him?"

"You think Kelsey has a crush on me…"

"Wait…what?"

"He likes you…a lot."

"Why are you telling me this?" Heather huffed.

Camden shrugged.

"How do you know? And why hasn't he said anything?"

"I don't know, Heather. We're not ten. There are no check yes or no notes to pass around. He's liked you for a while and the only reason I know is because we're good friends. He really is a stand-up guy. I've trusted him with my life a few times in the five years I've known him. I'm pretty sure he's scared you'll reject him. That's why he hasn't said or done anything."

"What am I supposed to do about it?"

Why is this shit so much easier with lesbians? Camden shook her head. "I don't know. Talk to him the next time you see him…about more than just the reason he is here. If you like him, show interest. Have a real conversation. Flirt, for God's sake."

"Is that how you get all of thc girls? Talking?"

"Why does everyone think I've had all of these women?" she snapped. "I don't sleep with everyone who shows interest." She rubbed her finger and thumb together on her forehead, staving off the start of a headache. "I need to get back to work. Just…I don't know. Do what you want with what I told you. It's none of my business anyway. Keep me updated on the otter," she said before walking out of the room.

"Camden…I could…uh, use some help feeding the animals," Kelsey said, seeing her in the hallway.

"I need to get back to the mountain. Maybe another time." She started to walk away and turned back around. "Kelsey, how old are you?"

"Twenty."

Camden swallowed the lump in her throat. "You know I'm old enough to be your mother, right?"

"So." The young girl shrugged.

Camden shook her head. "I'm flattered, but nothing will ever happen between us except a strictly professional relationship. If that is a problem for you, I suggest finding employment elsewhere, or avoiding me altogether when I am here."

"It's that woman, isn't it? The one you brought here."

"Yes and no."

"She's pretty."

"Yes, she is. And, so are you. You'll meet someone one day who completely knocks you out of your shoes. I promise. It just isn't me," Camden replied, before walking out of the building.

*

Camden had texted Leigh, asking if she wanted to meet for lunch not long after she'd left the conservatory, but a few hours had come and gone and she'd never heard back from her. She blew it off, figuring she was out in town somewhere, and went about the rest of her day.

She and Baker worked on a couple of illegal hunting cases and set some game cameras out to try and catch the culprits in the act. She never bothered telling him about her conversation with Heather. That was something they needed to work out on their own. They *were* adults after all.

"You feel like going to the Dirty Moose tonight? It's karaoke night," Baker said when their shift came to an end and she drove him to his truck at the station.

"Nah. I have a few things to do."

"What's going on with that pretty vacationer?"

"I've seen her a few times." Camden shrugged.

"You can bring her with you."

Camden smiled. "I'll ask her, but I doubt she'll want to go. Besides, I'm dead tired. I really need to just go home and sleep. If we get called out tonight, I'm liable to pass out on the side of the mountain."

"Yeah, I didn't get much sleep either, but I'm going to go have a beer."

"Why don't you invite Heather?"

"She doesn't live in town."

"That's never stopped you before," she chided.

He shrugged.

I give up. She sighed. "I'll see you tomorrow. Have a good night."

"You too." He grinned.

She rolled her eyes and drove away.

*

After a quick shower, Camden pulled on a pair of jeans and a black sweater and headed over to see Leigh. She'd called her on her way home, but it went to voicemail. She was a little worried since she hadn't been able to reach her all day.

As soon as she pulled into the driveway, Camden noticed two things. Leigh's car was gone, and the cabin was dark. "What the hell?" she mumbled, getting out to have a look around. A white envelope got her attention. It was sticking out of the doorjamb above the knob and deadbolt lock. Her name was scrawled across the front of it in loopy, feminine handwriting. She quickly tore it open.

Chapter 20

Leigh awoke to the sun filling the cabin with bright yellow light. She was alone and had been for a couple of hours, but she reached out anyway, running her hand over the cool sheets. She sighed, breathing in the faintest scent of Camden's cologne as she stared out the window at the massive fir trees. "I'm going to miss waking up to this every morning," she muttered.

Her phone lit up on the nightstand with Abby's smiling face, bringing her back to reality. She ignored it, but that was just the first of the tell-tale signs it was time to get back to her life in the city. She got out of the bed and ran a hand through her hair, shaking it out around her shoulders before pulling on her robe. She went downstairs to start a cup of coffee, then headed back up to get ready for the day. As soon as she was finished dressing, she retrieved her suitcase from the closet and began putting her clothes inside in no specific order. She added her bathroom bag and the couple of souvenirs she'd purchased, then zipped it closed. She turned around at the top of the stairs, looking back at the rumpled sheets on the bed. Her chest ached as flashes of making love with Camden flooded her mind. *It was never a mistake.*

After loading her suitcase in the car, Leigh went back inside while it warmed up. She grabbed a piece of paper and a pen from the kitchen drawer. A few tears rolled down her cheeks as she began writing.

Camden,

I don't know how to write this because I've never had to before now. As I look around this cabin for the last time, I feel like it was all a dream. There's never been anyone like you in my life. This week was supposed to be a journey to find myself and let go of the chains of my past that keep holding me down. In a way, I accomplished what I set out to do, but like all things, it came with a price.

When I decided to take this trip on a whim, the last thing I expected was to meet someone so charismatic, she knocked me off my feet without even trying. It had been so long since I'd let anyone get close to me. All I knew how to do was keep my family at arm's length, and push everyone else away, and suddenly the walls I'd carefully built around me, crumbled to the ground.

I know I'm a coward, but I couldn't bear to look into your eyes and tell you I'd fallen for you…and say goodbye in the same sentence. Our time together was short, but I'll never forget it, or you. You have no idea how much you've changed my life in just one week.

I'll never regret a second of my time here. I have a feeling I will remember our time together for the rest of my life. Please stay safe. I'll think of you always.

Leigh

She quickly folded the paper and stuffed it into an envelope. Then, on her way out, she tucked it in the doorjamb above the deadbolt lock. She never looked back at the cabin with fear she'd break down crying. Her phone beeped with a voicemail from Camden, which she ignored as she pulled out onto the main road and set her GPS to take her home.

*

Leigh wasn't supposed to return to work for another few days, but that hadn't mattered. Her decision to leave early had everything to do with falling for Camden. She'd only been in love one other time, and it was certainly nothing like this. She simply couldn't go through that again.

She overlooked the text messages and additional voicemail from Camden as she drove along the highway. She never wanted to hurt her, and felt horrible for doing so. *It's for the best. I'm sorry.*

Chapter 21

Camden sat in her truck in shock as she stared at the empty cabin. The letter lie on the center console next to her. When she'd left to get ready for her shift that morning, she had no idea it was the last time she'd see Leigh. It stung thinking back to the night they'd shared. Vacationers had come and gone, and she'd come and gone from their beds just as easily. However, this time was so different. It was so much more. *Leigh* was so much more. She smacked her fist on the steering wheel as a couple of tears escaped her eyes, sliding down her cheeks. "Damn it," she spat, wiping them away bcfore balling up the letter up and tossing it on the passenger floorboard of the truck. "I thought you were different," she whispered as she started the engine and drove away.

*

The Dirty Moose was a hole in the wall bar that sat on the edge of town, with a few pool tables, a couple of dartboards, a tiny stage in the corner, and a menu full of fried food. Several of the locals frequented it, leaving the resort bars to the vacationers.

Half of the double doors opened, whisking the cool air inside. A few heads turned, nodding in Camden's direction as she walked past. The air smelled like kitchen grease and stale beer, and the woman on the stage singing karaoke sounded like a cat who smoked two packs a day.

"I thought you weren't coming," Baker said.

"Changed my mind," she muttered, pouring herself a glass of light beer from his pitcher. She'd wanted something much stronger, but she was driving.

"She left, didn't she?"

"Don't they all?" Camden muttered, taking a long swallow from her glass. Then, she grabbed a pool cue and set a twenty-dollar bill on the table. "Best of three?"

"Deal." He pulled a twenty from his wallet to match hers.

"Rack 'em," she said, adding blue chalk to the end of her cue.

He knew better than to question her. This vacationer had been the closest he'd ever seen her get to dating someone, and he sensed it had ended abruptly. Especially after she smashed the balls so hard on the break, one went flying off the table. "I should just give her the twenty," he gulped under his breath.

"What was that?" she questioned, retrieving the ball.

"I'm good." He shook his head as if he hadn't spoken and moved to the other end of the table to take his first shot. She'd sunk a solid ball, so he had stripes. He easily sunk one ball, then missed his next shot.

Camden checked the angle of the shot, then lined up her cue. With a quick flick of the wrist, she drove the white ball into the red one, sinking it in a side pocket. Then, went on to sink three more balls before missing a shot.

"Are you singing tonight?" he asked, sinking two balls before missing.

"No." She moved around the table, eyeing her last two balls before easily sinking them both, plus the eight ball. She sat down on the stool. "Rack 'em back up," she said, pulling her glass to her lips.

"I'm a pretty good listener…if you ever want to talk about it," he said sincerely as he put the balls together in the triangle.

"There's nothing to say. We had a good time together and she left today." She shrugged, stepping up and blasting the balls again on the break. They all stayed on the table this time, and none of them managed to drop into the pockets. "Open table."

Baker added a little bit of chalk to his cue and searched around for the easiest shot. "You didn't know she was leaving, did you?"

"Nope." She finished her beer and set the empty glass down.

He finally took a shot, sending the yellow ball into the corner pocket, setting him up with the purple ball, which he sunk as well. His third ball missed the mark and bounced off the rail. Camden studied the striped balls for a second, then quickly sunk two of them before missing her third.

"Maybe she had an emergency at home or something," he said, preparing to take his next shot.

"Yeah," she sighed, knowing that wasn't the truth. Baker was a good friend, and he was trying, but honestly, there wasn't much to say to begin with.

He sunk three balls and missed his fourth, leaving two solids on the table, which set Camden up for an easy shot. She quickly sunk all of her balls, plus the eight ball, clearing the table once again.

"You're such a hustler," he laughed. "I don't know why I bother betting with you."

She smiled and shrugged.

"Double or nothing?" he questioned, leaning against the table with a grin on his face.

"Nah. I need to get home and get some sleep," she replied, shoving the cash in her pocket. "Thanks," she said, patting him on the shoulder.

"Anytime." He nodded in understanding.

*

Camden put a couple of thin logs in the wood-burning stove when she got home. Once it was glowing orange, she tossed the note inside and sat down in the nearby recliner. There was no sense in keeping it. She had it memorized, not that she cared to read it again anyway. The heat coming from the stove was warm and inviting. Before she knew it, she'd fallen asleep.

Grayish blue eyes looking back at her and soft lips on hers woke Camden with a start. She glanced around the room. The light on the stove hood was the only thing illuminating the room. The fire had been out for some time. There weren't even any embers glowing on the bottom. She sighed and got up, pouring herself a tall glass of water, before heading to her bedroom.

Chapter 22

Leigh wrinkled her nose at the stale air of the hospital. Her stethoscope bounced against her chest and her sneakers squeaked as she walked down the hallway, moving from one exam room to another in a long list of mundane patients when her phone began vibrating. She'd taken Camden's name out of her phone, but the number was recognizable. "I'm sorry," she whispered, wiping away a stray tear as she watched the call end before her voicemail picked up. She cleared the call and shoved it in her pocket. *I wish I could turn back time to the day we met and do it all over again.*

"I still can't believe you came back early," Abby said, bumping shoulders with her. "I want to hear all about it."

Leigh cleared her throat. "There's not much else to tell, and there was a storm coming. I didn't want to get snowed in or risk driving back in bad weather." She hated lying to her friend, but she wasn't interested in talking about it. *I'm a coward and I ran from the best thing that has ever happened to me because I keep letting my past dictate my future.*

"What about that smoking hot wildlife officer? Are you going to see her again?"

"I wasn't seeing her to begin with…so no."

"Really? It sure seemed like you were spending a lot of time together."

"We weren't dating, Abby," she stated. "I need to get some of these patients discharged before asshole gives me more of his bitch work. I'll catch up with you later."

Abby sensed the irritation in her friend and backed off. She knew there was something else bothering her besides the ridiculous antics of the hospital. She seemed to have been having the time of her life up at the cabin. Abby had no idea what had happened, but something had changed her friend.

"I'll have a bottle of wine ready to go when you want to talk," she said.

Leigh held her thumb up over her head in agreement before walking into the room.

*

Camden let a couple of days go by before she tried calling Leigh. It went unanswered and she hadn't bothered leaving a voicemail. She'd already sent a text a few days earlier and got nothing in return. "She probably has a husband," she muttered, staring at her phone. "It wouldn't be the first time." She didn't have any social media accounts, but she knew how to search it. That was how she and Baker found out about the majority of their illegal hunting cases. However, a quick search on Leigh's name yielded absolutely nothing. In fact, nothing came up at all when she put her name in the search engine altogether. *Are you a ghost?* "I'd think she gave me a fake name if I hadn't seen her license the day I pulled her over."

After a few more minutes of checking everything she could think of, she gave up and set her phone on the side table next to her recliner. There was nothing more she could do. Leigh had chosen to leave without saying goodbye and she wasn't taking her calls. "It's probably for the best," she told herself.

Chapter 23

As the days faded into weeks, Camden fell back into her old routine. Thoughts of the beautiful vacationer slowly drifted away, getting replaced by one SAR call after another as peak ski season rolled through the mountain.

She was on her way home after being called out on a rescue in the middle of her day off when a wildlife call came in for a sick moose who was tilting his head to one side and walking in circles, an indication of brain worm sickness, which literally was a parasitic worm in the brain. It happened from time to time, and the wildlife officers always put the animal down, out of its own misery.

She wasn't far away and although the idea of shooting an animal never sat well with her, it was the right thing to do. She grabbed the radio mic on the side of the computer in her truck. "This is Gorely. I'm two minutes out from the moose. I'll take the call."

"Copy," dispatch replied.

Camden pulled up on the scene and immediately saw the large animal walking in brisk circles with his head tilted all the way left. She sighed and grabbed her rifle from the case behind her seat. Thankfully, the people who had reported it were gone, leaving her alone to do her job. She leaned across the hood of her truck to take aim through the scope. "I'm sorry," she whispered. As the animal made another loop, she squeezed the trigger, firing a single shot into his head. He immediately dropped to the ground. She stowed her rifle and called dispatch to let them know he was down so they could send an officer on duty out to retrieve the carcass. Whenever they had to put an animal down or confiscate animal meat from illegal hunting, the meat was always given to low-income families and the nearby homeless shelter so that it was never wasted.

Once she was back in the truck, she dialed a number on her phone and enabled the speakerphone.

"Hey. I heard you go to that moose call," Baker said as he answered.

"Yeah. It wasn't far from the address. I figured why make it wait, you know?"

"I feel the same way."

"I was about to head home. I'm thinking of going to Ma and Pa's for dinner. You interested in stopping by?" she said.

"I would…but, I actually have a date."

"Really?"

"Yep."

"Well, enjoy your evening then. I can't wait to hear all about it."

"Aren't you going to ask me who it is?"

"Why? Do I know her?" she questioned. "Wait a second. It's not Heather…is it?"

"Uh-huh."

"Seriously? Way to go. So, you finally got up the courage to ask her out."

"She kind of asked me."

"Really?" she chuckled.

"Anyway, it's about damn time. I hope you two have fun."

"You too. Tell Ma and Pa I said hi."

"You're not taking her there?" she questioned in surprise.

"No. We're going to dinner at some Italian place."

"Oh, probably Mario's. It's not far from where she lives in Granville. It's pretty good actually. I've been there a few times. Well, don't let me keep you. Tell her I said hi."

"I will. Hey…do you have any plans tomorrow?" he asked before hanging up.

"I'm going over in the morning to help Uncle Pa change the garbage disposal at their house, but that's about it."

"I was thinking of taking my sled out. There won't be much snow on the ground soon. The forecast is already warming up next week."

"Yeah, I saw that."

"I'll touch base with you before I head out."

"Sounds good." She ended the call and headed down the road.

Her cabin was dark with nothing but the full moon overhead to illuminate the path to the small front porch. As soon as she unlocked the door, she stepped inside and slipped her boots and jacket off. The cabin had central heat, but she only turned it on when she was going to sleep since her room was in the back of the cabin. Otherwise, she preferred to sit in the recliner next to the wood-burning stove. She tossed a few logs inside with some kindling and lit it up before going to her room to change out of her uniform.

Once she returned, she contemplated opening a beer, but knew she was too tired to even finish it. Instead, she went to task heating up some leftovers for dinner since she was too tired to go back down to the restaurant. While she waited for the microwave to work its magic on the frozen, homemade dish, she glanced around at her living space. She'd grown accustomed to the bachelor life over the years and up until a couple of weeks ago, it fit her just fine. It flabbergasted her how quickly her entire life shifted in one direction overnight, then changed right back as if nothing had ever happened. She would be sure she had traveled backward in time, if the memories of her time with Leigh weren't so strong. "If everything happens for a reason, I'd sure as hell like to know the reason we met," she muttered, pushing off the counter to check the time on the microwave.

*

The sun was high in the sky just before eight a.m. when Camden pulled into her parent's driveway. They lived in town, in a small, single-story house only a few blocks over from the restaurant. When they moved off the mountain they were looking to downsize and the quaint house had fit them perfectly.

"Knock knock," she said, using her key to come in through the front door. "Uncle Pa?"

"In here," he called from the kitchen.

"You started without me?" she chided, shaking her head. "I can do that. Let me get under there."

"I've got it. Hand me that pipe wrench."

She did, as instructed. "You remembered to turn off the power, right?"

"I'm old, not dumb," he said, peering out from under the cabinet at her.

She smiled.

"There's fresh coffee in the pot. I just made it, *before* I turned off the power."

She shook her head and walked over, pouring a mug full. Then, she opened the fridge, looking for the cream container in the dark.

After a minute passed, Uncle Pa said, “It’s in the cow!”

Right! She began looking for the ceramic cow on the shelf and found it in the back. She tipped it forward and white cream flowed into her mug.

“You’d think you’ve never been here,” he uttered.

“It’s been a while.”

“I know. If it wasn’t for the restaurant, we’d probably never see you.”

She sighed, knowing he was right.

“I’m sorry, kiddo,” he said, sliding out from under the cabinet with the contraption in his hands. “We just miss you.”

“I miss you, too.”

“Come on, let’s ride over to Hawthorne’s. Hopefully, he has a similar one,” he said, referring to the local hardware store that also carried lawn and garden, and farm accessories.

Camden got into the passenger side of his late-model truck and buckled her seatbelt. The radio was on, but the volume was too low for her to recognize the song.

“Aunt Ma’s worried about you, kid,” he muttered as he backed out of the driveway and headed down the road. “Frankly, I am too. You haven’t been the same since that vacationer left.”

“I’m fine. I got a little more attached than I should have. That’s all.”

“A little more attached? Is that what you kids are calling it these days?”

"Calling what?" she questioned, staring out the window. She had no idea where this was going, but her Uncle Pa was known for his philosophical talks every now and then, and she enjoyed every minute of them, whether they made sense or not.

"Falling in love," he said.

Camden choked on the saliva she swallowed and went into a coughing fit, causing Uncle Pa to laugh and offer her a toffee flavored hard candy that he kept in a bag in the console.

"I'm fine," she mumbled, clearing her throat. "Besides, she's gone, so it doesn't matter anyway."

"Love isn't something you can see coming. There are no sirens or warning signs. Suddenly, bam!" He smacked his hands together. "It hits you like a damn two-by-four in the chest. Some people can take the hit, but there are people who can't handle it. They run like hell…and all you can do is let them go."

She nodded but didn't say anything.

"I was a lot younger than you are when I let the love of my life go. She was so young and innocent. But, man was she beautiful. I had no idea the yearning in my heart to see her, and the warmth spreading through me when she smiled, was love…until she was gone. I felt like she took a part of me with her and the rest of me was going to die without it."

"Wow, Uncle Pa. How did you move on?"

"I said when they run, you have to let them go, but I never said they were gone forever. Love is scary and unpredictable, but it's a hell of a lot easier to navigate together. Most of the people who run at first, they come back. Their broken heart catches up to them, and trust me, it hurts just as bad on their end."

"So…she came back?"

"Yeah." He smiled. "It took her a few weeks, but she ran back as quickly as she'd left."

"What happened?"

"I married her, of course!"

"Wait…Aunt Ma?"

"Almost sixty years." He looked over at her.

"That's…wow," she mumbled in surprise. "Somehow, I don't think Leigh's going to come running back," she sighed.

"If it's real love, it'll find a way," he said, pulling into the parking lot behind the hardware store. "Give her some time."

"Hey, did you and Aunt Ma know Heather and Baker are dating?" she said, changing the subject once they walked inside.

"Baker? Really?"

"Yeah. They had their first date last night, but I'm sure it won't be the last. They've been interested in each other for months and neither said anything. I finally put the bug in their ears."

He grinned and shook his head.

Chapter 24

Leigh opened the door of her apartment after hearing the loud knock. She was still dressed in her light blue scrubs since she hadn't been home long.

"Girl, go wash the stink of that shitty hospital off. I have a chilled bottle of wine with me," Abby said, walking inside.

Leigh smiled at her friend.

"Go on. This needs to breathe a little anyway."

"Alright, alright," she said, scampering off to the bathroom.

It only took her ten minutes to shower, towel off, and get dressed. She towel-dried her hair and combed the rest of the water out before turning the blow dryer on it. She didn't want to dry it completely, just enough to leave it slightly damp.

"Don't you feel better?" Abby asked when she walked back into the living room.

"Absolutely," Leigh replied, reaching for one of the glasses of wine as she sat down on the couch beside her. All it took was one sip to remind her of the mountains. Abby had obviously bought the same wine she'd drank while she was at the cabin. She closed her eyes, savoring the flavors on her tongue and the memories that followed. As much as she'd tried to get back to her life, she often found herself going back to the tranquility of the mountain and calming happiness she felt around Camden.

"You okay?" Abby asked.

"Yeah," Leigh sighed.

"You looked a million miles away."

A hundred and fifty-three to be exact. She smiled.

"You haven't been the same since you came back. What the hell happened up there?"

"We're going to need another bottle," Leigh laughed, sipping her wine as she put her feet up on the coffee table.

Abby stayed quiet, sensing her friend was finally about to talk to her.

"I don't know, to be honest with you. I felt so free…so happy. It's been years since that's happened to me, and it scared me." Leigh looked over at her friend. "I ran like hell…because that's all I know how to do anymore."

Abby nodded. "I felt a little bit of that happy freedom once I got over the hurt and anger from my divorce. It took me a while to accept that it was okay. I'm scared to death to fall in love again though. What if the next guy's a cheating piece of shit too? You know?"

"Yeah," Leigh sighed. *Exactly. What if history repeats itself? I will never ever go through that again.*

"Did that good-looking wildlife officer have anything to do with you finding happiness up there on the mountain?"

Leigh sipped her wine, letting the fruity flavors slosh around in her mouth before swallowing. "Yeah," she whispered. "I was falling for her."

Abby squeezed her friend's hand. "That's why you came home early, isn't it?"

Leigh nodded.

*

As soon as Abby left, Leigh dialed a number on her phone and curled her legs under her on the couch. It rang twice before a woman picked up.

"Hey, Mom," Leigh said.

"How was your trip? I was so worried about you up there all alone. I can't believe you didn't tell us until you were already there."

"It was good…great actually. I had more fun in one week than I've had my entire life. I rode on a snowmobile all over the mountain, got to watch animals being rescued, saw a lot of wildlife, and went on a hike. I felt so free and happy for the first time in years."

"Wow. It sounds like you had a wonderful time. You said a week. I thought you were going for two."

"I was, but I came home early."

The subtle shift in her daughter's voice was a red flag. "What happened, honey?"

"I met someone," Leigh sighed. "We had the most amazing time together, then I ran as fast as I could."

"Sweetie, you've been running for five years. At some point, you have to let yourself love again."

"I'm so scared of everything happening all over again," Leigh said, wiping a tear from her cheek.

"Unfortunately, that's a chance you have to be willing to take. Your father and I have been so worried that you would never open your heart again. You can't let your dark past ruin your bright future with someone else."

"I felt so free on that mountain. For those few days, I nearly forgot everything and was no longer running. As soon as I returned to the hospital, I felt caged."

"You can't keep living your life looking over your shoulder, honey. There's nothing there but an old, painful ghost."

"You sound like my therapist." She smiled to herself.

Her mom chuckled softly. "Well…I certainly went to my fair share of the appointments with you. Speaking of Dr. Sherry, have you called her?"

"No," she sighed. "I have to be able to get through this without her, or I'll never be able to move on with my life and let myself love again."

"Tell me about this person you met. She did all of those activities with you?"

"Her name is Camden, and she's... I've never met anyone like her, Mom. She's a fish and wildlife officer on the mountain, as well as a search and rescue team leader."

"She sounds busy," she laughed.

"Yeah. But, she's damn good at her job. In fact…I wasn't going to tell you this, but I got lost in the woods. She rescued me."

"Leigh Gertie Myer, why on earth would you keep that from me?!" her mother growled. "Thank God you're okay!"

"I'm sorry."

"Well, now I'm really glad you met."

Leigh laughed. "She took me all over the mountain on her snowmobile. That was the neatest thing I've ever done. We saw the rapids and had lunch at a ski restaurant at the top of the mountain. I also got to watch her rescue a baby bear, and I fed wild animals at the conservatory with her. She's just…"

"She sounds amazing, honey." It felt good hearing happiness in her daughter's voice.

"Yeah…and that's what scared me. Everything happened so fast. I let myself fall for her so easily." She wiped another tear. "I ran without saying anything to her."

"You're the only one who will know when you're ready to love again. I just hope and pray you see it and allow it to happen. You deserve to have love and happiness in your life."

"I've been miserable since I've been back home. I can't stop thinking about her, but also all of the people I met while I was there. The atmosphere was…I don't know. Just different. I fell in love with everything, she was an added bonus I never expected."

"Nothing is promised in this life and sometimes the risks you take are very rewarding. Other times, they're nightmares. You simply don't know until you take the chance."

"You're right, Mom. As always. I love you."

"I love you too, honey."

She ended the call and flopped back on her bed, staring at the wall. She missed the view of the giant fir trees covered in snow and the liberated feeling of being on the mountain, away from the ghosts of her past. But, she missed Camden most of all. *I can't get you out of my head. I see your eyes everywhere and I feel your gentle kisses in my dreams at night. I just don't know if I'm strong enough to take the chance on you…myself…or us.*

Chapter 25

Camden was happy to see the snow beginning to melt on the top of the mountain. The town at the base hadn't had snow on the ground in over a week. The trails had been closed for nearly two weeks. It wouldn't be long before they opened back up for UTV and four-wheeler season.

"I saw the report this morning about the dirt bikes out on the trails," Baker said, sipping his cup of coffee.

"Yeah, I got it too," she replied between bites of breakfast.

"How are things going with our niece?" Uncle Pa asked, refilling Baker's coffee. "We expect a wedding invitation."

"Uh…," he mumbled.

Camden laughed. "He's teasing you."

Uncle Pa chuckled and walked away.

"I had no idea anyone knew we were dating," Baker squeaked.

"It's been a few weeks. This is a small town. It doesn't take a genius to figure it out. Besides, Heather's mom and Aunt Ma are sisters. Not much gets past them."

Baker nodded.

"Are you happy?"

"Yeah."

"That's all that matters," she said, pushing her plate away. "Come on. Let's go see if we can bust some dirt bike riders. All of this happy talk has me wanting to write some tickets."

"Still haven't heard from her, huh?" Baker said, tossing some cash on the bar to cover his tab before following her out.

"No," she mumbled, holding the door for him.

"I can't believe she left without saying anything."

"She left a note."

"You didn't tell me that."

She shrugged. "It didn't say much. She didn't give a reason for leaving."

"I still can't believe with all of the social media today, you can't find her."

"I get the feeling she's someone who doesn't want to be found. When she was here it was almost like she was on the run in the beginning and then she let herself relax. I think that's what scared her and sent her packing. I don't know."

"I'm sorry."

"Thanks, but there's really nothing to be sorry about."

*

After a few hours of riding along the trails in Baker's UTV, he and Camden were about ready to call it a day when they spotted something orange in the distance. She quickly grabbed the binoculars and trained them on the area.

"Son of a bitch," she grumbled.

"What is it?"

"The dirt bikes!"

Baker quickly started the UTV and took off in the direction of the bikes while Camden kept her binos on them.

"There are two of them. If they split, go after the one on the left," she said, watching the bikes race through the woods. Sure enough, they parted. Baker followed her direction, choosing the one that continued going through the backcountry terrain outside of the groomed trail.

The dirt bike rider kept increasing his speed as he bobbed and weaved around rocks and trees. He turned to take a switchback, but was going too fast. He overcorrected and crashed into a tree. Camden watched him fly off the bike. They were twenty yards back, but made it to his location quickly. She jumped out, running up to him.

"My shoulder's out," he grumbled in pain.

"Is anything else hurting?" she asked, checking him over.

"No. My shoulder hurts like hell! Please put it back in," he cried.

"Why did you run from us?" she asked, rocking back on her heels.

"I don't know. I was stupid. Please…it hurts."

"What's your friend's name?"

"What friend?"

She looked at Baker and shrugged as she began to stand.

"Wait! Joe! His name is Joe."

"Joe…what?"

"Nettles."

Baker called the name in to get an address and search warrant for the dirt bike while Camden popped his shoulder back in. He screamed in pain for a split second, then sat up as if nothing had happened to him.

"You're lucky I don't arrest you," she snapped. "You're getting four citations: reckless driving, evading officers, out of date registration sticker, and riding on the trails when they're closed."

"Damn it," he grumbled. "How am I supposed to get this bike home? The handlebars are bent to hell."

"You probably should've thought of that before you decided to take off through the woods like a mad man."

Baker came back with all of the tickets for him to sign. He folded them up and shoved them in his pocket before getting on the bike and attempting to ride off with the crooked handlebars.

Camden laughed. "He's lucky he's alive."

"Yep. Idiot." He shook his head and started the UTV. "I have the address for the other guy."

"Great. Let's go pay him a visit," she said with a big smile.

*

The ride out of the woods didn't take too long and before they knew it, they were back at Baker's truck. They loaded the UTV onto the trailer and headed over to the address they'd gotten from dispatch.

"Wow," Camden said in shock when she saw the dirt bike parked in the yard. "I mean, at least attempt to not look guilty," she added, walking over to it while Baker went to the door.

"Joseph Nettles," Baker called, knocking loudly.

A young man opened the door. "I'm Joe Nettles."

"Were you just out riding this bike in the woods off Buckhead Trail with Jason Lyle? Don't lie to me. We saw you both together and we stopped him after he wrecked his bike into a tree."

"Oh, damn! Is he okay?"

"He's fine. So, you admit to being with him and running from us?"

"Joey, what's going on?" an older gentleman said, walking up behind him. He looked like he'd just gotten out of the shower. "I'm Wayne Nettles. Joe's father."

"Mr. Nettles, we are with fish and wildlife. We caught your son and another young man out on the closed trails today on their dirt bikes. They've been called in for riding several times. Anyhow, when we spotted them today, they both ran from us. The other young man was in a bad wreck, but is okay. He identified your son as the other rider…who got away from us."

"What have I told you about hanging around that loser? He's going to get you arrested…or dead! And why the hell are you out riding this bike? What happened to you working? I ought to kick your ass! Tell them what you've been up to. Don't lie."

Baker cleared his throat. "We don't need him to admit guilt. He's been identified by a witness, so we're just going to write up his citations. It'll take a couple of minutes."

"Why don't you haul his ass to jail? Maybe that'll teach him a lesson. He was supposed to be working a new job. I had no idea he was out hanging around that bum." He shook his head. "And you better not be smoking dope anymore, or I *will* kick your ass!"

"I haven't done that in months," he muttered with his head hung low. "I'm sorry, Dad."

Camden walked back up with the tickets. He only had three since his machine's registration was current.

"Sign these. The number on the back is for the magistrate. You'll need to call and set a court date."

The father shook his head. "Let this be a lesson to you, son. Get a job and get your life together."

"Have a good day," Camden said, walking back to the truck.

"I don't want kids," Baker muttered as he backed out of the driveway.

"Have you told Heather that?" Camden laughed. "I'm too old, so I don't have to worry about it. Besides, I can't have an accident anyway."

He rolled his eyes and shook his head as he drove down the road.

Chapter 26

Leigh had a little more bounce in her usual dreadful step as she walked into the hospital. A few doctors passed by as she walked around the ER.

"Myer, I need a cath in room two," one of the doctors said, passing by her in the hallway.

"I'm not on shift," she called back, continuing her path. She finally found what she was looking for when Abby walked out of room six.

"Hey! I thought you were off today," Abby said.

"I am. Listen…" she pulled her aside. "I want to buy your cabin. I spoke with the bank. I think I can make you a pretty fair offer."

"What are you talking about?" Abby asked, completely in shock. "Have you lost your mind?"

"I have to go back. That's the only place I feel alive and free…and happy. No, I haven't lost my mind, but I *have* been running and I'm ready to stop."

"I don't know what to say."

"Say you'll accept my offer."

"What about your job?"

"I have my resignation letter in my hand."

"Wow. You're really serious."

Leigh nodded.

"I don't even know what that place is worth."

"My bank looked it up and gave me a number, but I want to make sure it's fair to you."

"You know I don't care about that cabin, Leigh. Whatever the bank said, give me half of it."

"No way. I'm not screwing you over, Abby."

"You won't be. I'll be happy to have it off my hands. I don't need the rental income anyway. I got half of asshole's pension from the airline, remember? It's sitting in the bank waiting for me to retire one day. Go on, be happy. But, I'm going to miss you."

"I'll miss you too." Leigh hugged her. "I'll get the bank to draw up the papers today. It's a cash deal, so it should go to closing quickly."

"You can go ahead and move in. I'll call the rental manager on my lunch break and let her know everything. She'll leave the key for you."

"Thank you!" Leigh hugged her again.

"You owe me a bottle of wine!"

"I owe you a lot more than that. I promise to explain everything to you. You're my best friend. You deserve to know my story."

"I'm here for you…always."

Leigh smiled before heading back down the hallway towards the nurse's station to find the head nurse on duty.

*

Leigh felt like a little kid as she began packing all of her belongings. She couldn't help reminiscing about the last time she'd moved. It was the worst time in her life and after settling in a new city, she was sure she'd never be moving again. Now, here she was, boxing up her life all over again. Except this time, she was happy…and most of all, free.

"This is crazy," she kept telling herself as she walked around, tossing things into boxes and bags.

Her parents had offered to help, but there truly wasn't much to do. The apartment she'd been renting for the past five years had come furnished, and the cabin was also furnished, so she was only moving her personal belongings. In a space less than 900 square feet, there wasn't a whole lot of room for anything unnecessary.

When she finished taping the last box closed, she began taking everything out to her car. Squeezing everything in would be a challenge, but she was up for it. There was no way she was making two trips. The drive was three hours one way. She decided early on, if it didn't fit, it wasn't going with her.

Once the car was fully packed and nearly busting at the seams, she went back inside the apartment one last time. "I was broken when I first arrived here, and now look at me. I'm leaving to start the life I've chosen for myself. You weren't a bad place to call home, but you could stand to gain an extra closet or two." She grinned, looking around one last time. "You were good to me. I hope you're equally as healing to whoever comes in behind me."

She placed her key on the counter and walked out for the last time.

*

Anderson East played from the iPod hooked to the radio as Leigh drove along the highway. She thought about the dinner conversation with her parents before she left town.

"We just worry about you, honey. Are you sure moving there right away is what you really want?" her father had said. "How well do you even know this woman?"

"Dad, I'm moving for me…not her. She's an added bonus, but honestly, I've never been so happy. It's funny. I almost hated it at first, with all of that snow, but it quickly grew on me. There's something relaxing and serene about that mountain. I truly feel it's where I belong."

"You're certainly old enough to make your own decisions," her mother had said. "I know you aren't doing anything in haste. This is well thought out."

"Thanks, Mom."

"As soon as you're settled, we're coming up there. I want to check out this mountain and meet Camden," her father added.

"I'd love for you both to meet her, but there's no guarantee she'll want anything to do with me. I told her I was falling for her, and ran away at the same time."

"If it's real love, she'll welcome you with open arms."

"I sure hope you're right, mom," she mumbled.

*

It was nearly dark by the time Leigh arrived at the cabin and began unpacking her car. She was too tired to do anything other than bring her stuff inside. She was surprised to see the snow was already gone, meaning the warmer spring temperatures had begun making their way up the mountain.

Once she was finished with the car, she opened a bottle of wine to celebrate her new place, poured a glass and walked over to the couch. "Welcome home," she said, sitting down with her feet curled under her. Nothing had changed since she was there two months earlier except the trees were no longer covered in white powder. As she looked around inside, she realized there really wasn't anything she wanted to change or replace…other than the locks. *You're perfect just the way you are.*

She thought being a homeowner for the first time would scare her, but she was more excited than anything. Actually owning something other than her car, which technically the bank still owned for another 10 payments, was surreal. Knowing no one could ever take it away from her, was a feeling of pride and great accomplishment. "I have a feeling I've found where I belong," she whispered to herself.

*

Leigh spent the next couple of days changing the locks on the cabin, stocking the kitchen with food, as well as a couple of wine bottles, and buying other necessities. The general store owner had been surprised to see her and even more shocked when she'd told him she loved the town so much she decided to move there. He welcomed her with a hug and a big smile.

As soon as she was finished changing the utilities to her name, which was the last of her mundane tasks, she pulled on a pair of slacks, low heels, and a nice blouse, and headed back down the mountain. She drove through town and parked in the lot for the clinic. Dr. Eric John was waiting when she arrived.

"I must say, I was quite surprised when you called," he said, showing her to his office.

"Imagine my reaction when I decided to uproot my life and move here." She smiled.

"The city tends to burn people out. I worked in Burlington for some time after I completed med school. I honestly hated it."

She nodded. "So, obviously I'm here about the offer you made me a couple of months ago."

"Yes. I had a feeling that's what you wanted to discuss. Currently, it's just me and Belinda, the part-time nurse, Helen who runs the desk up front, and Cindy, the girl who handles the appointment scheduling and insurance billing. Since dad retired, I could really use a full-time nurse practitioner to see patients." He wrote a number on a piece of paper and slid it over to her. "This is my offer. I won't sugar coat things. It's full-time Monday through Friday at this salary. There's a lot of overtime and no extra pay for it. We do have full medical coverage at no charge, however."

She opened the paper and read the number. It was twenty-five percent less than her city salary had been, and her overtime was paid. The medical benefits were the same. She knew the pay would be lower, so it wasn't a shock. She folded it back up.

"I'll accept your offer and take the job under one condition," she said.

"Name it."

"I'm not interested in dating you. Not now…not ever to be honest. I'm a lesbian. Are you going to have an issue with that?"

He smiled. "I saw the way you looked at Camden Gorely and knew right away. She's a great person."

"Yes, she is. So, when do I start?"

"I'd put you on right now, but I'm sure you want some time to get settled in. Didn't you just move here?"

"A few days ago. I could use a couple more days to get settled."

"That's fine. I know our dress code is a little old fashioned. Feel free to wear scrubs if you feel more comfortable."

"Thanks." She reached across the desk and shook his hand.

As soon as she left, Leigh headed over to the restaurant to grab some lunch and was greeted at the door by Camden's Aunt Ma.

"I heard a rumor you were back," she said, placing a menu on the table. "Have you seen Camden?"

Leigh shook her head.

"You broke her heart, and you better not be back to do it all over again."

"I'm back for good. I moved here, actually."

Aunt Ma didn't look pleased.

"I know we have a lot to talk about. I never meant to hurt her," Leigh sighed. "There's so much she doesn't know."

"I'm sure you know how to find her. That is, if she even wants to talk to you. I've never seen her with anyone like the way she was with you," Aunt Ma said before walking away to get her drink order.

Knowing how much she hurt Camden broke Leigh's heart all over again. Suddenly, she wasn't feeling very hungry. She was gone when Aunt Ma returned to the table.

Chapter 27

Camden heard around town that Leigh Myer was back, but she hadn't seen her. Truth be told, she wasn't sure she even wanted to see her. If she really was back and hadn't tried to contact her, then it wasn't her business. So, she ignored the gossip mill and concentrated on getting the trails opened for the season. The rental shops were already booking UTV and four-wheeler tours, and locals and vacationers were itching to get out on the mountain and tear up the trails. The last thing she needed was some vacationing city girl playing games with her.

When she finally finished working for the day, it was dark outside. Most of the trails had been checked and were now open. She still had a couple more to deal with in the morning. She'd spent the better part of her afternoon searching for evidence of another illegal hunter, which had taken more than a couple hours of her time.

She noticed the car in her driveway as she rode down the street. "This isn't going to go well," she muttered, recognizing it as she pulled in beside it. She put the truck in park and got out.

"I know I'm probably the last person you want to see right now," Leigh said, stepping out of her car.

Camden nodded.

"Can we talk…please?"

"There's nothing to say," Camden muttered, walking up to her front door.

Leigh followed. "Aren't you going to ask why I'm here?"

Camden shrugged. "It's not my business."

"Damn it," Leigh groaned in frustration. "Will you at least let me explain myself? Then, if you never want to see me again, I'll understand."

Camden searched her eyes. Their color seemed paler than the last time she'd seen her.

"There's so much you don't know," Leigh whispered.

Camden let out a deep sigh before opening the door and tilting her head for Leigh to go inside. She followed behind her, turning on the lights as she made her way to her bedroom, where she stored her gun in the nightstand, and removed her heavy boots. When she walked back into the living area, Leigh was seated at the small dining table. Camden pulled out the chair adjacent to her and sat down. She thought about offering her something to drink, but had a feeling this conversation wasn't going to last long enough.

Leigh stretched her arms out slightly, clasping her hands together. "Ten years ago, I met a woman named Samantha Whitaker. She was charismatic, attractive, smart…everything anyone looks for in a partner. She swept me off my feet. I fell madly in love with her, and at the time, I was sure she loved me just the same. We were married less than a year later; bought a house; started our lives together." Leigh paused to collect her thoughts. The pain of telling her story never got any easier. Each time it was like a black cloud covering the light around her and a heavy weight crushing her chest, making it difficult to breathe.

"Not long after our first anniversary, I was held late at the hospital I worked at when several patients came in with trauma from a car accident. I had no way of calling home to let Sam know I'd be late. That night, I helped save the lives of four people, and two others passed away right in front of me while doctors worked rigorously to keep them alive. That wasn't the first time I'd seen death at work. Hospitals seem to be a magnet for it, especially in trauma, but it wasn't exactly routine for me to be so late," she sighed. "Anyway, I arrived home four hours later than when I should have. Sam was sitting on the couch in the dark. She jumped up, scaring the hell out of me when I flipped on the light. I tried to explain the trauma that had kept me at work, but she accused me of being out, whoring around with someone else. We argued back and forth. I'd never seen her so angry. Then, like a bolt of lightning and the rumble of thunder cracking across the sky, she back-handed me across the face. The metallic tinge of blood smeared across my split lip, running down my chin from where her wedding band cut me. I fell back against the wall, more so in shock than pain."

Camden stiffened in her chair. She had no idea Leigh's story was going to take this direction and wished she'd been warned. She kept silent, listening as she continued.

"Later that night, she held an icepack to my face while apologizing through heavy tears. I believed her when she said she loved me, and it was an accident, and she'd had a bad day, and she'd been worried about me. I listened to every excuse, believing every word…every time. That night was the first time she'd hit me, but it certainly wasn't the last."

Camden had never known anyone who had experienced abuse. She wasn't sure what she was supposed to do or say.

"It wasn't a daily, weekly, or even monthly occurrence… in the beginning. Little things would trigger it, setting her off. I learned quickly not to argue with her. I loved her, and I wanted our marriage and our life together to work. Someone who is experiencing abuse often blames them self, and I was no exception. I believed her every time she said she loved me and she was sorry. The crazy thing is when things were good, they were great, and that confused me."

She sighed softly. "I got good at contouring my makeup to hide the bruises. Then, three years into our marriage, we were trying to have a baby. We spent thousands of dollars on doctor visits, donor sperm, and insemination procedures, but I couldn't get pregnant. She didn't want to carry a child, so it was all on me. The doctor was able to get me pregnant twice, but both times my body refused it early on, ending them in miscarriages before ten weeks. After the second time, Sam got extremely angry. I don't know if it was the fact that my body wouldn't cooperate, or if it was the money we'd spent. Either way, I'd never seen her so mad. She slammed me against the wall and hit me with her fist, fracturing my orbital bones. She came to her senses and took me to a different ER than the one I worked in. They saw the bruises and asked me if I wanted to have charges pressed against her. I swore up and down I slipped and fell."

Camden shook her head.

"My parents started questioning me after that. They were living in a different city. So, they weren't close by. I made them believe the same lies I told everyone else. And, I believed the lies she told me once again. I blamed myself for not being able to have a baby for us. I actually went through a bout of depression for about six months.

Eventually, I pulled myself from the fog and together, we let go of the idea of having a family. Things were good. We started traveling here and there."

Leigh swallowed the lump forming in her throat as she gathered her thoughts. Then, she continued. "A couple of days before our fifth wedding anniversary, it was the birthday of one of my friends, who was also a nurse at the hospital. From what she told me, I sent a text to Sam that I was going out with her and a few other nurses for a drink to celebrate. I maybe had one glass of wine, then left." She wiped away a tear that fell from the corner of her eye. "I woke up in the hospital four days later after having been in a coma. My jaw was wired shut; the bones in my face were fractured; I had a concussion and four fractured ribs; and I'd had surgery to stop the internal bleeding from my ruptured spleen. If it wasn't for the pizza I'd ordered from the car on the way home, I would've died right there on our floor. Sam had beaten me badly, then threw me down the stairs. The delivery guy kept ringing the door bell, until she finally opened it. There was blood on her shirt and hands and apparently, he saw one of my limbs when he peered over her shoulder. He told her the ordered pizza had already been paid for, so he gave it to her and left. He called 9-1-1 from his cell phone as soon as he was in his car. That young man saved my life. I don't have any memory of it at all."

Camden bit her lower lip enough to taste the iron in her blood. She had no idea how anyone could do that to another person, much less someone they supposedly loved.

"Sam went to jail that night. My parents gathered all of my belongings and took them to their place, a couple of hours away, while I was in a rehab center recovering from my injuries. When I got out, that's where I went. I never stepped foot again in the house Sam and I shared. It was in her name, so I let the bank have it. I cleared out the joint account and filed for divorce. My parents had hired a great attorney while I was recovering and he made sure Sam wasn't allowed out on bail. She was charged with several felonies. I started a new job at a new hospital and eventually rented a studio apartment up the street from my parent's house. Our case finally went to trial about a year later. She was found guilty on all charges and sentenced to ten years in prison. Three years ago, after serving a total of two years, Sam hung herself with her bedsheets."

Camden sat back, utterly in shock.

"She refused to sign the divorce papers, so it was hung up in the courts, waiting to go in front of a judge. We were still married when she died, so I had to deal with her funeral and everything. Even from the grave, she was still controlling me. Once I got the death certificate, I changed my name back and began moving on with my life. The only somewhat good thing is, she never took it to the bedroom. I was never raped and she never forced me to do anything. Her anger was always directed in other ways."

"I don't…know what to say," Camden whispered. "I'm sorry. No one deserves what you went through."

"I thought I was over it. Lord knows I've had enough therapy to last a lifetime," Leigh said. "I've been with a couple of people since then, but it was one night stands only. I never exchanged pleasantries. I was always too scared it would happen again. I no longer believed in love, or really knew what it truly was. What we had wasn't real love. When I came here and you walked into my life out of the blue, the feelings I felt at the beginning of my relationship with Sam felt very similar to what I began to feel with you. It scared me, Camden. That's why I ran. I can't…I *won't* go through that again. I'm not saying you're an abuser, so please don't think that."

"I understand," Camden said.

"I actually came here to relax. I hated my job and was simply going through the motions of life. I'd started taking it out on those around me. My best friend, who knows nothing about my past, told me to take my vacation days and go to the cabin she owned after getting it in a nasty divorce with her cheating ex-husband. So, on a whim, I packed up and came here. I had no idea I would feel so liberated. I hadn't been that happy in a very long time. There's something serene about this mountain. Meeting you was a wonderful, added bonus." She smiled. "Anyway, after going back to my life…my job, I couldn't take it."

"What do you mean?"

"I quit and bought her cabin. I am an official resident."

"Really?" Camden raised a brow.

"Yes." She nodded. "I also got a job at the clinic. Abby, my best friend, thinks I'm nuts, but my parents are very happy for me. They saw firsthand what I went through and knew I was simply going through life instead of living it."

"Leigh…I don't want anything from you. I hope you know that. I'm fine with just being a friend. One thing is for sure, I've never ever hit anyone in my life. I'm definitely not a violent person, and I hold the people I love close to my heart."

"I like you, Camden. Honestly, it's a lot more than like, and it's scary. But, if I'm still being truthful, you are part of the reason I moved here. I'm not ready to jump into anything, but I'd like to get to know you and slowly see where it goes, if it's not too late. I never meant to hurt you. I'm sorry."

"Your leaving like you did certainly makes sense now." Camden grabbed her hands. "I feel strongly about you, Leigh. I've never had that with anyone. There's no pressure from me. I'll move at whatever pace you set."

"I can't make any promises," Leigh whispered.

"All I have is time," Camden replied. *I never knew what I was missing...until you came into my life, then abruptly left, taking a part of me with you.*

*

Camden watched Leigh's tail lights disappear. After she closed the door, she walked over to the kitchen counter and pulled a bottle of aged whiskey from the cabinet. She put a few cubes of ice in a rocks glass and filled it halfway. The first long sip burned all the way to her belly as she sat in the recliner next to the empty wood-burning stove, looking out into the darkness on the other side of the window across the room. She couldn't get the pictures out of her head that Leigh painted as she'd told her story. A tear rolled down her cheek, thinking about the horrors she must have endured for all of those years. "I'll never hurt you like that," she whispered, taking another long sip.

Leigh's running from the first feeling of affection was a good indicator that she was still broken. Camden had no idea if she was capable of allowing herself to love again. As she finished the last of the whiskey in the glass, she wondered if she'd be waiting for the rest of her life for something that may never happen, but it didn't matter. She knew she would wait.

She reached for the bottle, but thought better of it. She couldn't take away Leigh's pain or put her back together for that matter, and no amount of whiskey was going to change that. *All I can do is show you that I'm not her*. Getting up, she walked over to the sink to wash her glass out and put the bottle away. "As long as it takes," she sighed softly as she closed the curtains in the living area and headed to her bedroom.

Chapter 28

Leigh gulped the last of her coffee and shoved a breath mint in her mouth before getting out of her car. It had been a little over a week since she had told Camden the story of her horrid marriage. In such a small town, she was surprised at how easy it was to not see each other out and about. She hadn't expected Camden to call or stop by to see her. She was the one in charge of setting the pace…if there even was one.

She let the thoughts of Camden go as she walked into the clinic. The clean scent and calming atmosphere couldn't compare to the dinghy hospital she'd left. Most of the patients were kind and the only other staff members were Dr. John, a part-time nurse, and the woman who handled the front desk and the bookkeeping.

In the couple of weeks that she'd worked so far, no two days had been the same. Plus, she was actually diagnosing and treating patients, not taking orders from some doctor on a power trip. The new job had certainly been a welcomed change.

"Good morning," Dr. John said with a smile as he passed her in the hallway. "I brought donuts," he added over his shoulder.

Leigh shook her head. If she kept up with his pace and his sweet tooth, she was going to be overweight and addicted to sugar. *I already have vices in my life. They're called coffee and wine.* "No thanks," she called, walking into the small break room. There was a round table with a few chairs around it, a couch along one wall, a set of lockers, and a bookcase with several medical journals. She put her personal belongings into the locker she always used, and left the room, avoiding the donut box entirely.

"Mrs. Wilson, how are you this morning?" Leigh asked, walking into room four with her tablet in hand, scanning through the patient's electronic chart.

"I'd be better if this damn bunion would go away," she mumbled, reminding Leigh of an old hen with ruffled feathers.

"Let me take a look at it." Leigh donned a pair of latex gloves and pulled the end of the exam table up so Mrs. Wilson could stretch out. She'd already removed her shoe, so Leigh began checking the area on her left foot. "Tell me if any of this hurts, okay?" She began palpating around the spot.

"Ouch!" Mrs. Wilson screeched. "Hell yes, it hurts. All of it. The whole damn foot."

"I'd like to draw some blood and do a quick x-ray to get a better look," Leigh said, backing away from the table.

"X-ray? For a bunion? Maybe I should just wait for Dr. John. He'll give me some cream or something to put on it."

"Let me ask you something, Mrs. Wilson. How long has this been bothering you?"

"Oh, a few months, I suppose."

"In that time, would you say it has gotten better or worse?"

"The more I walk on it, the more it hurts."

"I believe you have a bone spur. The only way to know for sure is an x-ray."

"What the hell is a bone spur?"

"It happens when the body adds bone to an area. It sticks out and can rub against nerves or other bones, causing pain. Think of it like this, your body thinks your toe is hurt, so it begins the process of adding more bone to the hurt area to strengthen and heal it."

"I've never heard of such a thing. I'll just wait and see Dr. John."

"Okay…" Leigh said, trying to remain professional. "I'll tell you what. Let's do the x-ray, then Dr. John can come in and explain what he sees. How about that?"

"Fine."

Leigh shook her head and sighed in frustration once she was out in the hallway. Every day she had at least one patient who refused to listen to her and insisted on Dr. John giving the diagnosis, which was always the same. He'd told her several times already that he had years of growing a rapport with the local people and at first, they refused to let him treat them as well, asking only for his father. She knew he was right, which was why she retrieved the mobile x-ray machine and headed back into room four to prove her point to Mrs. Wilson.

"You know, my late husband's grandfather was kin to President Woodrow Wilson. That's where the name comes from," she said, carrying on a conversation mostly with herself while Leigh took a couple of pictures of her foot.

"Wow, that's pretty interesting," Leigh mumbled, trying to make sure she lined the machine up perfectly. "Alright, I'm going to step out into the hall and let it snap the photo. Don't move." Leigh walked out of the room and pressed the remote control. She heard it click, meaning it had taken the x-ray. Then, she went back in to adjust it for another angle.

"Why do you have to go out of the room? Are you pregnant?"

Leigh stared at her sideways. "Uh…no, ma'am. It's procedure." She wasn't about to go into the details about the radiation that comes with getting an x-ray.

"Oh. I always thought the women were pregnant and the machine would hurt the baby. I noticed you weren't wearing a ring, but you never know these days."

Leigh nodded. "Well…uh..." She cleared her throat. "I'll be back in a few minutes with Dr. John and a couple of pictures of the bones in your foot." She quickly left the room with the machine and waited for the printer in the back to produce the two images. Once it was complete, she placed them on the light board and turned it on. Mrs. Wilson's foot appeared in skeletal form. Leigh carefully looked at the image and found the bone spur quite easily on one of her toe joints.

"How's everything going?" Dr. John asked, seeing her walk out of the room with the x-rays in her hand.

"I was actually coming to find you. Mrs. Wilson has a bone spur on one of the toes of her left foot. She thinks I'm nuts and would like you to look at the x-rays. I haven't shown them to her yet."

"It won't stay like this," he said, walking down the hall with her while holding the x-ray up to the light above. "I see it right here, plain as day. What's your plan of action?"

"For now, ibuprofen and a cold compress. Corticosteroid injections may help, but she needs to see an orthopedic surgeon."

"I agree. I'll let you go over that with her. She's your patient."

"Thanks," she replied as they walked into the room.

"Mrs. Wilson." He smiled, coming over to give her a light hug. "Leigh tells me you're having an issue with your left foot."

"Yes. I think it's a damn bunion, but she's talking about some kind of bone spur thing. Can you take a look at it for me?"

"I just did actually, and she is correct. There is a bone spur on your toe joint. It's probably hurting because it is rubbing against the other toe, or perhaps a nerve. Here, let me show you. He held the picture up to the light and showed her how all of her toes looked the same except the one.

"What causes that?"

"Usually arthritis, but toes rubbing together in a tight shoe can sometimes cause it."

"How are you going to fix it?"

"Actually, I'm going to let Leigh handle all of that. You're in good hands, Mrs. Wilson. She and I have already discussed everything, and I agree with her completely."

"There is no immediate relief, I'm afraid," Leigh started as soon as he left the room. "However, ibuprofen and a cold compress may help ease the pain. You'll need to make an appointment to see an orthopedic surgeon. They will determine what the next step is. They may give you something to wear on your toe to stop it from rubbing, or it could require surgery to remove it altogether."

"Surgery?"

"Yes, ma'am. The procedure isn't too difficult and that might be the best way to alleviate your pain. Again, that's for the orthopedic surgeon to determine. I'm going to give you the referral paperwork before you leave. We'll forward it to your insurance, but you'll probably want to follow up on your end as well."

"Thank you," Mrs. Wilson said, getting down off the table. "Dr. John says you know your stuff. If he trusts you, I guess I do too."

"Great. Let us know how it goes," Leigh said, walking her to the front. She handed her off to Helen, who worked the desk. Then, she clicked on her tablet for the next chart and headed into another room.

Chapter 29

Camden was about to eat the apple she'd brought with her when her radio crackled to life. "Gorely, Crawford, we have a report of two teens who fell out of a raft in the rapids."

"Copy. Responding now," she radioed back, then called Baker on her cell phone.

"How in the hell are we going to find them?" he answered.

"I have an idea. Where are you?"

"Sitting on the side of the road off Duckbill Drive."

"Meet me at the entrance for Otter Trail. I just picked up my UTV from getting serviced. We'll take it."

"Be there in two minutes," he said, putting the truck in drive and speeding off.

"Dispatch, Gorely. Do we have a helo in the air yet?" she radioed as she pulled up at the trail head.

"We're working on it. ETA, ten minutes," dispatch replied.

"Copy." She quickly got out and began unloading the UTV from the trailer. By the time she had it ready to go, Baker pulled up next to her and got out.

"Where are we going?" he asked.

"There's a point where the rapids are really rocky. You can see it from the mountain side. It's off the trail and most people don't know about it. We're starting there and working our way up," she said, climbing in and starting the engine.

He nodded and clicked the five-point harness seatbelt. "I heard ten minutes on the helo."

"Yeah." She checked her watch. "Should be about six or seven now. They are starting at the top and working their way down. Either we'll see them or they will…I hope."

The machine raced along the mostly empty trail for close to two miles before Camden turned the wheel and left the groomed area. "Hold on. This might get rough," she yelled over the engine as they sped along, bouncing over the uneven terrain. The last time she was up there, everything was covered with pristine white snow and she had Leigh on the back of the snowmobile. They'd shared their first kiss that day.

"Do we know anything other than two teens fell out of a raft?" he asked, eradicating her wandering thoughts.

"Nope."

"Wonderful," he muttered, grabbing the door handle for dear life as Camden nearly had the UTV airborne as it raced along the various roots, rocks, and crevices covering the forest floor. "Have you seen Leigh?"

"A week or so ago."

"And?"

Camden brought the UTV to a skidding stop near a cliff.

"Holy shit!" he exclaimed, hearing the roaring water when she killed the engine. "I didn't know you could see the rapids from here."

"You'd be surprised at the secrets this mountain hides," she said, getting out of the UTV. "Come on. Let's see if we can spot those kids."

Baker followed her to a spot near the edge where they could peer over safely. Camden ran her binoculars up and down, looking for anything colorful. "I don't see anything," he said.

She grabbed the radio mic and squeezed the button. "Dispatch, Gorely. Where's that helo? We're on the south side near Devil's Bend. There's no sign of the teens."

"Copy. Still working on the helo. ETA unknown at this time," the dispatcher replied.

"Son of a bitch," she growled. Grabbing the mic again, she asked, "Do we know where they fell out at?"

"The other two teens that were in the raft said it was a really rocking turn."

"That sounds like Devil's Bend," she muttered to herself. "Copy. We'll keep searching here."

Baker had walked twenty yards south along the edge, but didn't see anything. When he returned to Camden, she was already headed further north.

"They had to have fallen out around this area. This is the most treacherous part of the rapids. The rest of it is class one and a little bit of two, but this section is a three." She kept walking with her eyes trained on the water. "There's no helo, by the way."

"You're kidding me."

"Wish I was."

"What the hell is going on?"

"You know how the county sheriff's office is. The Chester Police Department can barely afford the officers they have, so there's definitely no room in the budget for a helo."

"I don't see why we don't have one. We're the ones up here doing the same search and rescue." He shook his head. "And we're federal officers, not state cops. We should have better resources," he grumbled.

"Look!" Camden yelled, pointing down at the water. "Do you see something red?"

Baker followed her line of sight and looked through his binoculars. By the time he saw what she had pointed out, she was already running back to the UTV at full sprint. She raced to his position and backed the machine up about fifteen feet from the edge.

"I'm going to run the line off the UTV," she said, retrieving the bright yellow rappelling rope, harness, and bright orange helmet from the toolbox on the back. "When I'm ready, you'll have to pull us up."

"What happened to your winch?" he asked.

"It's a piece of shit. I don't want to risk it malfunctioning. I need to replace it."

He nodded. "Are you okay going down?"

She gave a thumbs up. They'd practiced this before with the search and rescue training they did twice a year. She removed her bulletproof vest and utility belt and emptied her pockets. She put on the body-hugging, orange life vest and attached her radio to it. Then, she pulled the Y section at the top of the harness over her shoulders and fastened the bottom section around each thigh, as well as her waist. He helped her connect everything and tighten the straps. A large D ring was attached at her chest level where the Y came together and another was at her waist level. She ran the line through the rappelling device and autoblock. Then, she clipped all of the loops to both of the harness D rings and tied the end of the line to the tow ring on the frame of the UTV, using a sturdy grapevine knot. For extra precaution, she also tied a second knot into a double figure eight around the trailer hitch that was rated to pull 2,000 lbs.

"I'll use the belay and autoblock to rappel down. Switch to channel six on the radio so we can communicate. Leave the radio in the UTV on with the volume up in case dispatch calls," she said. "Do you remember the hand signals in case my radio isn't as waterproof as they say it is?"

"Yes."

"Alright. I'm going down," she said, stepping over to the edge. She flung the end of the line over the ledge, watching it land in the water. Then she checked her weight on it before leaning back and going over the side.

Baker could do nothing but watch her slowly rappel down, all the way to the rocks jutting out along the edges of the racing water. He could see the two teens clinging to the rocks in the middle.

"Please let them be alive," Camden said to herself as she inched her way down as quickly and safely as she could. When she was about three feet from the water, she began hearing them yelling at her. "Oh, thank God!"

"We're over here!"

"I'm with mountain search and rescue. Are either of you hurt?" she yelled, realizing it was a guy and a girl.

"Not bad!" they replied.

"Is anything broken?"

"No!"

"I'm going to get into the water and swim over to you one at a time. When I get to you, you're going to put your legs through these straps on my harness and this upper loop connects around your waist. Then, we're going to get pulled up out of here. I'll come back down for the second one right after. Okay?"

"Got it!"

Camden knew the water was still freezing cold this early in the spring and they'd been in it at least an hour, possibly longer. She pushed along the wall of the mountain, moving her position so when she went into the water, it would flow her right to them. She let the line out enough to dump her into the rushing water. She was immediately swept right into the rock they were clinging to. She grabbed the female, who was closest to her and put the waist strap around her. "You have to try to get these over your thighs, or at least one of them."

The girl worked the loop over one leg while she clung to the rock, but she couldn't get her second one through.

"Okay listen, you're attached to my back, so you won't go anywhere. I need you to wrap your legs around my waist and hold onto the straps on my shoulders. Do not wrap your arms around my neck! Understand?"

"Yes," the girl said between chattering teeth.

Camden pulled the line tight through the locking block, bringing the girl up against her. "Here we go. Remember, hold onto the straps tightly. Do not let go. You will not fall. I promise." Camden grabbed her radio mic. "Baker, you copy?"

"Roger," he radioed back.

"I have a male and female, approximately eighteen years old. No visible injuries. I'm bringing the girl up with me."

"Copy."

"Ready when you are."

"Pulling now," he replied, putting the UTV in gear. The motor was already running and the four-wheel-drive was engaged. He pressed the gas slowly, allowing the machine to inch forward, hauling the weight up easily.

"Halfway," Camden radioed.

He kept going, listening to her give him measurements as the ledge grew closer and closer.

"Stop!" she radioed as they started going up over the edge.

Baker put the machine in park and set the parking brake before running back towards them. He tossed a rope to Camden and she clipped it to one of the D rings on her harness. Then, he wrapped it around the tree and began pulling to give Camden leverage as she climbed her way up and over the edge. Then, he rushed over and helped the young woman get out of the harness before backing the UTV up to the original spot.

Camden let the rope drop all the way to the water once more. "Give her a space blanket and tend to any wounds. She's borderline hypothermic. I'm going back down for the male."

Baker made sure she was over the edge safely, then he opened a space blanket that instantly heated from the solar rays of the sun, and wrapped it around her. She had cuts and scrapes from the rocks, but no serious injuries. He poured clean water on them and covered each one with a bandage.

*

At the waterline, Camden performed the task all over again, attaching the male to the harness loops behind her. "You have to hold on tight to these straps," she said before radioing Baker to pull her up.

He helped the girl into the passenger seat of the UTV and went to work hauling the rope back up like a makeshift wench. When Camden yelled into the radio, he stopped and ran back to help her come up over the edge.

"Get him into a blanket and clean up his wounds. I'll get these lines collected," she said, shivering from the cold water.

"Why don't you go get in a blanket? I can do this."

"I'm fine. We still have to get them out of here," she replied as she removed the harness and began rolling up the lines. "Dispatch, Gorely. We have the teens. They only have superficial wounds, but are semi-hypothermic. We have a twenty-minute ride out of the woods."

"Copy. Do you need EMS standing by?"

"Negative. It will be quicker for us to run them to the clinic. We already have them slowly warming with space blankets."

"Copy. We'll alert them of your arrival," the dispatcher said.

"We don't have four seats. How are we going to drive them out of here?" Baker asked.

Camden looked at the cab of the UTV as she finished stowing the lines in the toolbox.

"I'll ride in the back, they can double up in the passenger seat. Just don't toss my ass out of here," he said.

"Here, put this strap across you from one side to the other like a seatbelt. I'll go slow, but this will keep you from falling out if we hit rocks and roots," she instructed.

"You never answered me about Leigh, you know."

"I know," she sighed. "Let's get them out of here."

Chapter 30

"Leigh, we have an incoming trauma. Prep rooms one and two," Dr. John said. "Two teens fell out of a whitewater raft."

"Do we know the injuries?" she asked, rushing to get the rooms ready.

"Hypothermia is all I was told."

"Great," she muttered, mentally going over everything she would need.

Once the two rooms were set, it was a waiting game. Their last three patients were put on hold. Leigh heard the siren coming down the street and looked out to see a fish and wildlife truck pull in with its lights flashing. It came to a stop and the passenger door flew open.

*

Camden had driven her UTV up onto the trailer and left her truck parked. Since Baker's truck didn't have a trailer and was a crew cab with four full doors, they'd all fit easily and be able to get down the mountain and through town faster, so he drove.

When they arrived, the female was dehydrated and quite weak from lack of food and the early onset of hypothermia. Camden jumped out of the passenger side of the truck and opened the extended cab door to get her out while Baker helped the male out of the other side. He was able to walk on his own and was still wrapped in the silver blanket. Camden put one arm at the base of the girl's legs and the other just below her shoulders and picked her up, just as Dr. John and Leigh rushed out with wheelchairs. She quickly deposited her into the seat as Dr. John came over to her.

"They're both hypothermic and she's dehydrated. They were in the water for over an hour and took us nearly an hour to get them out and back down the mountain," she said, slightly shivering herself as she walked in behind them.

"Camden, you're freezing!" Leigh said, looking at the wet clothing clinging to her body.

"She rappelled over the side of the mountain, down into the water to get them, one at a time," Baker stated.

Camden shot him a glare. "I'm fine. Please take care of them," she said.

"Go to room three. One of us will be in there to check on you once we have them stable," Leigh insisted. Then, she went into the next room to tend to the male while Dr. John had the female in room one. His temperature was slightly low, but nowhere near hypothermic anymore. She gave him a gown to change into. Then, she started an IV and began giving him fluids while she checked him over for broken bones or deep cuts, but everything was superficial. "You're very lucky," she said. "Nothing needs stitches, and you're starting to warm up."

"Yeah, all thanks to that wildlife officer. I still can't believe she came down the side of the mountain on a rope to get us. She's badass."

Leigh nodded.

"If you need to go check on her, I'm fine. Can you check on my girlfriend while you're at it?"

"Sure," she said, walking out of his room.

"I can't believe they have no injuries," Dr. John said, meeting her in the hallway.

"Me too."

"How's Camden?" he asked.

"I was about to go in there now, but you can do it."

"No, you go ahead. I'll keep an eye on these two and have Helen get the waiting patients into rooms."

"Thanks," she murmured before walking into the room. "Damn it!" she snapped, seeing it empty.

Dr. John rushed in. "What's goi—"

"She left," Leigh grumbled, shaking her head.

He pursed his lips and nodded. "She's a grown woman, Leigh. We can't make her stay."

"I know that, but…" She shook her head. "She could be hypothermic, too."

"She wasn't in the water nearly as long. Besides, she's trained in emergency medicine and so is Baker Crawford. If she needed to stay, she would have. I'm sure she's fine."

She sighed and walked out of the room. She had patients to tend to.

*

"I don't know why you didn't stay and let them—"

"Let them do what, Baker? Tell me I'm cold and wet? No shit! I'll go home, take a warm shower, put dry clothes on, and eat some soup. I'll be fine. There was no reason to stay."

"I think it had to do with Leigh."

"I think you need to drive," she growled.

He shrugged and kept going down the road as they headed back up the mountain.

Leigh hadn't bothered calling or anything else for that matter, since the night she'd told Camden everything, making her wonder if she'd decided not to pursue anything with her after all. There was nothing she could do at this point and seeing her was like pouring salt on an open wound because Camden had no idea where they'd stood.

"Do you want me to come help you put the UTV away?" Baker asked, pulling up next to her truck and trailer.

"Nah, I've got it. I'll write the report up tomorrow when I get into the office. There's no need to do it now."

"I wonder whatever happened to the helo?" he said.

She shrugged. "I don't know, but I'll damn sure put it in my report. They may not have made it much longer if we hadn't found them."

"I agree. Have a good rest of your day, Spiderwoman," he teased.

"Nice," she laughed, shaking her head as she got out.

*

By the time Camden had arrived home, stowed the trailer and UTV, and taken a shower to warm herself up, it was starting to get dark outside. She was just about to sit down on the recliner when her phone rang. She contemplated letting it go to voicemail when she saw the number.

"Hello," she reluctantly answered.

"Why did you leave the clinic?" Leigh questioned.

Camden heard the sharp edge in her voice and calmly replied, "Because I was fine. You both had emergency patients, plus others in the waiting room. I didn't need to be there wasting anyone's time."

"You weren't wasting mine," she mumbled.

"Leigh…I promise I'm fine. I took a shower to warm up."

"Have you eaten?"

"Not yet."

"Come over for dinner."

"Are you sure?"

"Yes. I wouldn't invite you if I didn't want to see you, and it's not just because of today. I should've called you before now, especially after our last conversation."

"Can I bring anything?"

"I should have everything."

"Okay. When do you leave the clinic?"

"I'm home. We usually leave when the last patient is gone. Obviously, I can get called in for emergencies, but Dr. John will handle those unless there are multiple patients. Then, he'll call me in with him."

"Alright. I'll be over in a few minutes." Camden ended the call and stared at the dining table where Leigh had poured out her horrible past. As much as Camden wanted to see her and spend time with her, she was scared Leigh was going to break her heart all over again. Not because she wanted to, but because she simply couldn't help it.

She changed from sweatpants and a t-shirt to jeans and a baby blue polo shirt and pulled on a pair of dark gray, Merrell hiking sneakers, which were the non-work shoes she wore when there was no snow on the ground. As an afterthought, she grabbed a light jacket from the rack.

*

The green fish and wildlife truck had been parked in Leigh's driveway next to her car for the better part of five minutes. Camden leaned forward, placing her forehead against her hands, which were clasped to the top of the steering wheel. "It's just dinner," she sighed. The anger she'd felt when Leigh left abruptly without saying goodbye was long gone, and the sadness that had overcome her after finding out about the abuse she had suffered during her marriage had also passed, leaving her with a ball of nerves and unanswered questions. She'd never been around anyone who had endured the kind of cruelty and pure violence Leigh had been through.

She thought about driving away, making an excuse to do it again another night, but her phone rang. She swallowed the lump in her throat when she saw the caller ID.

"Are you coming in, or are you going to stay in your truck all night?" Leigh asked. "This isn't take-out."

"No. I'm coming in," she said, ending the call.

As soon as she was out of the truck, the front door of the cabin opened and Leigh stepped into the light. She looked casual in a white boat neck top with short sleeves, light-colored jeans that rested on her hips, and a wide, tan-colored belt. Her feet were bare and her hair was pushed back over her shoulders. She held a dark blue kitchen towel in her hand as she leaned against the door jamb.

God, she's beautiful. Camden shoved her hands into the front pockets of her jeans and smiled thinly as she walked up. "I was on the phone with the office, dealing with some stuff from earlier," she lied.

Leigh nodded and smiled. From her vantage point at the window, it definitely hadn't looked like she was on the phone. "Welcome to my home…officially. I signed the papers last week," she said as she closed the door behind her.

"Wow. Congratulations. Is this your first time as a homeowner? I know you'd mentioned a house."

"Technically…no. I was on the deed of the house when I was married."

Camden pursed her lips.

Leigh saw the uncertainty in her face and reached out, grabbing her hand. "It's going to come up and that's okay. *I'm* okay. I'm glad I told you."

Camden nodded.

"For so long, my parents handled me with kid gloves. I can't go through that with you. It's behind me. I know I'll always carry it with me to a certain extent, and that's what made me run from you. But, I'm here now and this is where I want to be. I need to know that you're okay with everything. I'll answer questions if you have any."

"You've already answered them for me," she said, looking down at their clasped hands.

"We've been intimate, Camden. I'm not going to freak out if you hold my hand or hug me, and I won't break. I promise." Leigh smiled. "The crazy thing is, sex has been the easiest thing. I guess because it was always no strings attached, so I never had to worry about falling in love and taking the next steps. Those are what terrify me."

Camden's eyes locked onto hers in a sort of mutual understanding. They knew they had feelings for each other, but no formal words had really been spoken.

"Is this why you were sitting in the truck?"

"I wasn't sure this was a good idea."

"Why lie to me?" Leigh let go of her hand and crossed her arms over her chest as she took a step back, almost in a defensive move that made Camden cringe inside.

"Because you've been through enough as it is," she sighed.

"Camden Gorely, you can be nervous about being around me or ask questions if you need to, but you cannot lie to me," Leigh said sternly.

"I'm sorry. I never meant to upset you. I just…I've never been around anyone who has gone through what you did, and I was unsure how to be around you. I know it's stupid. I have never and would never deliberately lie to you. Call it cowardice, but either way, I should've just told you how I was feeling."

"One thing's for sure, you're definitely not weak. The story those teens told today blew my mind. You're a hero to them, and you're so much more than that to me. What I told you, the hell I went through, it's a lot for anyone to take in. That's part of the reason I hadn't contacted you for a couple of weeks. I knew you would need time to digest all of it. Everyone does." Leigh grabbed her hand again. "Anyway, things have certainly changed between us, but I'm still the same person that was here with you three months ago. I just brought my life with me when I came back."

Camden nodded and smiled softly. "I'm glad you're here," she whispered.

"Me too." Leigh beamed.

"Is something burning?" Camden questioned, sniffing the air.

All Leigh smelled was her enticing cologne, until she walked towards the kitchen. "Damn!" she hissed, grabbing the mitt and flinging the toaster oven open. A puff of smoke came out. She quickly grabbed the baking sheet from the rack and tossed it on top of the stove. "That was supposed to be the garlic bread," she grumbled, shaking her head.

"Bread's overrated." Camden shrugged with a grin, causing them both to laugh.

"The rest of dinner is ready and waiting," Leigh said, removing a pan of veggie lasagna and another pan with prosciutto-wrapped asparagus from the oven where they were being kept warm.

"That part of it smells delicious. Are you sure you don't moonlight as a chef?"

Leigh chuckled. "I actually hate cooking. I'm just good at it. I started watching cooking shows when I moved into my apartment. I watched so many, I could probably open a restaurant."

"I'm not into cooking either. I usually make a big pot of spaghetti or something like that. Baker makes deer stew and chili, so we share a lot of meals."

The table was already set with plates, napkins, and flatware. So, all Leigh had to do was put the two dishes in the center. "Do you want some wine? I have red and white," she asked after getting everything situated.

"No, I'm good."

"I wasn't going to have any either, but I always offer it," she said, joining her as they sat down adjacent from each other. "I figured you ate at the restaurant a lot."

"I do, but only once a week, sometimes twice. I go there a lot more for breakfast, and lunch here and there. They won't let me pay for a meal, so I feel like I'm mooching off them. You know what I mean?"

"Help yourself, by the way. And yes. But, I'm sure you pay them back in other ways. Besides, they light up when they see you."

"That's part of the reason I try to stop in for breakfast. It's mostly just to see them." Camden waited for Leigh to add food to her plate before getting a square piece of lasagna and a few stalks of asparagus.

"Parents can be wonderful to have around, but they can always drive you crazy. When I moved back in with mine after rehab, I thought they were going to make me want to go to an insane asylum. I couldn't get up to go to the bathroom without one of them right there with me. I started seeing a psychologist while I was still in rehab and continued until about a year and a half ago. Both of my parents went to a number of sessions with me, so essentially, they went through the aftermath of it all as well. We were always close before, but I think that bonded us even more. They actually had to learn to let me go because they had latched on so tightly during that time. The doctor I was seeing helped them do that. She's amazing."

"Have you spoken to her at all with the move and everything?"

"No, actually. I'm in a different place in my life than I was two years ago even. She helped me see the light at the end of the dark tunnel. This move happened because of her and everything she did for me. I actually thought of calling her when I ran home from here, but a conversation with my mother brought back a lot of what she and I had discussed. Afterward, I no longer felt the need."

"My parents wanted to send me to a counselor when I was a teenager. They thought my rebellion had to do with my mother abandoning me and everything, but honestly, I was just coming to terms with being gay. It had nothing to do with them, but I pushed them away because I thought they would feel shame and perhaps disown me. Then, I would've had no one."

"Wow. How did you get through that?"

"They caught me kissing a girl."

Leigh put her hand to her face to hide her smile.

"I got a good lecture from them that day, believe me. It had nothing to do with what they'd seen, only the fact that I was keeping it from them. They were hurt that I felt like I couldn't come to them."

"They really are the sweetest people I've ever met."

"Yeah," Camden uttered in agreement.

"What happened with the girl?"

"She was here visiting for the summer. Her grandmother lived in town. I heard she got pregnant the following year. Either way, she never came back." She shrugged.

Leigh nodded. "So, I'm not good with desserts at all, but I did pick up some Ben and Jerry's ice cream. Would you like some?" she asked, removing their plates from the table to load them into the dishwasher.

Camden got up to help her. "I probably shouldn't."

"Don't tell me you're watching your girlish figure. Have you looked in the mirror lately? Besides, I'm sure you burned off enough calories today to eat an entire pint."

Camden raised a brow. "What flavor is it?"

"Half Baked, of course." Leigh grinned.

Camden couldn't resist. It was her favorite ice cream, and Leigh's smile was like oxygen for someone who was drowning. She found it impossible to say no to her. "Make it a small bowl," she said, grinning back at her.

"Bowl?" Leigh shook her head and pulled two pints out of the freezer, causing Camden to laugh hysterically.

"I'm not eating all of this."

"No one said you had to. It'll be here when you come back," Leigh replied between bites.

"Is that an invitation?"

"Sure. I promise not to burn the bread next time."

"Good. I promise to get my head out of my ass and come inside like a proper guest." Camden winked over the top of her ice cream pint.

Chapter 31

Leigh bobbed her head to the music playing on her iPod. The cell phone ringing on the counter grabbed her attention when the screen lit up with the caller's name and number. Leigh pressed the button to answer with the speakerphone after muting her iPod.

"Please tell me you're on the road," Leigh laughed, knowing her best friend all too well.

"Actually, I just pulled into town," Abby said.

"No way!"

"Yep. I got all jacked up on caffeine and snacks and hit the road just after eight o'clock. Not too shabby, huh?"

"I'm super impressed. Who are you? And what have you done with Abigail Curtis?"

Abby laughed, "Open your door. I'm here."

Leigh ended the call and ran outside to greet her friend with a big hug.

"This place is in the middle of nowhere," Abby muttered, hugging her back.

"Yes. That's why I love it so much. Get your purse. I've got your bag. Come on. I can't wait to show you around."

Abby had never seen her friend so genuinely happy. She couldn't help smiling at her.

Once they were inside, Leigh left the suitcase by the door and walked Abby around, showing her the entire cabin while pointing out the tiny things she'd changed to make it her own.

"Wow. This place is beautiful. No wonder Ron made it out to be a hole in the wall family cabin. He didn't want me knowing he had a sweet pad to bring his whores to." She shook her head. "I'm sorry. I'm really glad you've made it a home, though. You seem so much happier here."

"I am, actually. It's the happiest I think I've ever been. And, no worries about Ron. I'd forgotten all about that."

"Me too, honestly. So, what's been going on? I've barely spoken to you since you moved," Abby said, sitting down at the end of the couch. "That view is amazing."

"You should see it when there's snow on the ground," Leigh said, sitting in the middle of the couch and propping her feet up on the coffee table. "I'm sorry I haven't called much. I've been busy working and getting settled."

"Uh-huh…busy working that good-looking wildlife officer," Abby teased.

"Not likely," Leigh muttered.

"Oh no. Trouble in paradise?"

"I didn't move here for her, Abby. I did it for me. She's a nice addition, but we're not together. At least, not in that sense."

"Have you seen her at all? You've been here a month."

"We had dinner last week. That was only the second time I've seen her since I moved."

"I feel like I'm missing a pretty important piece of the story," Abby said.

"You are," Leigh mumbled softly. "Anyway, it's fine. We're just taking things slowly."

"Uh huh." Abby shook her head. "So, when do I get to meet her? And does she have any good-looking male friends?"

"I think most of the guys she works with are married, but I think her closest friend is single. I'll ask her."

"How's the job going? I can't believe you basically work banker hours with weekends off."

"It's nice unless we get an emergency call. Then, I have to go in and help deal with that."

"That sounds easy as hell."

"It is. I love it! I do just about everything the doctor does. We're the only medical facility in a forty-mile radius, so we get our share of emergencies, but we're just a local clinic, so there's only so much we can do. We are also the family physician for everyone in town and on the mountain."

"Can you give me a tour if it's closed?"

"It's not much to see. We have a waiting area with a reception desk out front. There are five exam rooms in the back, plus a break room, and the doctor's personal office. We also have portable x-ray and sonogram equipment that we are able to move from room to room. All of our lab work goes out daily with FedEx and we have to send people to the nearest hospital for tests. We refer a lot of people out to specialists because we simply can't treat everything in our small clinic."

"It sounds like a cakewalk compared to the dump you left behind. Which isn't getting any better by the way. They still haven't replaced you."

"Figures," Leigh muttered.

"So, what do you feel like doing? We can go into town and walk around. There are some neat places to see. The only thing up here on the mountain is the ski resort, unless you know the secret spots and have a way to get to them."

"Off-roading definitely isn't my thing," Abby laughed. "I am a city girl through and through. However, shopping sounds like a wonderful idea."

*

Camden leaned against her truck as the gas pump slowly filled the tank. It was Saturday afternoon, and thankfully, her last workday for the week. She adjusted her sunglasses and turned her head in time to see a black BMW pull in with out of state plates. The driver's door swung open and a long-legged brunette got out, pushing her long hair over her shoulder. She raised a brow and grinned like a sly fox when her eyes landed on Camden.

"Hi," she said, drawing the word out like she was saying it in slow motion.

Camden nodded.

"It's a sin to work on the weekend. I'm sure there are much better things you'd rather be doing."

Geesh. So, you wanna fuck in the back of my truck or your car? Camden shook her head. The vacationers were getting worse every year. She wasn't for rent as their plaything while they were in town. "I actually enjoy my job, so no, I'm right where I want to be. Have a good day," she said, putting the nozzle back on the pump before closing the tank cap.

"I'm staying at the resort up on the mountain. Maybe I'll see you again. I'd love a personal tour."

"I'm not a tour guide," Camden said, getting into her truck. She drove away without looking back. She thought about Leigh. Before meeting her, there was a time when she would've spent a week with that brunette's legs wrapped around her every night, doing everything for her that her husband couldn't. *I'm getting too old for all of this shit.*

"Dispatch to Gorely. We just got a call about a moose calf in someone's yard, possibly abandoned."

"Copy," she replied on the radio. "What's the address?"

"121 Wolf Landing."

"Responding now," she said, taking the main road up the mountain that led to the resort, but then turned off on another road that wound around, taking her right to Wolf Landing. She slowed down, trying to read the address numbers. "It should be a damn law for these numbers to be legible," she grumbled, pulling over next to a driveway with a truck and car in it when she saw the numbers 121.

"That was fast," a man said, walking over to her as she got out.

"I was nearby. Is the moose still around?"

"Yeah. He's over by the garage. He's been hanging around, almost like playing and calling for his mother with a whining sound."

"How long has he been here?"

"Two days."

"You haven't seen an adult moose around with him?"

"No," he said. "I wonder if someone killed her."

Camden shook her head. "I wouldn't be surprised."

"It takes a real piece of shit to kill an animal's mother. Don't get me wrong, I'm a hunter myself, but you can't be that hungry. There's a grocery store down the damn street."

"I agree with you. Plus, it had to have happened nearby if her baby is here. He would've run off, but not too far. You're a hunter, so I'm sure you know the regulations."

The man nodded.

"If someone killed her, it was a lot less than 500 yards from here," she stated.

He shook his head in disgust.

"Let's go see if he's still here," she said, nodding towards the garage.

The man led the way and she followed quietly. Sure enough, there was a brown moose calf hanging out, calling for its mother. He startled a little when he saw Camden. She noticed right away how shaky he was.

"He looks like he was born only a few days ago," she whispered.

"That's what I thought, too."

"I'm going to come around from this way. If you go that way, I'm hoping to trap him nice and easy. Be careful. Don't try to grab him. He won't hurt you, but he may try if he feels threatened."

"Got it," he said.

Camden put on her gloves and pulled some leaves from a nearby bush and walked closer with her hand out. "Hi, buddy," she cooed softly. The animal raised his head up, looking at her. She continued moving slowly. His nose twitched, sniffing the air. He looked maybe three feet tall and being newly birthed, and probably didn't weigh thirty pounds. He was a cute little guy with fuzzy dark brown fur.

When he began sniffing the leaves in her hand, she reached over, petting him softly. "It's okay. I'm going to take you somewhere safe," she murmured, sliding close enough to grab him when she let go of the leaves.

The man watched her wrap her arms around his front and back legs, hefting him up off the ground. “Holy shit,” he exclaimed.

Camden ignored him as she walked out to her truck. The door was open to the metal cage in the back, and she easily slipped him inside, making sure he was lying down since he was too tall to ride standing. Once she had him in a safe position, she closed the door and locked it.

“Would you mind if I took some leaves with me? We have about a half-hour ride out to the conservatory,” she said. “I’m not sure if he’ll eat them, but it’s worth a try.”

“Sure.”

Camden walked back with him and they tore a couple of handfuls of branches from the bushes together and snatched the leaves off. “Thanks,” she said, wrapping her hands around them.

“No problem. What will happen to him now?”

“They’ll put him in the wildlife sanctuary where no predators can get to him and once he is old enough, they’ll release him back into the wild.”

“That’s good.”

“I’m off tomorrow, so I may not be available, but someone from our office will be back to get a statement and search around for the carcass or kill spot of the mother. In the meantime, if you happen to find anything, please call our office,” she said as they walked back to the truck.

“Sure thing.”

Camden put all of the leaves inside the cage where the calf could get them. Then, she got into the truck and drove off.

*

Leigh and Abby had spent the afternoon walking around, talking and sipping malts they'd gotten from the local shop. Abby had bought a few neat trinkets in one store, and Leigh had given her a quick tour of the closed clinic.

"You were right," Abby said as they walked along the sidewalk, heading back towards the car.

Leigh raised a brow. "About what?"

"This being a Hallmark movie town." Abby shook her head. "It's neat to visit."

"But, you couldn't see yourself living here."

"Don't get me wrong…"

"No. I know it's different. It certainly isn't for everyone," Leigh sighed. "But, I knew right away. It was like filling my lungs with a breath of fresh air for the first time in a long time. When I got back to the city, I felt like I was breathing through a straw."

"I was actually going to say it somehow suits you. I don't know. You seem so relaxed and easy-going. I've never seen you like this."

"Must be the mountain air." Leigh grinned.

"Uh-huh…" Abby shook her head. "So, is there a good place to eat around here?"

"There's a pizza joint and a couple of other specialty places, but Ma and Pa's is the best, hands down."

Abby laughed. "You're kidding. It's really called Ma and Pa's?"

"Yep. It's right up here."

Abby shrugged. "Might as well get the whole experience."

Leigh smiled and shook her head. "You act like I moved to Mayberry."

"I'm pretty sure you did," Abby replied as they walked into the restaurant.

Chapter 32

The restaurant was small, but quaint like the town. Abby looked around at various pictures and memorabilia on the walls dating back over a hundred years. She was equally surprised to see it was run by an older couple who looked like they were well into retirement age.

"Abby, this is Camden's Aunt Ma. She and her husband own and run this place," Leigh said. "This is my best friend from the city. She came to check up on me. Everyone thinks I've lost my mind by moving here." She smiled.

"Some people just need a change of pace every now and then," Aunt Ma replied with a shrug as she showed them to a table. "I did hear you'd bought the cabin you were staying in and are working with Dr. John."

Abby's brows rose in surprise.

"Small town. News travels fast," Leigh said.

"Isn't that the truth," Aunt Ma uttered. "I'll be back in a few to take your order."

"So, Aunt Ma?"

"She's her aunt, but also her mother. Her aunt and uncle adopted her when she was little."

"Oh, wow."

"Yeah. They're super nice people. To be honest, I haven't met anyone yet that hasn't been nice."

"What about her? I bet she's naughty," Abby teased, seeing a woman walking across the room, having just come in through the front door.

"Are you sure you're straight?" Leigh laughed, turning around. Her eyes landed on Camden, standing in the middle of the room, speaking to her father. She was casually dressed in jeans and a black, zippered cardigan sweater with a gray-colored shirt underneath. She couldn't help smiling. Camden Gorely stirred something deep inside her. "That's Camden," she whispered.

"Get out. Are you serious? Go invite her over."

"Why?"

"Because I want to meet the woman who stole my best friend."

"She didn't steal me," Leigh muttered, shaking her head. "Hold on. I'll be right back."

*

"You're kidding," Uncle Pa laughed. "I bet that was a sight."

"I'm so lucky that thing didn't take off running. I probably would've never caught it," Camden said, telling him about the moose calf.

Uncle Pa saw Leigh approach and stepped to the side. "How are you this evening?"

"I'm fine. Thanks," Leigh replied with a smile.

Camden turned around, surprised to hear her voice. "Hey."

"Hi. I don't know what your plans are, but my best friend is in town from the city. Would you like to meet her and join us for dinner?"

"I have tables to get to. Go on," Uncle Pa said, encouraging her.

Camden grinned and shook her head as he walked away. "Are you sure you want company?"

"She's dying to meet you. She thinks you stole me away."

Camden laughed. "Does she know you?"

"Yeah, but she knows nothing about my past. I don't talk about it…ever."

"I understand." Camden nodded. "After you." She tilted her head.

Leigh led them over to the table on the other side of the room. Abby had piled her bags and purse in the seat next to her, leaving Camden and Leigh to sit side by side across from her. Leigh did a quick introduction before they sat down.

"It's nice to finally meet you," Abby said. "I've certainly heard a lot about you."

Camden looked at Leigh, who simply smiled at her before turning her attention to the menu.

Aunt Ma came by, getting their order. She hugged Camden when she saw her and hid it if she was surprised at her choice of tables.

"So, call me a naive city girl, but what does a wildlife officer do?" Abby asked.

"We basically police the woods and protect the animals." When Abby gave her an odd look, she explained it a little more. "Local and state police enforce the laws of the town or state making sure people are safe and follow the laws, rules, and regulations. We are federal officers who sort of do the same thing, but with hunters, fishermen, and recreational vehicle riders, and in the woods instead of the city streets. We also help sick or injured animals and remove nuisance animals. As a matter of fact…" she paused, looking at Leigh. "I had to capture a moose calf today and take him to the conservatory because he's too young to be on his own. I'm pretty sure someone killed his mother on residential property. He was in these people's backyard calling for her."

"Oh, my God!" Leigh exclaimed.

"He was maybe three feet tall and covered in fuzzy brown fur. He let me pick him up and carry him to the truck."

"Awe. I wish I could've seen him. How Cute!" Leigh cooed.

Abby watched the exchange between the two of them. She'd never seen Leigh light up like she had the moment her eyes landed on Camden, and now, she seemed like a giddy kid while talking about an animal. "What happens with him now?" she asked.

"They'll raise him and keep him safe until he's big enough to return to the wild. He was born two, maybe three days ago at most, so he has a lot to learn. The good news is, he seemed to be in good health."

"That's great," Leigh said. "I still can't believe you saw a baby moose and got to hold him." She shook her head.

"I assume you know of her little hike…" Camden said, turning her eyes to Abby.

"Uh…yeah. Who do you think called 9-1-1?"

Camden raised a brow.

"She called me instead of someone who could help her," she stated.

"It was your cabin. I thought you might know how to get back or something. I don't know. I panicked."

Abby laughed. "I'd never been to the cabin before today, and I've certainly never gone hiking. Anyway, I'm just glad you were there to rescue her." She watched Leigh and Camden exchange glances and soft smiles.

"I was just doing my job. I also work with search and rescue on the mountain," Camden said, turning her attention back to Abby as their food arrived. "So, are you a nurse, too?"

Abby nodded. "She left me behind at that dump they call County General Hospital."

"To be fair, you were there before me," Leigh teased.

"Touché," Abby chuckled.

"I took her around town today," Leigh said, changing the subject as she looked at Camden.

"Really? What did you think?"

"She hates it," Leigh laughed.

"No. I never said that." Abby smiled and shook her head. "It's different. Leigh described it as a Hallmark movie town and she was right. It belongs on a postcard or something."

"I've never thought of it like that, but yeah…you're probably right," Camden muttered, wiping her face with her napkin. "We're mostly a tourist destination. People flock here in the winter for the ski slopes and others come in the summer for the river rafting, hiking, and other outdoorsy adventures. Us locals tend to stay away from the areas they're in, but we generally don't mind them because, without the tourism, the town wouldn't thrive."

Abby nodded. "That makes sense."

"You know, Leigh isn't the first city girl to vacation here and make it their home. We've actually had a lot of people do it," Camden said.

"Must be something in the air," Leigh replied playfully.

"Yeah." Camden grinned.

When the check came, all three of them went for it.

"Please, let me get it," Camden said.

"I invited you to sit with us and she's my guest. I've got it," Leigh said.

"It was my idea to eat out. I know you were planning on cooking. The least I can do is pay for dinner," Abby interjected.

"My parents own this place, and they refuse to let me pay for a meal or leave a tip, so my dinner isn't even on there."

"Let's pay our own ways then. That seems easy enough," Abby declared, looking at Leigh.

"That's fine." Leigh handed her card to Abby, who put them together in the bill folder.

"Thank you for inviting me to join you both. Abby, it was nice meeting you," Camden said before standing to go.

"You as well," Abby replied.

Camden placed her hand on Leigh's shoulder. "Call me tomorrow if you're not busy. I'd love to take you both out to see the moose. That is if you want to."

"I'd love to."

"Count me out. I'm heading back home in the morning. I have to get caught up on laundry and clean my house, but thank you though," Abby replied.

"See you tomorrow, then." Camden smiled at Leigh before walking away.

*

"Okay. What's really going on?" Abby said as soon as they were inside the cabin. "Because it looks like you two are in love with each other."

Leigh closed and locked the door, then sighed as she leaned back against it. She knew her friend deserved the truth. It was difficult to tell her story, but what bothered her most were the sympathetic looks she got afterwards. It was as if people changed right in front of her. She pushed off the door and walked into the kitchen, where she grabbed a bottle of wine and two glasses.

"You're right," Leigh said, opening the bottle and filling the glasses halfway. She carried the two glasses in one hand and the bottle in the other as she walked into the living area where Abby was seated on the couch. She'd removed her jacket and shoes and made herself comfortable. "I don't talk about this much because I've tried very hard to put it behind me and keep it there," Leigh continued as she began telling Abby her story.

*

An hour later, the bottle of wine was empty and Abby's face was a wet mess from shedding numerous tears. She was finally able to pull it together knowing her friend was okay and that darkness was gone from her life. She began to understand why Leigh always seemed to be on edge, letting the smallest things bother her. She'd been to hell and back and miraculously lived to tell about it. It also made sense that she picked up and moved her life to a place where she felt free of the darkness and ghosts that haunted her.

"I see why you are keeping Camden at arm's length," she said, patting Leigh's hand. "You're afraid the past will repeat itself."

Leigh nodded.

"Honey, that's a risk you may never be able to take. Does she know that?"

"Yes. She knows everything."

"Can I ask you something?"

"Yeah."

"When you were first with your wife…before everything, did you feel what you feel when you're around Camden?"

Leigh pulled her lower lip into her mouth between her teeth and sighed. "I've asked myself that same question a hundred times. The answer is always: I don't know. I remember being happy in the beginning, but it was overshadowed for so long, it's really hard to pinpoint the details. I will say this, when I'm with Camden, it's like time stands still. I feel like I am happier than I've ever been, but I can't say for sure. Sam had me so mentally broken that I accepted her abusing me. That's a level of vulnerability I never want to get to again. I worked very hard with a psychologist for a number of years. I'm in a good place and I'm happy."

"What has your therapist said about you getting into a relationship again?"

"She doesn't know I moved here or anything. I haven't seen her in about two years. However, during our sessions she reiterated many times that what transpired between Sam and I wasn't real love, or real life. I think she'd be happy to know about Camden and trust me to pick up on the warning signs I so blatantly missed with Sam, if they were to arise. Part of my therapy in the end was recognizing them and telling myself I was strong enough to walk away."

"She sounds like she knows her shit. What have your parents said?"

“They want me to be happy, and if this place is what does it, then they are all for it. They know I’ve been going through the motions of life for years now, but haven’t actually been living it. My mother is similar to my therapist in a lot of ways. They both said I will know if and when I am ready to let myself love again. I honestly think my parents want to see me happily in love with someone who is genuine and caring. They still handle me with kid gloves at times. I promise, I won’t break. I really am okay. That time is behind me.”

“It seems like it’s just below the surface, though.”

“It is now. But, it wasn’t before I came here on vacation. Yes, it was there. It will more than likely always be there. It’s a part of me…a part of my life. I can’t erase history. Nevertheless, I’d learned to live without it being a thought in my mind. Then, I arrived on this mountain, and for the first time I felt liberated from my past. The light was so bright, the darkness disappeared. That’s when I let my guard down with Camden unknowingly. I was living in the moment and before I knew it, I was falling for her. Having a good time on vacation quickly went to making love with someone. It scared the hell out of me, and I ran as fast as I could.”

Abby wiped away another tear. It broke her heart to hear what her best friend was going through. She wished she knew how to help her. “What has Camden said about all of this?”

“She’s been very understanding. She’s willing to wait as long as it takes, even if we never make it past friends again.”

“She sounds perfect.” Abby smiled. “It will take an astronomical amount of courage and trust for you to love someone again after what you’ve been through. I think you'll know when you're ready and when you've found the right person."

"I guess one of the big things is, I don't want to constantly be watching for the warning signs. You know?"

Abby nodded. "Maybe when it's real love, you won't need to."

"Yeah, maybe." Leigh smiled thinly and hugged her friend. *I hope you're right.*

Chapter 33

Camden watched the steady stream of steaming hot coffee pour from the percolator into the glass pot beneath it. Dark liquid slowly rose as it filled. The slightly caramelized, nutty aroma drifted into the air, waking her senses as she inhaled.

Once it was finished, she stepped outside with a freshly poured cup, sitting on the homemade bench she'd made out of a downed tree on her property a couple of years earlier. It sat in front of the round fire pit she'd made out of mountain stones around the same time. It was her day off, but she was up in time to watch the sun rise over the trees in the cloudless sky, gradually casting everything in an orange hue. It was turning into a beautiful day to be down at the riverside, fishing for pike and crappie with her favorite jig lures. She'd tried to learn to fly fish like Uncle Pa, whom she considered a master at it, but that was one trait of his that hadn't rubbed off on her. Still, she went with him and gave it her best try anytime he'd invited her. However, she'd made other plans for the day, so fishing wasn't happening.

She checked her watch, wondering when would be a good time to call Leigh. *Maybe we can grab breakfast before heading over to the conservatory*, she thought, before remembering her friend was visiting from the city. "I probably should've offered to take her a different day," she muttered to herself.

*

"I hate that you're leaving so soon," Leigh sighed, sounding as bummed as she looked, watching her best friend gather the minimal things she'd brought with her.

"Me too," Abby pouted. "On a lighter note, aren't you going to see a baby moose today?"

"Yes, and I can't wait!"

"Have fun with that," Abby laughed. "Send me a picture."

"You could go with us and leave a little later."

"Nah. I'm good." Abby wrinkled her nose and smiled.

Leigh shrugged. "Suit yourself."

"I still can't believe you've turned into this small-town mountain girl who gets lost looking for wild animals and can't wait to go play with them in the zoo. I would wonder what you'd done with my city girl best friend, but honestly, I've never seen you happier. You're different, but in a very good way."

"Thanks." Leigh pulled her in for a hug.

"Thank you for telling me," Abby whispered. "I know you didn't have to. I feel honored that you chose to."

"You're my best friend, Abby, no matter how far apart we live. I should've told you a long time ago."

"I've never been in your shoes, but I hope it works out with Camden. I somehow get the feeling she'd never let anything happen to you, much less cause it herself. I hope one day I find someone who looks at me the way she looks at you."

"Thanks," Leigh said softly.

Abby smiled and took one last look around. "I think I have everything. I'm sure you'll send it to me if I left anything."

"Yeah," Leigh laughed, walking her out. "Be careful driving back."

"I will. You enjoy your day with that good-looking animal cop…and the baby moose too, of course," Abby teased as she got into her car.

Leigh shook her head and laughed. "Get out of here."

Abby waved as she backed out of the driveway and Leigh returned the gesture as she watched her head down the road. She couldn't help being excited about seeing the moose, but she knew some of the butterflies had to do with spending time with Camden. Knowing she was awake with the sun that had come up two hours earlier, she grabbed her phone from her pocket and called her.

It rang twice before the voice on the other end picked up.

"Hey, I assume you're on your second cup of coffee and contemplating what to do for breakfast," Leigh said.

"You think you know me so well," Camden replied, watching a hawk circle in the sky.

"Am I right?"

"Maybe."

Leigh chuckled.

"I was actually thinking of calling to invite you and your friend to breakfast. She's more than welcome to come with us to the conservatory, by the way."

"She just left, actually."

"Oh."

"I mean if you'd rather have breakfast with her I can call her to come back," Leigh teased.

"You're funny. What's got you all giddy this morning? It certainly can't be me."

"Not unless you're three feet tall and covered in fuzzy dark hair," Leigh replied.

"Nope, at least not the last time I checked. Although, I do smell a little better."

Leigh laughed. "I won't argue with that." *Your scent is intoxicating.*

"So, would you like me to swing by and get you now? We can stop at the restaurant on the way out of town. Or, if there's somewhere else you'd rather go…"

"No, they have the best food in town, hands down."

"Okay. So…see you in ten?"

"Sounds good." Leigh ended the call and went inside to finish getting ready. She was already wearing jeans and a lightweight, dark-blue sweater.

*

Breakfast went by quickly. They sat at the bar and ordered right away. Uncle Pa served them while Aunt Ma worked the dining tables. As soon as they were finished, they got back into the truck and headed towards the next town over, where the conservatory was located.

"I really appreciate you doing this," Leigh said.

"You're welcome, but it's really not a big deal. I wanted to come check on him myself, and I know how bad you've wanted to see one. Why not see one you can pet and feed?"

"What happens if I want to keep him?" Leigh smiled.

"He'll be close to 900lbs when he is full grown. Good luck with that," Camden laughed. "Honestly, you'd be surprised at how many people try to domesticate wild animals. All it does is make them unable to return to the wild. Several of the animals at the conservatory are there for that reason. Most of the others will be rehabilitated and returned to the wild. The rest have suffered injuries that make it difficult for them to be in the wild, so they remain as well."

"I'm actually glad we're going today, whether the moose is there or not. I've been wanting to talk to Heather about maybe volunteering there."

"Really?"

"I know being a human nurse is nothing like being a veterinarian or even a vet tech, but if she could use the help, I'd certainly enjoy helping the animals. I never realized how much I'd love being around them. Every morning I look out to see if I have any visitors in the back yard. There's been a couple of deer and rabbits recently, but nothing else."

"It's spring. Everything is waking up and babies are being born. If you keep it quiet and don't make any drastic changes, you'll probably see more. Just make sure your trash isn't kept outside. That's what attracts bears. You definitely don't want to see one of them on your back patio."

"I'm sure I'd freak out!"

Camden nodded in agreement.

"So…on a different note, I told Abby about my past last night," Leigh blurted while looking out the window.

"Really? I guess I was under the assumption she knew."

"No." Leigh shook her head. "No one knew except my parents, my attorney, the judge and jury, and my therapist. At least, until you. And now, her."

"Did you tell her because of me?"

"I owed it to her. She's my best friend. I should've told her years ago. But, yes, telling you definitely had something to do with it."

"Oh."

"She thinks we're in love."

Camden veered off the road and swerved back on.

"Oh my God!" Leigh shrieked.

"Damn raccoon in the road," Camden muttered. "Did you see it?"

"Uh…no." Leigh glanced at her.

"Yeah, so anyway, what did you say to her?"

"I explained that it wasn't that easy for me, and subsequently told her my story." She bit her lower lip in thought. "I'm glad I did though."

"Does it lighten the weight at all when you tell someone?"

"I'm not sure I'd call it that. I mean, everyone found out during the worst of it, except you and Abby. My parents went through hell alongside me during the recovery and trial. Then, again when I tried to put my life back together, or what was left of it anyway." She paused for a moment thinking about when she'd first told Camden a couple of weeks earlier and then just telling Abby the night before. "I definitely feel better after telling you both. I'm no longer carrying a dark secret, so yeah, I guess some weight has been lifted in a sense. What about you with your birth mother and everything? Do many people know about that?"

"I'm sure the whole town knows," Camden laughed softly. "At least the ones who have lived here the last forty or so years. The newcomers might've found out if they'd asked someone. It's a story with a sad beginning and a happy ending. In a way, I guess yours is too."

“Yeah,” Leigh nodded in agreement.

“I like Abby. She seems like a nice person and a good friend.”

“She really is. I tried to get her to come along, but she’s definitely not an animal person, much less a wild animal.”

“Well, she’s missing out because we’re about to go hang out with a moose!” Camden said as she turned into the parking lot of the conservatory and drove around towards the veterinary building.

Chapter 34

"Hey." Kelsey smiled politely "Dr. Sullivan is finishing an exam. She said she'll catch up to you."

"Thanks," Camden replied, nodding for Leigh to follow her.

"She seems different," Leigh uttered.

Camden simply shrugged.

Leigh remembered the layout from the last time they were there. When they passed by the cage the fawn was kept in, she paused, looking for the little deer.

"His leg is better. He's out running around the sanctuary," Camden muttered, sensing her stop. "We can go see him though. The baby bear is out there, too. He's a lot bigger now and will be released soon."

"Oh, wow. Yes, I'd like to see them."

"I think you'll like this even more," Camden said, walking her over to the next enclosure where a small, black moose was standing near a tree and bushes.

"Oh, my God," Leigh whispered. "He's just a baby."

"About four days old, to be exact," Heather said, walking up to them. Camden gave her a quick hug. "He's doing really well. I don't want him to get too used to humans, otherwise, we can't release him to the wild, but you can go feed him some grass-milk. Just don't stay in there too long."

"When are you putting him out in the sanctuary?" Camden asked.

"Probably in a few days. He doesn't have any injuries or ailments, and he's starting to eat leaves and twigs, instead of just grass-milk. I think he'll be fine."

"I had a feeling he was just abandoned and not in distress. I'm sure someone killed his mother," Camden said.

"That's awful," Leigh added.

"I agree. It happens quite a bit, actually. Anyway, here's the bottle," she said, handing it to Camden. "It's a concoction of animal milk and grass, blended into a smoothie."

Leigh was nervous and it showed.

"He won't hurt you," Camden reassured, looking into her eyes. "I'll be right beside you."

Leigh took her offered hand and followed her inside. The calf made a whining sound and walked around for a second.

Camden held out the bottle and slowly moved towards him. He sniffed the air and whined a few more times before coming close enough to grab a hold of the long rubber nipple protruding from the bottle. She pet him with her other hand. "Hey, Buddy. Remember me?" she murmured.

"That's amazing," Leigh whispered.

"You can pet him. He won't bite you," Camden said, showing her where to put her hand.

Leigh rubbed the fur between his ears and down the back of his neck. Camden watched her face light up with excitement when she put Leigh's free hand on the bottle. She stepped back slightly, taking a couple of photos of her.

"He's almost finished," Leigh said, looking at the side of the bottle. The moose hadn't moved. He continued eating from the bottle while Leigh pet him over and over, talking softly to him.

"He likes you," Camden said. Leigh's huge smile was genuine and contagious, reminding her of the innocent happiness of a child. It was a mental picture she never wanted to forget.

"I'm pretty sure it's the milk," Leigh laughed.

Camden shook her head. She knew the animal had sensed her insecurity at first, but they showed vulnerability to each other and it bonded them right away. *I don't want to take you away from him, but it's for the best.* "We should probably get going," she sighed.

"Yeah," Leigh agreed, pulling the bottle free. She walked over to Camden who was a few feet away and the moose followed, whining at her. She turned around, petting him one last time. "You grow up to be big and strong and stay hidden from the hunters," she said, wiping a tear from the corner of her eye. "I'll think of you often."

Camden grabbed her hand, interlacing their fingers as they walked out of the enclosure and shut the door. The moose's continued whining was drowned out as they went to another area.

"Well, what did you think of him?" Heather asked.

"That was the neatest thing I've ever done. This place is fascinating, and what you do here is incredible," Leigh replied. "I was actually hoping I could talk to you about volunteering. I'm not sure my skills as a nurse practitioner would be any service to you since I'm used to humans, but I'd love to help out with the animals in any way that I can."

Camden glanced at Heather.

"Really?" Heather questioned.

"Absolutely." Leigh smiled and nodded.

"You'd be surprised at how easily your skills will transfer from a human to an animal and vice versa," Heather said. "I could definitely use the help."

"Obviously, I can't be here all the time, but I'd really like to do what I can."

"I'm actually about to do surgery on a bobcat with a nasty abscess in his cheek. Would you like to watch? I always have extra pairs of scrubs if you want to help out."

"Definitely," Leigh exclaimed.

"Are you talking about Billy Bob? I haven't seen him around."

"Yeah, he's been hiding more than usual because his cheek hurts. We're going to remove the puss and irrigate the wound," Heather said.

"You two have fun with that," Camden replied. "I need to run by our FWC office here in town anyway. They're supposed to have some information for one of my illegal hunting cases. I'll swing back by to get you when I'm finished."

"We'll be thirty minutes, maybe forty-five at most," Heather replied.

"Sounds good," Camden said, checking her watch before walking away, leaving the two of them to go get Leigh a pair of scrubs to change into.

*

The large bobcat was sedated and lying on his side on the metal table with a tube protruding from his mouth, filling his lungs with oxygen to keep him breathing. Thick fur covered his cheeks.

"This is Billy Bob."

"He looks just like a really furry house cat, only he's a lot bigger," Leigh said. "He's gorgeous."

"These animals are strong enough to take down a deer, but they mostly feed on hare, mice, and squirrels. Look at his teeth. See how they're rounded and filed down?" Heather pulled his gums back so she could see them better.

Leigh nodded. "What caused that?"

"A human who found him as a baby and domesticated him. She also had his claws removed," Heather added, showing her his large paws. "Sadly, he really is a big house cat."

"Oh, my God. Why would someone do that to him?"

"She wanted him as a pet. He came to live with us here at the conservatory about two years ago. He roams around here just like a regular cat, playing with things, climbing on everything, and sleeping wherever he feels like it. He's a sweetheart. He and Sly are like brothers. He's the red fox that runs around here like a dog. You probably saw him the last time you were here. Anyway, they both went through the same domestication by two different humans and have to live here like house animals because of it. Anyway, he has an abscess right here." She pointed to his cheek, just above his jaw. "You can touch him. I promise he's not going to wake up and maul you to death."

Leigh smiled and reached over, touching the walnut-sized knot. "Did he have an infection in a tooth?"

Heather shook her head. "Funny story, actually. We had a loon in here, you know what that is right?"

"Yeah, they're kind of like a large goose, I think."

"Sort of. So, the loon was here because it was being treated for lead poisoning, which is quite common with the river and creek fishing nearby. Anyhow, the loon was on the mend, so we let it walk around a little bit while we prepared to move it to a regular enclosure instead of the incubated unit it was in. Billy Bob decided to play hide and go seek with the damn thing and jump up on the countertop in the open triage area that we use for large animals. Bobcats like to be up high to stalk their prey. Well, he dove off of there, scaring the loon half to death, which in turn freaked out, scaring Billy Bob. He took off running in the opposite direction and ran into the corner of a metal cabinet. It left a tiny gouge, but he seemed fine."

"Wow," Leigh laughed. "That had to have been a sight."

"It was nuts in here for a hot minute," Heather chuckled. "Nonetheless, I was petting him a few days later and noticed a pea-size knot there. I figured his body would absorb it, but it has continuously grown. I want to get it taken care of before the infection gets any worse. He's been on antibiotics for about a week now, so we're good to go."

"Great. I'll follow your lead, just tell me what to do," Leigh replied.

Heather began by shaving the thick fur from the protrusion. Then, she grabbed a scalpel and lanced it open. Milky white puss with a putrid smell poured out. Leigh was glad she had a facemask on to help ward off some of the stench. She grabbed surgical paper towels, sopping up the mess as Heather squeezed the remainder out of it.

"So, we also have a part-time vet, two techs, and about a half dozen animal handlers who volunteer as well. The hours are all jumbled around because of different schedules. It would be nice to have another person in here with any sort of medical knowledge," Heather said while checking to make sure she'd gotten all of the infection out.

"Is Kelsey a tech?"

"She's a handler, but she assists the techs sometimes."

"She seems different, friendlier than the last time I was here."

"That's because Camden told her she wasn't interested in her and never would be."

"I see," Leigh said, watching Heather irrigate the wound and swab the interior with a Q-tip full of antibiotic ointment.

"Speaking of my cousin, what exactly are your intentions with her because she has strong feelings for you. I've never seen her like this, and I don't want her to get hurt. Everyone has run away or left her, starting with her own birth mother, and continuing with everyone she's ever dated or cared about. I'm not sure if she'd told you that or not. She might not show it, but the abandonment hurts a lot more than you think. I'm pretty sure she is reliving it over and over through other relationships that kept ending the same way, with someone leaving her behind. She deserves better," Heather stated as she stitched the wound closed.

Leigh felt the breath escape her lungs as her chest began to tighten. She had no words. She'd been so focused on herself and her own pain for so long, the idea that someone else could be in pain…and that it would be caused by her, had never crossed her mind. The person who had caused all of her sorrow was dead and gone, but for Camden, there was no closure. *I'm sorry.* She swallowed hard, trying to keep her watery eyes from dropping tears down her cheeks.

"Hey, are you about finished?" Camden asked, popping her head in.

"Yeah. We're about to wake him up. Want to watch?" Heather called over her shoulder. "Think about what I said before you go down this road with her," she murmured, looking across the table at Leigh, who simply nodded.

"Aww, poor Billy Bob," Camden said, walking up and petting him.

"Why didn't we see him last time we were here?" Leigh questioned.

"A bobcat's nature is to hide and hunt. He walks around like he owns the place...when he feels like it. But, mostly he hides in his enclosure, watching from his vantage point up high on the tree. The door is open so he can come and go as he pleases. If he doesn't know you, he'll hide in there," Heather answered. "Okay, everyone, back up. We're going to keep him in the enclosure until the anesthesia wears off so he doesn't hurt himself." She picked him up, carrying him out of the surgery ward and down the hall. Inside his enclosure, she removed the breathing tube and gave him a shot in his hindquarters to counteract the anesthesia, similar to a shot of adrenaline. He woke instantly and tried getting up, but his limp body was wobbly. "It'll be okay, boy. We'll check on you and bring some treats in a little bit," she said, backing out and closing the door.

"Thank you for letting me assist, although I didn't do much." Leigh smiled.

"True, but now you know *what* to do and *how* to do it. You could probably read a few animal biology books and take the state test to make you a master vet tech. That's similar to a nurse practitioner on a human."

"That's a good idea. I'll look into it."

"Great." Heather passed her a card. "Here's my number. Let's touch base next week and figure out when you're available. I'll make sure you get to shadow all of the handlers and get used to the animals, then you can work with me and the other vet, his name is Troy. We'll help you learn what you need to know for the test…if you decide to take it."

"I look forward to it. Thanks again…for everything," Leigh said, biting the edge of her lower lip. "Give me a minute to change and I'll be ready to go," she added, smiling at Camden.

"We can go through the park on the way out and see the deer, if you still want to."

"Oh, yeah! I'd forgotten all about that."

*

"Everything okay?" Camden asked. "You've been quiet the entire ride back."

Leigh looked over, smiling at her. "Yeah. What an unbelievable day."

"I'm glad you had fun. I guess things worked out with you wanting to volunteer, which I think is amazing by the way, and then her allowing you to help with the surgery."

"Yeah, I was surprised she asked me to assist, but she pretty much did everything. I enjoyed it. I don't have a whole lot of time to give, but I'd like to do what I can."

"Do you think you'll take that test she talked about?"

"Definitely. It'll allow me to be a lot more involved."

"Somehow, I didn't see you as just a handler, taking orders from Kelsey," Camden laughed.

"Not likely." Leigh grinned. "You know, I have you to thank. You're the one who took me there and opened my eyes to wildlife."

"I saw the way you looked at that bear cub, and knew you'd be intrigued by the conservatory."

"You were right," Leigh laughed softly.

"If you don't have any plans, I'd like to make you dinner at my place," Camden said, pulling into her driveway.

"Sure. Give me time to shower off the animal stench."

"I'll warn you, I'm not a self-made chef, but you won't die."

"How do you know?" Leigh chuckled.

"Baker is still alive. We eat together often, trading the cooking duties."

Leigh nodded. "I remember you saying that. How is he? I haven't seen him since I've been back."

"He's good. All of his free time is spent with Heather these days."

"What? Your cousin, whom we were just with?"

"Yep. They're dating."

"Really?"

"Yeah. It's been a long time coming."

Leigh grabbed her purse and swung the door open. "I'll see you in about an hour and a half. Is that okay?"

"Fine with me." Camden smiled.

*

Camden tore through the kitchen, piecing together the meal she'd invited Leigh to share as the radio played a block of Tina Turner songs. She'd settled for spaghetti since it was the easiest and tasted pretty good, or at least she and Baker thought so anyway. She opened a bottle of white wine and set it in the metal chiller she never used, to keep it cool. Then, she set the table for two spaces adjacent to each other.

"You must understand, the touch of your hand makes my pulse react," she sang, bobbing her head as she walked around the main room of her cabin where her living area, kitchen, and dining table were all located in the open space. She kept her cabin neat, so there really wasn't anything to pick up. Still, she made sure anyway.

She saw the headlights shining through the curtain as Leigh pulled into the driveway. A soft knock on the door followed. Camden pulled it open, greeting her guest in jeans, a light blue t-shirt and bare feet.

Leigh smiled. She'd never seen her look so casual. She had a feeling she was going to like this side of her even more. "Is that Tina I hear?"

"Yeah. They're doing a greatest hits block on the radio. I forgot to turn it off."

"It's fine. I love her music," she said, setting her purse down on the futon couch. The alluring scent of Camden's cedar and magnolia cologne hung lightly in the air, tickling her senses. "I wish I could sing like her," she added, closing her eyes as she breathed in.

"Me too," Camden agreed. "I tried one night, but I can't hit those high notes to save my life."

Leigh laughed. "Where was this?"

"The Dirty Moose. It's a hole in the wall bar Baker and I go to a couple times a month to play darts or shoot pool. They have karaoke on Thursday nights."

"Wait. You sing?"

"Only karaoke and I'm not that great at it. We usually have a few cocktails first," she chuckled. "Don't get excited."

"I'd love to join you some time."

"Can you shoot pool?"

"You'll have to invite me along and find out," Leigh teased with a raised brow.

"Let's start with dinner and see how that goes." Camden grinned. "I hope you like spaghetti," she added, walking over to the table.

"Who doesn't?" Leigh uttered, feeling her stomach growl as she followed behind her. She waited for the wine to be poured before sitting down.

Camden stepped over to the counter and put a large helping of food on both plates. She set one down in front of Leigh, and the other on her placemat before taking her seat. She grabbed her wine glass. "To the moose?" she shrugged.

Leigh nodded, clinking her glass against Camden's. "To the moose."

*

Both women had kept the conversation light while eating. As soon as they were finished, Camden carried the nearly empty plates over to the counter, clearing them off in the trash before placing them in the sink to be washed.

"I can help with that," Leigh said, getting up.

"It's fine. I'm just running water on them. I'll wash everything later."

"You don't have a dishwasher?" Leigh questioned, looking around.

"I have two," Camden replied, holding her hands up.

Leigh laughed. "You cooked. The least I can do is help you with the dishes. Slide over," Leigh insisted. "You wash. I'll rinse."

Camden obliged, giving her space at the sink. She squirted soap on the sponge and began scrubbing the plates and silverware. She'd already washed the cooking dishes as soon as she'd finished, so there wasn't much to do. Once she finished, Camden dried her hands on the dish towel and noticed Leigh's hips swaying slightly to the beat of the music. She bit her lower lip and pulled her eyes from Leigh's ass. *She has no idea what she does to me.*

"You don't entertain much, do you?" Leigh asked, looking at the recliner and adjacent futon, sitting a few feet away along the wall by the front door, almost as an afterthought. The recliner was obviously where Camden spent her time.

"Only Baker. He's happy with the futon and a beer."

Leigh laughed, shaking her head as she sat down on the futon. "What about your parents or Heather? Do you have other family in the area?"

Camden sat next to her. "I usually go to my parent's house, and I can't tell you the last time I spent time with Heather when it wasn't work related or a family function at someone's house. Her parents live in Berkshire. It's just outside of here and next to Granville, where the conservatory is. They used to have a large dairy farm, but sold the cows, then the land piece by piece years ago. I used to spend a lot of time there, playing with the cows when I was little. Her dad and Uncle Pa are brothers, and my birth mother and Aunt Ma are half sisters. Gorely is Aunt Ma's maiden name and my given name, so when they adopted me, they kept it instead of changing it to Sullivan, which is everyone else's last name in the family."

"Is Heather an only child, too?"

"No. She has a brother named Kyle. He and his wife live in a different town, closer to her family. They have two little girls, Nellie and Winnie. He's an electrician for the power company," Camden said.

"Oh, wow."

"I see them at the holidays. That's when we all get together at my parent's house or theirs usually."

"It's just me and my parents in Vermont. The rest of our family is in New Hampshire. We visited a lot when I was a kid, but my grandparents are all gone now. My parents visit my aunts and uncles once or twice a year though."

"Yeah, my grandparents are deceased as well. They were kindhearted people who worked hard with their hands all of their lives and were always there to help someone in need. I think they were big influences on all of us," she said, referring to everyone in the family.

Leigh nodded, understanding a little more about Camden's work ethic and compassion. She was intriguing, and Leigh enjoyed getting to know more about her. There was something about Camden that made Leigh want to be near her. Throughout her entire marriage, Leigh craved the intimacy that should've been shared between two people in love, but never once experienced it. She found it surprising how intimacy came natural to Camden. It didn't matter what she was doing or who she was with, she always showed genuine interest, giving the person her full attention. She had a way of making Leigh feel like she was the only person on the planet when they were together, without even knowing it. This drew Leigh closer to her than anything physical ever could.

However, sitting less than a foot apart, sipping wine and listening to soft music in the background made their conversation about family feel way more romantic than it actually was. Leigh was sure it was the mere presence of the woman next to her, and not her surroundings, causing her mind to wander elsewhere.

"It's been a long day. I should probably get going," she blurted. "I had an amazing day. Thank you."

"I'm glad. I had fun, too. I doubt tomorrow will compare."

"Why is that?"

"I'm working," Camden laughed.

"Don't you usually have back to back days off?"

"Most of the time, but I'm trying to track down what happened to the mother of that moose calf. I'm not going to stop until I find out what happened to her. I know whatever it was, it was illegal."

"I love that about you," Leigh said softly.

"What?"

"Your incredability."

Camden raised a brow. "I don't think that's a word."

"Sure, it is. It means your ability to be incredible," Leigh teased.

Camden laughed.

"Anyway, thank you again for a really nice day," Leigh murmured, looking into her eyes. "I like spending time with you."

"Me too," Camden said, then leaned in to hug her lightly. Leigh pulled her closer, pressing their bodies together for an extra long minute before letting go and stepping back. Camden searched her eyes.

"I have to go before I kiss you because I won't be able to stop," Leigh whispered.

Camden's chest tightened with the familiar ache of desire. "I know," she sighed softly.

*

Leigh got into her car and started the engine. Then, she placed her hands at the top of the steering wheel and laid her forehead against them. "I can't believe I almost said goodbye to you forever. I came back for a reason. I had to know if the tranquility I felt was because of this place, or my time spent with you. Now, I know it was both." She looked up at the cabin as she leaned back in her seat and put the car in reverse.

Chapter 35

Leigh went from one patient to another, methodically reading charts, diagnosing one ailment after another, but her mind was on Camden. It had been a week since their day at the conservatory. She'd replayed their goodbye in her head a hundred times and in every single one of them, the outcome was the same. She should've kissed her and let Camden take her to bed. That was what she'd wanted, and still did days later.

"Mrs. Coleman, let's take a look at this rash," she said, pushing the thoughts to the back of her mind as she walked into the next room on her list.

"It's bad," the woman said, fidgeting around on the exam table she was sitting on. "I can't stop itching. It's making me crazy, literally."

"Where is it?" Leigh asked, looking at her arms, face, and neck. Everything appeared normal. Suddenly, the woman hopped off the table and dropped her pants and underwear, putting all of her nakedness on display. Leigh gasped when she saw the red skin covered with tiny little blisters all over her butt and vaginal area.

"What is it? Do you know? I really don't want to show this to Dr. John. Please say you know what it is?"

"How long have you had it?" Leigh asked. "You can pull your pants back up."

"About four days. I was out in the woods with my husband when he was hunting. It started that night and keeps getting worse."

"Did you do anything in particular while you were out there? Like maybe have sex?"

"No. Definitely not." She shook her head. "I pretty much sat in the blind with him. It was boring as hell. I don't know how he does it. And after this, I am damn sure never going again."

Leigh couldn't imagine the discomfort she was in. "Did you use the bathroom at all?" she asked, trying to pinpoint what happened.

"Yes. Twice."

"Where, exactly?"

"In the woods between two bushes. He doesn't keep toilet paper in his hunting pack, so I had to wipe with leaves," she snapped, shaking her head. "He said that's what he does."

"Has he ever come home with a rash like this?"

"No."

"It looks like poison ivy or poison oak, perhaps even both. You're obviously allergic to the oil on the leaves. Your husband probably isn't, so he can wipe with them all day long."

"Oh, my God. I never thought of that."

"I'm going to give you oral prednisone. That will help, as well as a steroid cream. A colloidal oatmeal bath and calamine lotion may help soothe it as well. I'm also going to give you an antibiotic just in case. I'm afraid you're going to have to work through it. All of this together should begin to help within six to eight hours. Maybe sooner. It'll probably take a full week for it to completely run the course, but the worst of it should be behind you after today."

"Thank you," Mrs. Coleman said.

"I'm going to get these prescriptions. I'll be right back," Leigh said, stepping out of the room.

"There's someone here to see you. He said it's very important, so I put him in my office," Dr. John said, catching her in the hall.

"Who is it?" she questioned in surprise.

"Camden's father."

"Okay. Let me run these back into Mrs. Coleman. She has poison ivy and oak all over her lady parts and needs to start this prednisone right away."

"Good call. But, ouch," he cringed. "If it's serious, you can go. I can handle the rest of the afternoon," he added, nodding towards his office.

"Thanks."

*

Camden had just come out of a quarterly meeting when she noticed she had a voicemail. "Officer Gorely, this is Hank Mackey. You removed a moose calf from my property a week ago. Anyway, I found the mother…or at least her carcass. It's about a hundred yards from my house and stripped of its meat like it was slaughtered. It looks like it's been there at least a week. I'll be home for the rest of the day if you want me to show it to you. My address is 121 Wolf Landing."

"Son of a bitch," she growled, starting the truck and taking off in the direction of his house. "Please let there be evidence so I can bust this guy's ass!"

The mountain roads rarely had traffic, which made the quick trip up from town only a few minutes long. She parked in the driveway and got out, retrieving a pair of gloves and a couple of evidence bags.

"I guess you got my message," the man said, stepping outside. She recognized him from the last time she was there.

"Yeah. Let's go take a look at it. You didn't touch it at all, did you?"

"No, ma'am. I saw it, realized it was a moose carcass, and came in here to call you. I was out riding in my UTV with my son. That's how I found it."

Camden nodded.

He opened the shed and backed a solid black UTV out. "I programmed the location in my GPS, so we should be able to go right to it," he said.

Camden got into the passenger seat and buckled her safety belt. Then, they took off across the property. The smell was atrocious once they arrived. The remaining skin and meat was spoiled and covered with flies and maggots. She felt the urge to puke several times as she walked around taking pictures of the scene with her phone. It was most definitely a mature female moose.

"Does your property connect with other private land owners, or state land?"

"Both," he said, "depending on which direction you go."

Camden nodded as she searched around for any clue as to who did this and why. She was about to give in and head back to the office to print the pictures she'd taken when she spotted something metal half underneath the carcass. She took a couple of pictures. Then, together, they pulled the animal to the side slightly, allowing her to pick up the discarded knife. She quickly took a few more pictures before placing it in an evidence bag.

"Hopefully, there will be something to go on," she said, marking the location on her phone's GPS.

*

The police station was rarely busy, so Camden was able to get the knife looked at by a forensics expert who found a thumb print and a little bit of blood that was human. She had them go ahead and run the print in the local database since she was there and the blood was sent out to a lab for further testing that would reveal a DNA profile. She talked to a couple of officers she knew through her SAR work, while she waited.

The system didn't take long to come up with a name, picture, and address. *Owen Pruitt.* He'd been arrested for drug charges less than a year ago and was on probation. "This ought to be good," she muttered, looking at the printed information the officer had just handed her. "Crawford, Gorely. What's your 10-20?" she radioed, wanting to know his location.

"I was about to grab some lunch. Want to join me?"

"Go ahead without me. I have to serve an arrest warrant. I'll take a black and blue with me," she said.

"Copy."

"Can you spare someone to go with me to pick him up and carry him to the county jail?" she asked the officer who was assisting her.

"I'll go with you," he replied, adding, "here's the last known address from his probation officer."

"I need to type up this warrant. Give me your cell number. I'll call you when I'm ready to go," she said.

*

"Owen Pruitt," Camden said, when a man who looked like the mug shot, opened the door. If he was surprised to see a police officer and a fish and wildlife officer on his porch, he didn't show it.

"Yes."

"Were you out hunting a week ago on the eastern side of White Tail Trail?"

"No. I don't even know what that is."

"It's a parcel of government-owned property that butts up against a piece of private property. How about a moose? Have you seen any of those lately?"

"No." He shook his head. "I don't hunt. I'm on probation and not allowed to have a weapon of any kind."

"There was a moose killed out on that private property about a week ago. She had a newborn calf with her. Know anything about that?"

"No."

"Listen, Owen. I'm going to be honest with you, so I need you to be honest with me. Did you kill that moose and slaughter it for the meat?"

"What? No. You have the wrong guy. I didn't kill anything. I'm not supposed to have any weapons. Probation. Remember?"

"Then you won't mind us searching your house," she stated flatly.

"Yes, I mind. Do you have a warrant?"

Camden smiled and handed it to him. "I sure do. I also have the knife you left at the scene with your fingerprints and blood on it."

The color in his face drained.

"How do you think I found you?" she questioned. "Owen Pruitt, you're under arrest for shooting a gun on private property and within 500 yards of a dwelling, as well as hunting without a license. You're also under arrest for illegally possessing a gun and knife while on probation."

The police officer put him in handcuffs and held him at the door while Camden searched around. Within five minutes, she'd found the rifle he'd used to kill the moose, plus another knife, as well as a freezer full of moose meat, all of which she bagged up as evidence.

"Luckily, the moose calf survived," she said. "He's the reason I found you."

"I had to feed my family," he grumbled as she walked past him to put everything in her truck.

"If you're not allowed to hunt, then that's not the way to do it…is it?" she replied sarcastically, then turned towards the police officer. "You can head down to the jail. I'm going to finish up here and lock the door. I'll be right behind you."

Chapter 36

It had taken two hours to get Owen Pruitt booked in the county jail. Camden had to meet with his probation officer to go over all of the charges, including the three that were felonies, so he could submit them directly to the judge who had presided over his previous felony charges, which had him out on probation to begin with. By the time she'd finished, all she'd wanted to do was go home and shower off the disgust of the day.

She knew something was wrong as soon as her cabin came into sight. Uncle Pa's truck and Leigh's car were parked in her driveway. She pulled haphazardly in behind both of them, making sure her truck was off the road. Before she even killed the engine, her parents and Leigh were standing nearby, waiting to greet her.

"Is everything okay?" she asked, getting out.

"We all decided to visit at the same time," Aunt Ma said.

"Uh-huh…" Camden uttered, eyeing them suspiciously. She tried making contact eye with Leigh, but she'd kept her eyes on Camden's parents. She shrugged and walked over to the cabin door. Everyone followed her inside. "What's really going on?" she asked, closing the door behind them before removing the utility belt that held her gun, ammo, radio, and handcuffs. Then, she pulled the bulletproof vest up and over her head. She placed them both on the dining table on the opposite side of the room.

"You should probably sit down," Uncle Pa said as he sat on the futon between his wife and Leigh.

"Alright," she mumbled in confusion, walking over to her recliner.

"There's no easy way to say this, so I'll just give it to you straight. I know that's how you'd prefer it," he said. "Your birth mother was killed in a car accident a couple of weeks ago."

"What? Where?" Camden's brow scrunched and she shook her head, mentally trying to digest what he was saying to her.

"She was in Canada. Apparently, she's been living there this whole time. The guy she was married to tracked down Aunt Ma because she was listed as her next of kin."

"I'm so sorry, honey," Aunt Ma said, wiping tears from her face.

"I don't know what to say," Camden sighed, running her hand through her hair.

"We're here for you. Whatever you need. We love you, kiddo," Uncle Pa said.

"Thanks."

"He told us he would send down some of her things. He had her cremated and held a simple ceremony in a park where he spread the ashes," Aunt Ma said.

Camden nodded. "Did he know about me?"

Uncle Pa shook his head.

"I think she let go of this life when she left. None of us will ever know why she felt the need to do so."

"There's nothing any of us can do about it now. She's dead and gone," Camden said. "I'm sorry Aunt Ma."

"Don't be sorry, honey. That woman hurt you, but she gave me the greatest gift in the world."

"I love you both." She got up, hugging them.

"We'll let you and Leigh talk. We asked her along to help where we couldn't. Give her a chance," Uncle Pa whispered.

Camden gave him a half-smile, then walked her parents out. When she stepped back inside and shut the door, the mental glue she was using to hold everything together, suddenly failed. She sunk down to the floor with her back against the door as tears flowed down her cheeks. Leigh jumped up, rushing to her side. She wrapped her arms around the sobbing woman and held her close.

"Thirty-eight fucking years!" she cried. "She left me thirty-eight years ago and never looked back. Never once called or wrote to check on me. She just left me. How do you do that to your child then start your life over like she never existed? She obviously never loved me."

"I don't know, baby," Leigh whispered, kissing the side of her head.

"I hate her. God, I hate her so much," she sobbed.

Leigh simply held her while she let it all out. Camden's birth mother was breaking her heart all over again from the grave. She had no idea what to say to her. She understood now why Heather had confronted her about her intentions. The pain Camden had carried all of the years was deeper than she let on. She knew that feeling all too well. The devastating pain she'd suffered was completely different, but it hurt all the same.

"I promise, I won't leave you," she murmured, holding Camden tighter. "Never again." Leigh felt a couple of tears slide slowly down her cheeks.

Camden pulled back slightly, turning tear-soaked eyes on her.

"I'm so sorry she hurt you."

"It's okay," Camden sighed. "Thank you for being here."

"There's nowhere else I'd rather be."

Camden adjusted her position so that she was sitting next to Leigh instead of cuddled in her arms. "I thought I'd put that woman behind me a long time ago." She shook her head and let out a heavy breath. "I just don't understand how she could have this whole other life and forget all about me like I was nothing." Her tears were gone, but the sadness remained in her voice.

"If she really loved you, she would've never left to begin with, or at least realized it and came back to have a life with you."

Camden looked into her eyes. "You're the only one who ever came back," she whispered.

Leigh ran her hand over Camden's cheek, wiping away her wet tears. "I had to. I realized…" she said softly, her voice fading away. Nervousness began to build in the pit of her stomach, but the gentleness in Camden's sad, questioning eyes staring back at her made her forget all about her apprehension. "I'm in love with you," she said, biting her lower lip. "I fell for you and I ran out of fear history would repeat itself. I came back because this was the only place that made me feel free, like I could live again. And a big part of that was you, Camden. *You* made me feel like I could live again. I'm sorry it has taken me so long to say this to you, and I know the timing isn't ideal. I just…I want you to know I love you, and I'm never running again. This is where I want to be. Where I *need* to be." She let her hand fall from Camden's cheek as she searched her eyes.

Without saying a word, Camden leaned over, closing the distance between them as her lips met Leigh's in a gentle kiss. Her mouth lingered, waiting for Leigh to either continue, or pull away. As if reading her mind, Leigh's lips claimed Camden's in a heated exchange that left them both wanting more. Camden saw the look of desire burning in her eyes. Her own tongue snaked out, licking her lower lip subconsciously. She'd never wanted anyone as bad as she wanted Leigh in that very moment. Every fiber of her body ached with the need to touch and be touched. She moved to her feet and held her hand out.

The hunger in Camden's gaze was unmistakable. Leigh swallowed hard. Her chest heaved with excitement as adrenaline began coursing through her veins. She felt like she'd just ran a mile. She held her hand out, allowing Camden to pull her to her feet and into her arms. Their lips met again and this time, Leigh spun her around, backing Camden up against the door. She ran her hands up and down the front of her lithe body as she kissed her hard, insinuating the heavy need built up inside of her. She'd never taken the lead with anyone except strangers, a learned behavior from getting beaten for displaying that sort of dominance in her marriage. But, Camden made her feel safe and open to be herself for the first time ever. There wasn't a timid thought in her mind as Leigh snatched Camden's uniform shirt open. The buttons popped off, hitting the floor with tiny clinking sounds as she pushed the garment over her shoulders, dropping it in a heap behind her. Without hesitation, Leigh pushed her undershirt up, sliding her hands along Camden's warm flesh at the same time. She reached around, unclasping her sports bra, then pushed it up over her head along with the undershirt. With Camden's upper body free of impeding clothing, Leigh was able to run her hands all over her, feeling every inch of her smooth skin.

Camden was on fire, burning from the inside out. Her senses were on overload from Leigh's fervent kisses and the carnal way her hands were roaming her half-naked body. It was threatening to explode at any moment. She was too far gone to do anything other than allow Leigh total control, something she was almost certain she'd never had before and that was okay. Who took the lead, who touched who where, none of that mattered to Camden. All she wanted was to be with Leigh, teetering on the edge of desire while hanging on by a thread. Just as she was in that moment. She'd never experienced anything so erotic in all of her adult life.

Leigh's hands moved down to Camden's waist, lingering for a split second before loosening her belt, opening the button, and sliding the zipper down. She playfully bit Camden's lower lip, pulling back to see her heavy-lidded eyes while her fingers teased the waistband of her bikini briefs.

"I need you," Camden whispered.

Leigh pressed her lips to Camden's once more, drinking from her kisses like a parched lover while tugging her pants and briefs slightly off her waist with both hands. Camden's legs spread as far as they could go. Leigh moved her hand down from Camden's belly button, sliding lower and lower until she cupped her, coating her fingers with hot, silky wetness as she pulled them back through the folds.

Camden trembled when Leigh's fingers grazed her swollen clit. She sucked in a breath, pushing her legs further apart, not caring if she tore her pants in half. Leigh pressed two fingers in circles around her throbbing center before sliding them deep inside of her. Camden groaned with pleasure as Leigh's fingers swirled around, then pulled halfway out before pushing in deep again. Her eyes slammed closed and her hips bucked in rhythm with Leigh's slow, satisfying thrusts.

Leigh had only touched complete strangers in this way and had never taken the time to really feel what she was doing…until now. The muscles around her fingers were hot and squishy, and silky smooth, allowing her to glide back and forth.

By the time Camden tightened around her, drawing her fingers in deeper, Leigh was practically holding her up with her other arm and part of her own body, pinning her against the door. Camden's hips stilled and she let out a guttural moan as she shuttered in Leigh's arms.

"I love you," Leigh whispered, pulling her fingers free and sliding them up her torso, coating Camden's midsection with her own wetness.

"I've never loved anyone the way I love you," Camden replied breathlessly. "I know I never will again."

Leigh moved her clean hand up on Camden's chest above her left breast with her fingers barely touching her collarbone. She softly rubbed her thumb side to side over her breastplate. "You don't have to because I'm not going anywhere."

Camden smiled, then kissed her softly. "Can I talk you into going to my bedroom before I fall down?"

Leigh laughed and backed away, allowing Camden to peel herself off the front door. Her pants were slung low on her hips with the front fly spread open, and she was nude from the waist up. "You are sexy as hell," she muttered.

Camden smiled and shook her head as she led Leigh to her bedroom. Once inside, she pulled her shirt over her head, revealing a tattoo down her left side that wasn't there before. "This is new," she uttered, running her finger over the script. "What does it mean?"

"Free," Leigh said. "I got it when I went back to the city. After coming here…and subsequently being with you, I realized I was finally able to be free from the ghosts that haunted me and fear that held me back from living my life. I had this done as a reminder to myself."

"Liberation looks very good on you," Camden whispered, bringing her arms around her waist as she went in for a sensual kiss.

*

Leigh sighed, taking in a deep breath as she opened her eyes. For the first time in a very long time, the anxiety and fear that always caused her to run wasn't there. It was wonderful to wake up feeling love and happiness instead. She smiled, rolling her head to the side to look at the slumbering woman next to her. Beautiful hazel eyes fluttered open.

"Hi," Camden mumbled, yawning.

"Hi." Leigh smiled and curled onto her side, kissing her lips softly.

"I can make breakfast. Or, at least I think I can. I usually just stop at the restaurant," Camden rambled. She wasn't used to waking up with a woman in her bed. In fact, she couldn't remember the last time that had happened. Her cabin was great for a single person, but not much for entertaining company.

"Move in with me," Leigh blurted.

Camden raised a brow and sat up. The blanket and sheet spilled around her waist, revealing her breasts.

"I'm serious." Leigh rose in the same manner and grabbed her hand. "I know what we have is real love and I don't want to waste another minute without you. I'm tired of letting my past run my life. I'm ready for my future. Camden, *you're* my future. I want a life with you."

Completely shocked, Camden could think of nothing but yes. "Yes," she said, smiling like a little kid before kissing her.

Leigh lied back, pulling Camden down with her as their lips parted in a passionate kiss.

Epilogue

One Year Later

Camden looked through the large, picture windows at the massive trees that just two weeks earlier, were covered in pristine white snow. She hated getting out of bed and leaving the woman lying next to her. In all honesty, she could call in sick and take the day off, but she'd just run out of sick days and vacation time at some point. The life she'd built with Leigh was nothing less than perfect, if there were such a thing. She tried to remember them having a disagreement, but couldn't think of one. As she watched her sleep, she thought about all of their conversations while cuddled together on the couch, and many nights they'd made love in front of the fireplace.

"You look lost in thought," Leigh murmured, smiling at her.

"What do you think about getting married again one day?" Camden questioned, taking her slightly off guard.

Leigh cleared her throat and sat up a little. "I've thought of that a lot lately. I never knew being in love could be like this."

Camden reached into her nightstand and pulled out a gold ring with a decent sized solitaire diamond. It was old-fashioned and not as flashy as the new designs that had multiple diamonds or colored stones, but when she'd bought it, she had a feeling it would be perfect for Leigh. She turned back to her, leaning up on one elbow.

"There's no pressure," Camden said, showing it to her. "You can wear it or we can put it away and never bring it up again." She cleared away the nerves that seemed to ball up in her throat. "We hadn't really talked about it. So, I wasn't sure if—"

Sensing her hesitation, Leigh placed her hand on Camden's cheek. "Ask me," she whispered.

"What?"

"Ask me, Camden," she said, looking into her eyes.

"Uh…" She licked the dryness from her lips and smiled at the beautiful woman staring back at her. "Leigh Myer, you were a stranger who walked…wait, more like sped, into my life and quickly became my whole world. I couldn't imagine my life without you. Will you marry me?"

"Yes! Yes! Yes!" Leigh exclaimed with a big smile and soft chuckle. "I love you so much."

"I love you, too," Camden said, sliding the ring onto her finger while kissing her tenderly.

Leigh wrapped her arms around Camden and lied back, pulling her down for a more voluptuous kiss that had them both breathless and craving more…until her alarm began beeping on the nightstand. "Ugh…" she groaned as Camden reached over, silencing it.

"Son of a bitch!" Camden shrieked, noticing the time. "I'm going to be late for work."

Leigh laughed. "At least you have a good reason."

"It would've been better if we could have continued," she replied, leaning down, kissing her again.

Leigh pushed her away. "I'll be late as well if we keep this up."

"You're right. We have to go be responsible adults," Camden pouted.

"Yes, but responsible *engaged* adults!"

"I like the sound of that." Camden snuck in another kiss before getting out of bed. "Want to meet for lunch at the restaurant?"

"Sure. Noon?"

"That works for me."

*

The hearing for Own Pruitt, the man who had broken several laws in killing the mother of the moose calf, had been sentenced to serve seven years in prison. The assistant district attorney had been shooting for ten, which was the maximum. Camden found out the news as soon as she walked out of the quarterly staff meeting at the office.

"Got big plans for lunch?" Baker asked.

"As a matter of fact, I'm having lunch with my fiancée," she said with a grin.

"No way! Congratulations!"

"Thank you, and if you tell Heather before I do, I'll skin you like an animal," she stated.

"My lips are sealed...only if I can be your best man, or whatever you call it."

Camden shook her head and laughed as she got into her truck.

*

Leigh went into the restaurant and Aunt Ma waved for her to choose her own table. Leigh smiled and picked the very first one she and Camden had sat at together. A minute later, Aunt Ma appeared with a menu and a glass of iced water. She was about to ask if Camden was joining her when she saw the shiny rock on her finger.

"Oh, my word!" she exclaimed, quickly calling for her husband to come over. "I'm so happy for both of you!"

"What's going on?" he said, rushing up next to her.

Aunt Ma pointed to the ring and shook his arm.

"Wow. It looks like our girl did good," he said, smiling and winking at her.

"She sure did." Leigh smiled. "I can't wait to be a part of your family."

"Oh, honey, we knew you'd be a part of our family the day she brought you in here and introduced us," Aunt Ma said. "We've looked at you like that ever since."

"Thank you. You have no idea what that means to me," Leigh replied.

Aunt Ma patted her hand as Uncle Pa walked off to deal with his tables. "I'll be back in a few minutes. I assume she's joining you?"

Leigh nodded.

By the time Aunt Ma disappeared into the kitchen, Camden walked through the door. Their eyes met from across the room and both women lit up with huge smiles.

"You have the radiance of a woman who is madly in love," Camden teased as she sat down across from her.

"I am, actually…with a sexy wildlife officer. Do you know her?" Leigh replied playfully.

Suddenly, Camden's radio crackled to life. "Gorely, dispatch. What's your twenty? We have a deer hit by a car on Forrest Lane. It's still alive and trying to get up."

She looked at Leigh and smiled thinly. "I'm sorry."

"Don't be. I'll see you at home," Leigh replied, adding, "our home. The place we plan to spend the rest of our lives together, loving each other."

Without hesitation, Camden got up from the table and kissed her cheek softly, then she walked away.

Aunt Ma stepped over to the table, having just witnessed the exchange. “That’s the life of a wildlife officer who gives everything she has to her job,” she sighed.

“I know,” Leigh replied, still smiling as she watched Camden already responding on her radio before she was even out the door.

About the Author

Graysen Morgen is the bestselling author of several bestselling lesbian fiction titles. She was born and raised in North Florida with winding rivers and waterways at her back door, as well as, the white sandy beach. She has spent most of her lifetime in the sun and on the water. She enjoys reading, writing, fishing, coaching and watching soccer, and spending as much time as possible with her wife and their two children.

You can contact Graysen at graysenmorgen@aol.com; like her fan page on Facebook.com/graysenmorgen; follow her on Twitter: @graysenmorgen and Instagram: @graysenmorgen

Other Titles Available From Triplicity Publishing

Enticed by Love by Lynn Lawler. Henrietta Bailey is a mysterious woman who has spent her entire life living in the town of Crescent, a sleepy beach community in central coastal California. She loves the beach, the ocean air, and the town itself. Her simple life fulfills her. However, she spends much of her time reminiscing about her long-lost love, a woman who left her devastated. Now, another woman awaits on the horizon; a wise, intelligent, and sexy lady who is sophisticated beyond her years. This woman yearns for her soul mate and lover. Will she be able to win Henrietta's heart, or will Henrietta be fated to live the rest of her days alone?

Love Undercover by Domina Alexandra. Remi Stone never expected to get the opportunity to work undercover for narcotics. But, when the chance arrives, she takes it. With drugs coursing through a high school, Remi has only until the end of the school year to find the suspects responsible. Undercover, Remi plays her role, moving one step further into the drug industry. She never thought she'd be moving one step closer to the woman who would change her life and take hold of her heart. There is just one issue. Remi Stone is undercover as an eighteen year old high school senior. And the woman she can't seem to ignore is her History teacher. There will be a lot of challenges along the way, including one that could cost Remi her life and her heart.

Playing the Game by Graysen Morgen. Randi Rojas is a professional soccer player who seemingly has it all, a successful career, a long-term girlfriend, a loving family, and a great group of friends…until a chance meeting with an attractive woman sends her way offside, and into a whole new game. Berkley Ward lives her life to the extreme, spending her days either in the gym or four-wheeling in the woods, and her nights patrolling the streets as an officer. Affairs with taken women are easy, but after years of playing games, she's finished…until she meets a beautiful woman and a game she can't resist. Both women play a dangerously seductive game of cat and mouse, teetering on the edge of friendship and affair.

Rebel Sweetheart by Sydney Canyon. When a headstrong, country music superstar starts getting threatening letters while on tour, her manager has no other choice but to hire someone to investigate the threats, and keep her safe. Haley Nielsen is as stubborn as it gets. She does things her way, and her way only. The last thing she needs or wants is a babysitter following her every move and controlling everything she does. Shane Crowley isn't your typical private investigator, or bodyguard, for that matter. She's a former U.S. Deputy Marshal with a lot of experience, and an all or nothing attitude. Tempers flare and the energy burns red hot between the two women as they spend weeks together cooped up on Haley's tour bus, traveling the country. Will they stop resisting each other long enough to see eye to eye? Or will the letter writer make good on his threats?

A Tale of Spiders and Canned Soup by Kathy L. Salt. Living on your own can be hard, but even more so when you're dealing with haphephobia; the death of a twin sister; and a crush on your teacher. Mika is still in contact with her foster family who homes the loves of her life, three young children she would do anything for, when she begins attending University of Aberdeen and meets Pauline, an Australian that teaches Viking history. Neither woman is used to breaking the rules, and their way to each other is a hard one, especially when Mika vows to get custody of the children, whether she is ready to be a parent or not. *A story about growing up. A story about dealing with grief. A story about Mika and Pauline.*

A Night Claimed by Domina Alexandra. Bonnie Collins had plans. And being a werewolf wasn't one of them. Attacked by a rogue who was out to claim her, and facing what she now has no choice of becoming, Bonnie can't let go of her human life as a Paramedic. The last thing Bonnie needs is more challenges. However, Rikki, the Alpha of Mill City will be just that. Finding her to be possessive and ruling, Bonnie begins challenging the Alpha's every breath. Finding out her attack was no accident only makes her more angry at the situation. A group of rogues are out to get her. With no clue why, Bonnie has no choice but to seek help from the alluring Alpha and her pack, accepting the new world she was forced into.

Stunted by Breanna Hughes. Professional stuntwoman Jessie Knight takes her job very seriously and although she works in the entertainment industry, she has zero desire for fame or notoriety. She also has a very strict no-dating policy when it comes to coworkers. That is, until, she meets famous actress Elliot Chase on the set of her new film. The adrenaline rush of the stunts is nothing compared to the sparks that fly between them. After a passionate night together, a sex tape is leaked that sends Jessie and Elliot's private and professional lives into a spiral. Will the fallout be too much for them to last? Or will they find a way out of the mess together?

Mission Compromised by Graysen Morgen. Natalia Moreno is thrilled when she arrives in Fiji for a relaxing vacation. However, she soon discovers the overwater bungalow she's staying in has been double booked for the entire stay, and the resort is full. Annoyed and frustrated, she has no other choice but to share her hut with a stranger. Christian Garnier is sent to Fiji for what she refers to as a working vacation, until she finds out she has an ornery roommate for the next two weeks who is dead set on making her job twice as hard. Soon, all hell breaks loose and the two women are sent around the world on a wild goose chase.

Stargazing by Kathy L. Salt. Lissa stared open-mouthed at the GIF that played over and over on the screen in front of her. Heat flushed to her face, igniting her skin. Her heart started pounding in her chest. *Stupid internet, it should really come with a warning label.* She's never been interested in relationships or sex and as the years have gone by she has retreated more and more into her work. Everything changes when she meets Star, a porn actress with a heart of gold and a troubled childhood. *They say that opposites attract, but how much of that is true? What chance do they have when one of them is a virgin and the other one star in pornography?*

I Belong with Her by Domina Alexandra. Tajel Pierce loves the thrill of being a paramedic. Every call she goes on gives her a rush. She makes no time for a personal life. No one can ruin her love for her career. Then there is Arianna Castaldi, who just transferred to her new paramedic position in a whole new state. All she needs is a new start without any distractions. Arianna and Tajel's relationship doesn't start off perfect. Embarrassed of the one night stand Arianna believes she had with Tajel, she wants to pretend they never met and make their relationship strictly business. The only choice they have to keep from strangling each other is to go from denying their feelings to accepting them as they work through intense 911 calls.

Awakened by Fate by Lynn Lawler. Jackie is a woman living life according to her own rules. She's married, but it's the unspoken, open kind. She can have as many female lovers as she likes; she just can't talk about them. After a bizarre encounter turns her world upside down, things slowly begin to change. She finds herself in desperation as she searches for answers. What she discovers is nothing is delivered in a neatly wrapped box. Now that everything has been brought out into the open, she finds she can't run away from her truth anymore. With her new life, comes new responsibilities and a different outcome than what she was expecting. Jackie isn't alone in the story. She meets several new people who help her along her journey.

Nautical Delights by S. L. Gape. Lady Elizabeth Barrington has spent her entire life trying to please her family; constantly opting for a quiet life, she utilises her profession as a doctor to keep out of her families' clutches; bar the annual two-week Caribbean private cruise, where there is simply no budge. Confined to two weeks on board the Iconica super yacht, she intends on keeping her head down and enjoying as much of the holiday as she can, whilst keeping her family at arm's length. Until a crew member catches her eye.

Worlds Apart by S.L. Gape. Hollywood A-lister Heidi Spencer-Brady is everything you'd expect of an Idol. Loved by all, the British Beauty is graceful, talented, humble and so far removed from the 'typical' LA scene. When her husband's infidelity with his new 'leading lady' is leaked, Dawn, Heidi's best friend and manager, goes all out to protect her. She arranges for Heidi to go back to the UK and stay on her cousins farm they had visited as children, much to the disappointment of the animal fearing Heidi.

Castor Valley (Law & Order Series Book 2) by Graysen Morgen. Jessie Henry is torn when she reads about the capture of the Doyle brothers, two young men who were part of her old gang. Unable to let them hang for a crime she's sure they didn't commit, Jessie leaves her wife and the Town of Boone Creek behind, and sets out on a journey back to the one place she thought she'd never see again, *Castor Valley*. Ellie Henry watches the love of her life leave, not knowing if she will ever return. When she gets an odd telegram, nearly a week later, she fears Jessie is in trouble. With no other choice, she goes to the one person who can help her.

Fight to the Top by S. L. Gape. Georgia is a forty year old, single, Area Director from Manchester, UK who is all work and definitely no play. Having no time to socialise or spend time with her family she prides herself on being fit and well-polished. Erika is an Area Director for the same company, but in the United States. Whilst she is concentrating so heavily on the promotion she has been fighting for, she's starting to feel like her life outside of work is falling apart. The two women are exceptionally different, and worlds apart. Both of their lives are turned upside down when their jobs are snatched from under their noses, and they are suddenly faced with being thrown together by their bosses for one last major project...in Texas.

Boone Creek (Law & Order Series book 1) by Graysen Morgen. Jessie Henry is looking for a new life. She's unknown in the town of Boone Creek when she arrives, and wants to keep it that way. When she's offered the job of Town Marshal, she takes it, believing that protecting others and upholding the law is the penance for her past. Ellie Fray is a widowed, shopkeeper. She generally keeps to herself, but the mysterious new Town Marshal both intrigues and infuriates her. She believes the last thing the town needs is someone stirring up trouble with the outlaws who have taken over.

Witness by Joan L. Anderson. Becca and Kate have lived together for eight years, and have always spent their vacation in a tropical paradise, lying on a beach. This year, Becca wanted to try something different: a seven day, 65-mile hike in the beautiful Cascade Mountains of Washington state. Their peaceful vacation turns to horror when they stumble upon a brutal murder taking place in the back country.

Too Soon by S.L. Gape. Brooke is a twenty-nine year old detective from Oxford, who has her life pretty much planned out until her boss and partner of nine years, Maria, tells her their relationship is over. When Brooke finds out the truth, that Maria cheated on her with their best friend Paula, she decides to get her life back on track by getting away for six weeks in Anglesey, North Wales. Chloe, a thirty three year old artist and art director, owns a log cabin on Anglesey where she spends each weekend painting and surfing. After returning from a surf, she stumbles upon the somewhat uptight and enigmatic Brooke.

Never Quit (Never Series book 2) by Graysen Morgen. Two years after stepping away from the action as a Coast Guard Rescue Swimmer to become an instructor, Finley finds herself in charge of the most difficult class of cadets she's ever faced, while also juggling the taxing demands of having a home life with her partner Nicole, and their fifteen year old daughter. Jordy Ross gave up everything, dropping out of college, and leaving her family behind, to join the Coast Guard and become a rescue swimmer cadet. The extreme training tests her fitness level, pushing her mentally and physically further than she's ever been in her life, but it's the aggressive competition between her and another female cadet that proves to be the most challenging.

Never Let Go (Never Series book 1) by Graysen Morgen. For Coast Guard Rescue Swimmer, Finley Morris, life is good. She loves her job, is well respected by her peers, and has been given an opportunity to take her career to the next level. The only thing missing is the love of her life, who walked out, taking their daughter with her, seven years earlier. When Finley gets a call from her ex, saying their teenage daughter is coming to spend the summer with her, she's floored. While spending more time with her daughter, whom she doesn't get to see often, and learning to be a full-time parent, Finley quickly realizes she has not, and will never, let go of what is important.

Pursuit by Joan L. Anderson. Claire is a workaholic attorney who flies to Paris to lick her wounds after being dumped by her girlfriend of seventeen years. On the plane she chats with the young woman sitting next to her, and when they land the woman is inexplicably detained in Customs. Claire is surprised when she later runs into the woman in the city. They agree to meet for breakfast the next morning, but when the woman doesn't show up Claire goes to her hotel and makes a horrifying discovery. She soon finds herself ensnared in a web of intrigue and international terrorism, becoming the target of a high stakes game of cat and mouse through the streets of Paris.

Wrecked by Sydney Canyon. To most people, the *Duchess* is a myth formed by old pirates tales, but to Reid Cavanaugh, a Caribbean island bum and one of the best divers and treasure hunters in the world, it's a real, seventeenth century pirate ship—the holy grail of underwater treasure hunting. Reid uses the same cunning tactics she always has before setting out to find the lost ship. However, she is forced to bring her business partner's daughter along as collateral this time because he doesn't trust her. Neither woman is thrilled, but being cooped up on a small dive boat for days, forces them to get know each other quickly.

Arson by Austen Thorne. Madison Drake is a detective for the Stetson Beach Police Department. The last thing she wants to do is show a new detective the ropes, especially when a fire investigation becomes arson to cover up a murder. Madison butts heads with Tara, her trainee, deals with sarcasm from Nic, her ex-girlfriend who is a patrol officer, and finds calm in the chaos of police work with Jamie, her best friend who is the county medical examiner. Arson is the first of many in a series of novella episodes surrounding the fictional Stetson Beach Police Department and Detective Madison Drake.

Mommies (Bridal Series book 3) **by Graysen Morgen.** Britton and her wife Daphne have been married for a year and a half and are happy with their life, until Britton's mother hounds her to find out why her sister Bridget hasn't decided to have children yet. This prompts Daphne to bring up the big subject of having kids of their own with Britton. Britton hadn't really thought much about having kids, but her love for Daphne makes her see life and their future together in a whole new way when they decide to become mommies.

Rapture & Rogue by Sydney Canyon. Taren Rauley is happy and in a good relationship, until the one person she thought she'd never see again comes back into her life. She struggles to keep the past from colliding with the present as old feelings she thought were dead and gone, begin to haunt her. In college, Gianna Revisi was a mastermind, ring-leading, crime boss. Now, she has a great life and spends her time running Rapture and Rogue, the two establishments she built from the ground up. The last person she ever expects to see walk into one of them, is the girl who walked out on her, breaking her heart five years ago.

Second Chance by Sydney Canyon. After an attack on her convoy, Marine Corps Staff Sergeant, Darien Hollister, must learn to live without her sight. When an experimental procedure allows her to see again, Darien is torn, knowing someone had to die in order for this to happen.

She embarks on a journey to personally thank the donor's family, but is too stunned to tell them the truth. Mixed emotions stir inside of her as she slowly gets to the know the people that feel like so much more than strangers to her. When the truth finally comes out, Darien walks away, taking the second chance that she's been given to go back to the only life she's ever known, but she's not the only one with a second chance at life.

Meant to Be by Graysen Morgen. Brandt is about to walk down the aisle with her girlfriend, when an unexpected chain of events turns her world upside down, causing her to question the last three years of her life. A chance encounter sparks a mix of rage and excitement that she has never felt before. Summer is living life and following her dreams, all the while, harboring a huge secret that could ruin her career. She believes that some things are better kept in the dark, until she has her third run-in with a woman she had hoped to never see again, and gives into temptation. Brandt and Summer start believing everything happens for a reason as they learn the true meaning of meant to be.

Coming Home by Graysen Morgen. After tragedy derails TJ Abernathy's life, she packs up her three year old son and heads back to Pennsylvania to live with her grandmother on the family farm. TJ picks back up where she left off eight years earlier, tending to the fruit and nut tree orchard, while learning her grandmother's secret trade. Soon, TJ's high school sweetheart and the same girl who broke her heart, comes back into her life, threatening to steal it away once again. As the weeks turn into months and tragedy strikes again, TJ realizes coming home was the best thing she could've ever done.

Special Assignment by Austen Thorne. Secret Service Agent Parker Meeks has her hands full when she gets her new assignment, protecting a Congressman's teenage daughter, who has had threats made on her life and been whisked away to a Christian boarding school under an alias to finish out her senior year. Parker is fine with the assignment, until she finds out she has to go undercover as a Canon Priest. The last thing Parker expects to find is a beautiful, art history teacher, who is intrigued by her in more ways than one.

Miracle at Christmas by Sydney Canyon. A Modern Twist on the Classic Scrooge Story. Dylan is a power-hungry lawyer who pushed away everything good in her life to become the best defense attorney in the, often winning the worst cases and keeping anyone with enough money out of jail. She's visited on Christmas Eve by her deceased law partner, who threatens her with a life in hell like his own, if she doesn't change her path. During the course of the night, she is taken on a journey through her past, present, and future with three very different spirits.

Bella Vita by Sydney Canyon. Brady is the First Officer of the crew on the Bella Vita, a luxury charter yacht in the Caribbean. She enjoys the laidback island lifestyle, and is accustomed to high profile guests, but when a U.S. Senator charters the yacht as a gift to his beautiful twin daughters who have just graduated from college and a few of their friends, she literally has her hands full.

Brides (Bridal Series book 2) by Graysen Morgen. Britton Prescott is dating the love of her life, Daphne Attwood, after a few tumultuous events that happened to unravel at her sister's wedding reception, seven months earlier. She's happy with the way things are, but immense pressure from her family and friends to take the next step, nearly sends her back to the single life. The idea of a long engagement and simple wedding are thrown out the window, as both families take over, rushing Britton and Daphne to the altar in a matter of weeks.

Cypress Lake by Graysen Morgen. The small town of Cypress Lake is rocked when one murder after another happens. Dani Ricketts, the Chief Deputy for the Cypress Lake Sheriff's Office, realizes the murders are linked. She's surprised when the girl that broke her heart in high school has not only returned home, but she's also Dani's only suspect. Kristen Malone has come back to Cypress Lake to put the past behind her so that she can move on with her life. Seeing Dani Ricketts again throws her off-guard, nearly derailing her plans to finally rid herself and her family of Cypress Lake.

Crashing Waves by Graysen Morgen. After a tragic accident, Pro Surfer, Rory Eden, spends her days hiding in the surf and snowboard manufacturing company that she built from the ground up, while living her life as a shell of the person that she once was. Rory's world is turned upside when a young surfer pursues her, asking for the one thing she can't do. Adler Troy and Dr. Cason Macauley from Graysen Morgen's bestselling novel: *Falling Snow*, make an appearance in this romantic adventure about life, love, and letting go.

Bridesmaid of Honor (Bridal Series book 1) by Graysen Morgen. Britton Prescott's best friend is getting married and she's the maid of honor. As if that isn't enough to deal with, Britton's sister announces she's getting married in the same month and her maid of honor is her best friend Daphne, the same woman who has tormented Britton for years. Britton has to suck it up and play nice, instead of scratching her eyes out, because she and Daphne are in both weddings. Everyone is counting on them to behave like adults.

Falling Snow by Graysen Morgen. Dr. Cason Macauley, a high-speed trauma surgeon from Denver meets Adler Troy, a professional snowboarder and sparks fly. The last thing Cason wants is a relationship and Adler doesn't realize what's right in front of her until it's gone, but will it be too late?

Fate vs. Destiny by Graysen Morgen. Logan Greer devotes her life to investigating plane crashes for the National Transportation Safety Board. Brooke McCabe is an investigator with the Federal Aviation Association who literally flies by the seat of her pants. When Logan gets tangled in head games with both women will she choose fate or destiny?

Just Me by Graysen Morgen. Wild child Ian Wiley has to grow up and take the reins of the hundred year old family business when tragedy strikes. Cassidy Harland is a little surprised that she came within an inch of picking up a gorgeous stranger in a bar and is shocked to find out that stranger is the new head of her company.

Love Loss Revenge by Graysen Morgen. Rian Casey is an FBI Agent working the biggest case of her career and madly in love with her girlfriend. Her world is turned upside when tragedy strikes. Heartbroken, she tries to rebuild her life. When she discovers the truth behind what really happened that awful night she decides justice isn't good enough, and vows revenge on everyone involved.

Natural Instinct by Graysen Morgen. Chandler Scott is a Marine Biologist who keeps her private life private. Corey Joslen is intrigued by Chandler from the moment she meets her. Chandler is forced to finally open her life up to Corey. It backfires in Corey's face and sends her running. Will either woman learn to trust her natural instinct?

Secluded Heart by Graysen Morgen. Chase Leery is an overworked cardiac surgeon with a group of best friends that have an opinion and a reason for everything. When she meets a new artist named Remy Sheridan at her best friend's art gallery she is captivated by the reclusive woman. When Chase finds out why Remy is so sheltered will she put her career on the line to help her or is it too difficult to love someone with a secluded heart?

In Love, at War by Graysen Morgen. Charley Hayes is in the Army Air Force and stationed at Ford Island in Pearl Harbor. She is the commanding officer of her own female-only service squadron and doing the one thing she loves most, repairing airplanes. Life is good for Charley, until the day she finds herself falling in love while fighting for her life as her country is thrown haphazardly into World War II. Can she survive being in love and at war?

Fast Pitch by Graysen Morgen. Graham Cahill is a senior in college and the catcher and captain of the softball team. Despite being an all-star pitcher, Bailey Michaels is young and arrogant. Graham and Bailey are forced to get to know each other off the field in order to learn to work together on the field. Will the extra time pay off or will it drive a nail through the team?

Submerged by Graysen Morgen. Assistant District Attorney Layne Carmichael had no idea that the sexy woman she took home from a local bar for a one night stand would turn out to be someone she would be prosecuting months later. Scooter is a Naval Officer on a submarine who changes women like she changes uniforms. When she is accused of a heinous crime she is shocked to see her latest conquest sitting across from her as the prosecuting attorney.

Vow of Solitude by Austen Thorne. Detective Jordan Denali is in a fight for her life against the ghosts from her past and a Serial Killer taunting her with his every move. She lives a life of solitude and plans to keep it that way. When Callie Marceau, a curious Medical Examiner, decides she wants in on the biggest case of her career, as well as, Jordan's life, Jordan is powerless to stop her.

Igniting Temptation by Sydney Canyon. Mackenzie Trotter is the Head of Pediatrics at the local hospital. Her life takes a rather unexpected turn when she meets a flirtatious, beautiful fire fighter. Both women soon discover it doesn't take much to ignite temptation.

One Night by Sydney Canyon. While on a business trip, Caylen Jarrett spends an amazing night with a beautiful stripper. Months later, she is shocked and confused when that same woman re-enters her life. The fact that this stranger could destroy her career doesn't bother her. C.J. is more terrified of the feelings this woman stirs in her. Could she have fallen in love in one night and not even known it?

Fine by Sydney Canyon. Collin Anderson hides behind a façade, pretending everything is fine. Her workaholic wife and best friend are both oblivious as she goes on an emotional journey, battling a potentially hereditary disease that her mother has been diagnosed with. The only person who knows what is really going on, is Collin's doctor. The same doctor, who is an acquaintance that she's always been attracted to, and who has a partner of her own.

Shadow's Eyes by Sydney Canyon. Tyler McCain is the owner of a large ranch that breeds and sells different types of horses. She isn't exactly thrilled when a Hollywood movie producer shows up wanting to film his latest movie on her property. Reegan Delsol is an up and coming actress who has everything going for her when she lands the lead role in a new film, but there one small problem that could blow the entire picture.

Light Reading: A Collection of Novellas by Sydney Canyon. Four of Sydney Canyon's novellas together in one book, including the bestsellers Shadow's Eyes and One Night.

Visit us at www.tri-pub.com

Made in the USA
Monee, IL
12 October 2020

44866213R00184